BIG
BEN

1

USA TODAY BESTSELLING AUTHOR
NANA
MALONE

Big Ben
COPYRIGHT © 2020 by Nana Malone

Cover Art by Najla Qamber
Photography by Wander Aguiar
Model: James Klipinger
Edited by Angie Ramey
Proof Editing by Michele Ficht
Published in the United States of America

BIG
BEN

ONE

Livy
Present Day

Darkness wrapped her arms around me like a lover I'd grown tired of. Too heavy, too cloying. If I'd had my pick of hiding places, I wouldn't have chosen a freaking closet.

But beggars and choosers and all that.

Only a sliver of light underneath the door made my coffin seem like less of a permanent void. My heart kicked inside my chest, each beat like a punch against my ribs.

But it wasn't fear.

Oh no. It was something deeper. Darker. *More worrisome.*

And it felt a hell of a lot like excitement.

The heat of the man who held his hand pressed over my mouth completely enveloped me, wrapping itself around me, not like the stifling shroud of a wet blanket but more like the safe cocoon of a weighted one.

I should have been terrified. Screw getting caught. I needed to kick, and scream, and raise hell because I could very well die in this closet.

No, you won't.

Okay, maybe not, but it sure as hell felt that way. That was what I got for literally running away from a party. But in my defense, I was escaping Fenton Mills, my boyfriend's boss. That man had far too many hands and had consumed far too many gin and tonics to care who saw him try to grab my ass.

If I was in the mood to be honest, I had to admit the crowd had started to get to me too. Dexter had promised to stay by my side, knowing how crowds made me crazy, but true to form, he'd gotten caught up talking to someone, had some scotch, and left me alone like a sitting duck.

So I'd gone looking for a little reprieve. A moment to breathe. Somewhere to hide. The office door was open, and then I'd leaned against the stupid statue, a ceramic of what looked like bodies intertwined. How was I supposed to know how fragile the damn thing was? I'd been startled by a noise and bumped the stupid thing and had to scramble to catch it.

I'd grabbed onto what looked like a handle just in time. Problem was, when I righted the statue…the handle came off in my hand. Only it wasn't a handle at all. It was a dick. I had statue dick in my hands. *Statue Dick.*

As if that hadn't been enough cause for panic, the noise I'd heard only drew closer with footsteps outside the door. Cold, clammy sweat popped on my skin, and I had to make a literal fight-or-flight, game-time decision. There was no fighting in my party shoes, so I'd chosen to flee. But I couldn't very well go out the door I'd come through because then I'd have been caught, so I hid in the closet, in the dark. And I'd been prepared to stay there for however long I needed to.

I didn't have to wait long. After minutes, the door opened and light spilled in, practically blinding me and giving me only a one-second glimpse at what I was certain would mean a trip to jail when a man so broad that he blocked out the direct light put me in darkness again.

He was well over six feet. His blond hair was a little too long. And his ice blue eyes pierced directly into my soul, freezing me where I stood and sending heat licking over my skin. I caught just enough of a jaw so square that it would make Henry Cavill jealous before he stepped into the shoebox-size closet that was definitely too small for one of us, let alone two.

His broad shoulders took up far too much room and made it difficult to breathe. Our bodies pressed up against each other, and the heat of him chased away the chill of my fear. But my thundering, tripping, skipping heartbeat stayed. My breath became shallow and thin. Probably because he was hogging all the damn oxygen.

I should have been afraid, but it was excitement that made my belly do flips and injected that hint of euphoria that lied to me and told me I could fly.

"What do you think—" I didn't get to finish my statement because the Viking god in Armani placed his damn hand over my mouth and leaned ever so close. A wash of heat spread over my body as I molded against him because, quite frankly, I had nowhere else to go. I was hot and flushed and worried, but somehow, not scared.

"Be still." The gruff, grumbly growl sent a spike of heat through me. But I did as I was told. I could hear movement in the office beyond. I didn't want to be caught. The more I moved, the more noise I made. And the last thing I needed was evidence of the broken sculpture to be found. Evidence I still held in my hand.

So, I was stuck like that, pressed up against a total stranger with a chest broad enough to obscure me from view and tall enough to tower over me. Christ, he was big.

The voices and footsteps drew closer outside.

I held my breath. *Oh shit. Oh shit, oh shit, oh shit.* I couldn't be caught in here. No way in hell could I explain any of this. There was no easy way to say, "Hey, sorry I broke your priceless statue's dick as I was running away from your party." So I was stuck. In a closet, in the dark. With a guy who could only be described as a Viking in a tux.

And was that his very large erection pressing against my belly? I swallowed hard. Oh yes, that was also most certainly his hand on my ass. I opened my mouth to bite his hand, and he admonished me with a whispered, "Shut up. Neither one of us wants to get caught, love."

He had a point there. But his hand flexed on my ass, and I was not okay with it.

Except… Somewhere deep down inside, my inner libido was absolutely fine with it. It had been six long months since I'd had sex, boyfriend notwithstanding, and I was craving a man's touch. But it was still wrong. The Viking wasn't Dexter. I needed to get the hell out of there.

But there was one slight problem; whoever was in the office wasn't going away, so I was stuck there with one of the Viking's hands on my ass and the other on my mouth, and I was too afraid to breathe.

"You need to moan. You had better be a damn good actress."

He couldn't see me, but I still furrowed my brow before I opened my mouth to protest. Then suddenly, he lifted his hand off my mouth, but he didn't release me. Instead, he slid that hand into my hair, angling his head so his face was in the crook of my neck. "You're going to have to moan now."

"What the—"

His mouth on my neck sent a spike of pure need that tugged low in my belly, and the moan that followed was completely involuntary. It felt good. Too good. His lips trailed along my collar bone. His teeth nipped my skin. I wanted to argue. To fight. To tell him to get his hands the hell off me because I had a boyfriend. But I was distracted by his mouth and the hand in my hair tugging it to the side, making a mess of what had taken me hours to artfully straighten and arrange.

But still the footsteps and voices grew closer, and the Viking whispered again. "Fake it till you make it, princess. Make me *believe* you."

His hand tightened on my ass, squeezing and pulling me flush against him. The hard length of his erection was like steel against my belly.

He throbbed against me, and before I could wiggle away, the door cracked open and light streamed in like a ray of sunshine. I finally understood what he was doing.

This was for show. This was our way out. Our way to keep from being caught. We had to fake this and fake it well.

I moaned loud enough to be heard. The door opened a little wider, and I ducked my head into his neck too. My breathing was ragged as he ravaged my neck. Later, when I came to my senses, I would tell myself I hadn't rocked against his erection.

All I heard then was a chuckle from someone, and muffled words as the door closed again and any hint of light was gone.

The Viking Adonis should have released me then, but he trailed his nose up the column of my throat again until he hit the shell of my ear, and then his lips whispered, "Very well done, princess."

He released me suddenly. But his jacket caught on my pin as he shoved open the door, and I squeaked. "No, no, no." But I heard the soft *ping* as my pin hit the floor, and the sound made tears well in my eyes. "Shit."

"Are you okay?" His voice was brusque, distracted.

I fell to the ground, trying to find it. "No, I am not okay. You broke my p—"

He tapped his ear as he gave me a hard look. "I'm really sorry. But I've got to go." And then he was gone, leaving me completely alone with my mother's broken pin in the palm of my hand. I wobbled in place, unable to get a sense of my bearings as tears welled in my eyes

What the hell had just happened?

@

Ben

I'd never been one to run from trouble, but there was a first time for everything. Once I escaped the closet into the outer office with the Picasso on the wall, I hurried down the hall and into the stairwell then leaned against the cold concrete of the wall.

I hadn't expected to find anyone else in that office, let alone a woman whose body imprint I could still feel along mine like she'd left a thermal heat signature beneath my skin.

I forced air into my lungs with a series of slow inhalations. I needed to get my shit together. People were fucking counting on me. Now was not the time to get distracted.

I knew my sins.

Greed. Pride. And my two personal favorites, wrath and lust.

I knew them all. I had cataloged them appropriately.

I was a rogue. A rebel. I didn't believe the rules applied to me, or rather, I was tired of playing by them.

It was a night for revenge, not for getting tangled up with a beautiful woman.

It didn't matter if my palms still itched from the feel of her arse in my hand. And that fucking scent... coconut and lime, all light and citrusy. I could still smell her even though she wasn't near me any longer.

East Hale, my tech support and best mate, broke the silence

on the com unit in my ear. "If you're done snogging the random woman in the closet, we have a plan to carry out." Luckily, he was only mildly irritated.

"I'm already on the move, East," I muttered as I hurried down the stairs. This was the problem when you were working with your mates on different activities.

"You'd bloody well better be."

"Only fucking Ben Covington would get sent in to copy files and meet a woman," said Bridge Edgerton. His goddamn voice was always distinctive. The years at Eton had smoothed out his East End accent, but a light edge always slid back in when he was giving me shit.

"Swear to God if you two don't shut it, you're in for an arse kicking."

The deeper laugh was all Bridge, and I could only shake my head. *Twat.*

East spoke again. "Move your arse. Cameras will only be down another thirty seconds."

"On it." I didn't want to have to explain what I was doing anywhere near Bram Van Linsted's office when those cameras came back online. If I fucked up, we were back to square one. None of us wanted that, so I had to make this work.

"Don't forget, drop the flash drive into the potted plant by the main exit. We have someone on the cleaning crew who will pick it up."

The Van Linsted family was security crazy, which happened when you owned a diamond empire. Every guest at this little party would be searched before leaving. I didn't want to get caught with the files.

The stairwell dumped me out in a hallway downstairs. My shoes made a soft *click-click* sound on the marble floors. I glanced around. Fortunately, there was no security in sight.

I could hear the harp music clearly from down the hall when East said, "Incoming, Ben. Turn left."

I took the door immediately to my left, slipping in and closing it behind me.

A woman shrieked, and the man pumping his hips between her thighs turned with a snarl. "You fucking mind, mate?"

I bit back my chuckle. "Sorry. Didn't know this room was taken."

In my ear, around a laugh, East told me the hallway was clear, and I grinned at the couple I'd interrupted. "I do have to say... running off to shag in an empty conference room is not really that inventive, is it?" I ducked back out when the bloke glared like he wanted to hit me.

I managed to make it down the hall and into the main foyer. "Okay, I'm in position."

"Ahh, pretty boy has remembered he has a job to do."

"Shut it, Bridge. Don't be mad at me because you're about to tie yourself to a ball and chain." I grabbed a glass of champagne from a passing waiter. "Don't be jealous because the ladies love me. You too could have all the pussy in the world, but you're giving that up."

East sounded bored when he said, "If you two are done acting like children, we still have another device to copy."

The first part of my assignment had been to sneak into Bram Van Linsted's office and copy the data on his laptop. I was familiar enough with the Van Linsted estate to make that happen. After all, I'd spent enough time there as a child and then later when we were classmates at Eton.

Van Linsted Senior hadn't been much of a fan of me or my mates. Having to be in charge of our instruction for the Elite had been a chore he clearly loathed. And he'd made his disdain known. He'd made it clear he didn't want any of us anywhere near his son. But his hands had been tied, so he'd had to tolerate us and we'd had to tolerate him.

But the time for tolerance was almost over.

CHAPTER 2

Ben

I sipped my champagne, doing my level best to blend into the crowd. Easier said than done when my face was so damn recognizable.

As James Covington's son, it was difficult to be inconspicuous. After all, this was a fundraiser. Marcus Van Linsted had supported my father as Prime Minister, so I was expected to attend. And there were more than a few people who wanted to speak with me, or, at the very least, be *seen* speaking to me.

I knew how to do approachable but aloof. After all, I'd been doing it for years. It was just a matter of slipping on the mask. My gaze scanned the crowd and found our host easily enough.

"I've got him."

"Okay. Remember, you have to get close to him. It's going to take a full two minutes, maybe three. But once you have it, get the fuck out."

"Nothing more specific than that?" As plans went, sometimes East was lacking in detail.

"It's not an exact science. Remember we don't want anyone to know what you're doing."

"Right. Remind me the next time we steal sensitive

information from our own secret society to put one of you in the field."

East chuckled. "Then who would be on tech? You? That's a recipe for disaster."

Technology and I got along fine as long as I didn't have to rely on it for anything. I liked relying on myself. It was safer.

Relax. Don't rush. Take your time. Play the part.

Bram Van Linsted was in the middle of the crowd as the man of the hour. He was smiling and shaking hands. I needed to get this done now.

With dark hair and blue eyes, he was a charming git. Even in the middle of the crowd, it was easy to spot him. He was surrounded by people. After all, they wanted to curry favor. Van Linsted was filthy fucking rich with excellent political prospects. His family had served in politics for years until leaving for the private sector. Rumor was he'd be making his own political bid soon enough.

I knew what most of these people didn't know though. Van Linsted wielded more power outside of politics than in it. And if there were to be any kind of elections, they wouldn't be *by the people*. They would be only by the people he looked upon as peers.

People like me, like my friends, were the kind of people he wanted to strip power from.

But now I had money. Not my father's money, my own. Between Bridge, East, and myself, we had enough power to dismantle the Elite. If we were smart.

Everything had to go right, or the dominoes wouldn't fall the way we needed.

I bumped into a waiter as I marched toward my target, deliberately causing a minor crash. The guy had only two glasses on his tray, so the spill wasn't too bad. "Mate, I'm sorry."

I made a show of attempting to help him and having to be saved by him instead. It would be better if everyone thought I was pissed. They'd make assumptions that I was useless. Insignificant.

When I was back on my feet, I pulled my jacket back into place and leered at Van Linsted's date, Cassandra something or other. She was a model. There was something so familiar about her in the jawline. Had I shagged her? It was hard to remember that kind of thing. As much as I was doing this for show, playing the luxury-stricken playboy, there was some truth to the carefully constructed exterior. After all, I'd been playing the part for a very long time.

When Van Linsted caught sight of me, he frowned as if he'd tasted something bad. "Covington, I see nothing has changed."

I forced my gaze to meet his. "Arsehole," I said with equal parts of disdain and irreverence. "Still a prick, I see."

Cassandra raised her champagne glass to her mouth, but I could see the corners of her lips twitching as she bit back a laugh. It wasn't like I was lying. Everyone knew he was a dick. Just because his family owned a diamond empire, he thought his shit didn't stink. Well, that was going to change.

He rolled his eyes then drained his glass of champagne. "You really are predictable, Covington."

I whisper-shouted loudly enough for the nearby groups to overhear. "Ladies, you know that him *being a dick* does not equate to him *having a big dick*, right? I know that's confusing."

In my ear, East cursed. "Can you get closer, mate? You're too far away."

One of the redheads in the group gave me an appraising look from top to bottom. Her gaze slid over me as if calculating exactly how much I was worth by what I was wearing. Tom Ford shoes, the slick Armani tuxedo, the classic Tag Heuer, even the

Hermes tie all rang up the cash machine in her head. When her gaze met mine, I winked at her. "Care to jump ship, love?"

I inched closer to Van Linsted as I sidled up to her. I thought I might still be too far away, but East's voice reassured me. "That's it, right there. Don't move. Closer if you can, it's a little slow to download."

I leaned in to whisper. "I'm Ben. You can call me *Big* Ben if you prefer." She chuckled at that, and I nudged even closer to her.

Van Linsted scowled. "What do you want, Covington?"

"I wanted to say hello. It's been a while. Obviously, things are moving in the right direction for you."

From my peripheral vision, I saw security inching their way through the crowd, trying to be discreet as they sliced through the people like a Damascus steel knife. I was running out of time.

I was going to have to agitate him. East's frustration was clear as he growled, "Mate, closer. Something is wrong."

Bugger.

I needed Van Linsted to initiate prolonged contact. And there was only one way I could think of to do that. "How is it hiding under Mummy's skirts, Bram? Your family did always bail you out of problems. Rumor has it she's going to skip you for inheritance. Is that true?" I turned my attention to the crowd. "Ladies, did you know that Bram here doesn't actually control his purse strings? Mummy does. Those diamonds you see draped around her neck are solely controlled by her. You're better off trying your luck with Miles, his younger brother. Bram here has no say in Van Linsted holdings." It was true.

Marcus Van Linsted, Bram's father, might have been the head of the mines on paper, but marrying April had been the infusion of cash, all told in the billions, that the business needed.

All eyes were on me. I spread my arms. "I, on the other hand, am a self-made billionaire with a *B*." I mock-stumbled forward. "So that should help in your decision making."

In my ear, East chuckled and egged me on. "That's it. It's working. Also, you're a right git. Thank God you're not on the side of evil."

I was going to have to physically climb the fucker if the download didn't go any faster.

The other women in the group didn't even bother casting Van Linsted a goodbye glance as they stalked over to me. The tallest one with the dark auburn hair grinned. "My name is Fiona."

"Ah, like the princess. I'm Ben. You can call me Big Ben though. I don't falsely advertise. Bram here, well, he's known for having a little prick. And, you know, generally being a prick. Just his Mummy's errand boy."

I knew Van Linsted. He didn't get his hands dirty. He didn't know how to fight. Not like I did. I could afford to take a few calculated risks. But security was close.

In my ear, Bridge growled. "You're going to have to get right up next to him. We still have at least a minute and a half left."

I needed to push him. I stepped closer still. If I could get him to attempt to run at me, that might help.

"How does it feel, Bram? When everybody in your life chooses someone other than you, including your mother?"

The muscle in his jaw ticked.

Come on, you fuck. Get in my face. I needed it to be showy. I needed him to think he had the upper hand.

He did step to me then, a sneer twisting his lips, turning him into a Disney villain in stark contrast to his perfectly ordinary features. His voice was pitched low when he said, "How is your friend, Toby?"

And we had lift-off. In my ear, East said, "Yup, almost there. Thirty seconds."

The good news was my reaction wasn't forced. Everything I felt was real. Every emotion, the anger, the hatred... I just had to play it up, let it loose. Unleash it.

"I will fucking kill you," I ground out.

"Sure you will." And then he started to move away. Fuck. I still needed another few seconds. Running out of options, I charged ahead and rushed him. Security was dangerously close, but I landed a satisfying straight jab to his nose.

Blood splattered everywhere, and then I grabbed him by his very expensive Armani jacket. "You always thought you were too good for us. You think being a Van Linsted makes you any better than Toby? He was the best of us, and you're envious because you will never be as good as he was."

"If you say so. I beg you to kindly take your hands off me."

And then it was over. Hands grabbed me from behind. "Sir, you'll have to come with us."

Shit. Another couple of seconds.

God, I hated Bram. At that moment, I could've killed him.

I had no choice. I had to struggle. To my right, my eye caught a shimmer of red, and something made my skin prickle. It took my attention off of Bram for a fucking second. A swath of red. A distraction. My attention was divided, and a crack came out of nowhere.

It was the sting I noticed first, then the sound. And then my head jolted to the right. I continued to struggle. I needed my arms to defend myself. Who was I kidding? I needed my arms to kick his arse.

I saw the lady in red, her eyes wide with shock and horror as she rushed forward. Bugger. I didn't need her next to this. She was going to get hurt.

East tweeted in my ear. "We got it. Get out of there."

The guards were starting to pat me down, restraining my arms. Oh, this was definitely going to hurt.

Angling my body to the right, I rolled my shoulder up and slid my arm out of the grip of one security guard. She was getting so close. Too close. Could I do this?

She ran up to us. "Stop it. Release him instantly. You're making a scene."

Her gaze met mine. Midnight eyes looked straight into my soul, twisting me up at the most inopportune time. If they patted me down before they handed me to the police, they were going to find the drive.

Performing the drop wasn't going to happen. There was too much attention on me, and I needed to hand it off. Ditch it. *Something.*

The woman. She was my only hope. They might not look too closely at her purse. The guard grabbed for my arm again, but not before I elbowed him in the gut and lunged for her.

I had no idea who she was, but she'd be on camera, so we'd be able to get facial recognition and find her later.

The guard reached for me again and I stumbled forward deliberately. She reached out for me as if she'd known the plan the entire time. As if we'd orchestrated this synergistic clusterfuck.

In the scuffle, she almost went down. One of the guards reached for her and tried to help her. I took hold of her purse and slid the device in and then let myself be taken down. "Fuck. All right, all right, all right. I'm going."

She glowered at me. "He's the prick who broke my pin, but this is overkill."

I prayed to God that no one had noticed the transfer. I'd fucked this up. All of it was completely fucked up. If we lost our chance to dismantle the Elite, there would be no justice for Toby. Not now, not ever.

@

Livy

So much for minding my own business.

I'd gone my whole life following the rules. Playing by them. A year ago, my mother had told me to start living like I was only going to get one take.

Somehow, I didn't think this was what she meant.

Two grown men fighting... at a political fundraiser? Who the hell would do such a thing? It was asinine. I had meant to find the Viking and give him a piece of my mind for breaking my pin

I'd found him all right. Right in front of me. In an actual fight.

In the span of thirty minutes, I'd broken what was likely a priceless artifact, then hidden in a closet with a man so hot I could still feel his warmth wrapped around me. He'd whispered things to me that I'd only ever imagined someone saying. And then, I'd witnessed that very same man in a fistfight with Bram Van Linsted, firstborn son to one of London's most elite families.

Who the hell was this Viking guy that he didn't fear the wrath of the Van Linsted family? To hear it told, if everything went the right way, Bram would be prime minister in a decade or so. That would be enough time to make his foray into politics.

I shook my head and searched the crowd for Dexter, the only man I *should* be concerned with. But as usual, he was MIA. He loved a party. Me, not so much.

Did he ditch you?

I swallowed my annoyance. Before leaving our flat, we'd made a deal. He was to lay off the booze and not overindulge.

I couldn't find him though. The Viking caught my eyes

again as security engaged him. Who the hell was he? And what did he have against Bram Van Linsted? More importantly, what the hell had he been doing in the closet?

"I will say, it's never a dull occasion when the Van Linsteds are involved," a voice whispered from behind me.

With a shudder of disgust chasing away my curiosity, I stepped back. "Mr. Mills. Have you seen Dexter? I can't find him anywhere."

He grinned at me broadly and leaned into my personal space. "You are all right, aren't you? Not injured at all? I was worried as I watched you walk into that fray." He reached out an arm to wrap around me, but I ducked just out of reach as I searched the crowd again.

"You know Dexter. Working the crowd. He's really made himself an invaluable asset at the firm."

I gave him a wan smile. Dex loved his job. All he wanted to do was make partner. I'd ruined his first shot, so I had to play nice, no matter how badly Fenton Mills made my skin crawl. "His career is so important to him. And he has my full support."

He stepped closer, not quite touching me but standing so close that the gin and tobacco on his breath were mostly what I smelled. "Not everyone has someone as supportive as you. I know Emily doesn't always understand my *drive*. My *need*."

I forced myself to swallow the bile that tried to rise. The last thing I wanted to hear about was his *need*. "Well, it's a very demanding career. If you'll excuse me, I'm going to text Dexter and head back into London. I've got a hell of a migraine looming."

His brows furrowed as his gaze searched mine for any hint of falsehood. He wasn't going to find any because I was done. Ready to bolt.

His frown eased, and he nodded. "I'll send you in my car. As a matter of fact, I can join you."

Oh hell no. Not happening. "So kind of you, but what about Emily? I know she said she had to travel in the morning, and she can't very well ride the shuttle if you send the car with me."

His lips pressed together in annoyance. He knew I was right. He couldn't leave his wife behind. "Of course, you're right. Remember, I count you as part of the Mills family and will do anything to look after you."

"Uh, thank you, sir." I eased back, plastering a smile on my face that I hoped seemed genuine but aloof. He gave off strong level-five creeper vibes, and the less time spent in his presence the better.

Thankfully, the security line was almost empty, and I handed my clutch to a guard while I was patted down. The guard was so busy staring at his monitor and talking to someone on his walkie about how cameras in a sector were down that he barely looked at me. "Have a good night, miss."

Once outside, I dragged in all that blessed fresh air, crisp and clear, and I felt like I could finally breathe for the first time all night. The estate was located in the village of Virginia Water, close to the city, and it sat on an acreage of sparkling green. Automatically I glanced around, hoping I'd still catch a glimpse of the Viking, but he was already gone. *And you were going to, what? Interrogate him about what he was doing with you in the closet? Get real.*

I didn't know him. He didn't owe me anything. Except a new pin. And I had a boyfriend. *One who abandoned you at the party, knowing full well crowds make you crazy.*

I squashed the voice of discontent. It wasn't useful right now. My social anxiety had gotten worse since mom's passing. Well, really since the car accident. I knew how to manage on my own. Depending on anyone was a recipe for disaster.

I snapped open my purse to find my shuttle ticket then pulled out the stiff cardstock. I frowned when I noticed what looked like a black tube of lipstick in the bottom of my clutch. My lipstick was in a silver tube.

The hairs on the back of my neck stood at attention, and I glanced around. I'd made it through the security check point with no problems. But something had made me wary.

I was a firm believer in our evolutionary cues that warned us of danger. Maybe some of that came from micro expressions, maybe a change in the air, but something told me to wait until I was on the shuttle back to London to investigate.

My feet dragged as I boarded the black limousine party bus with three other people. I chose a position close to the back where it was dark. The whole time I could feel the lipstick tube burning a hole in my purse. How had it gotten there?

Once the bus had been moving for ten minutes, I pulled out the black tube and examined it. It was only then that I realized it wasn't lipstick. I tugged on it and it separated into two parts. It was a flash drive. What. The actual. Fuck?

Think, Livy. Slow it down. That was a game my mother had played with me as a kid when I would get so worked up about a social situation that I couldn't function. It always worked. Once I got over my initial fear, I could always think more clearly.

One deep breath. The lingering scent of various perfumes clung to the air. Another deep breath. The chill had me pulling my shawl tighter around myself. A final breath. My mind played back the end of the party, those last moments when I'd tried to play hero.

The Viking.

He'd done this. He'd made me his accomplice. But to what?

CHAPTER 3

Livy

As the seconds ticked by, my brain speed processed the seven stages of mental ass kicking. I was desperate for answers. Had I been targeted? Did he do this on purpose? Was this some kind of game? Was he someone who assumed, that like my mother, I was a diplomat?

He'd be very disappointed. I was an executive assistant. I had no access to anything or anyone important.

I'd changed industries after moving back from the states to be with my mother, and I hadn't been able to find an operations position. And unlike my mother, I had zero taste for the diplomat's lifestyle.

Denial came quickly. Because no way was this happening to me. There was clearly some kind of mistake. I hadn't just broken a priceless artifact then unwittingly smuggled out some kind of flash drive. Even I wasn't that stupid. Dexter was going to be furious. How the hell did I get myself into these kinds of situations?

Guilt lingered. I should go back and turn myself in. The anger though, that was surprising. I wanted to put on the gloves I used to have when I did Krav Maga and go to town, grounding and pounding this flash drive. I hadn't asked for the disruption in my life. The other stages followed quickly after the denial and guilt, and finally, I was left with the flash drive still in my palm.

The shuttle pulled up to St. Pancras station. For fear of being searched again, I shoved the drive into my bra, using my shawl to cover the misshapen bulge.

My stomach knotted and tightened as I stepped down off the shuttle with not a cavity search in sight. It was disturbingly easy to walk away with whatever this was. I was in such a tag that I took no notice of the glass arch above. Or the inky blankness only broken by crystals of water as it drizzled. What was on the damn thing? What if this was all some kind of horrible misunderstanding? And why had the Viking handed it to me? I was a total stranger. Naturally, I flinched as I thought about how we'd actually first met. I was in such a fog I almost walked into The Meeting Place Statue. The bronze statue of the couple only served as a reminder of how my evening had ended.

I laid my head back against the glass as my train passed Victoria station. I could almost see myself talking to my mother about what had happened earlier and her saying, 'At last, some adventure.' I blinked my eyes rapidly, dissipating the sting of tears.

This was no adventure. The Viking screamed danger. And while I wanted some excitement in my life, I didn't have a death wish. Not to mention, Mom had loved Dexter. The two of them had been thick as thieves. But then Dex was always a charmer.

When I reached my station, I stepped off the train, pulling my shawl closer around me to ward off the wet chill. With my clutch tucked under my arm, I started the four-block trek home. On the street, my shoes made soft suction sounds as they tread on the wet roads. My phone rang, and I pulled it out from my purse, smiling when I saw who it was. "Hey, Telly."

Telly Brinx was a legitimate walking, talking badass and had been since Uni. We'd shared a flat with two other girls and then promptly moved out on our own. "Hello, gorgeous. How's the event? How are you feeling? Tense? Anxious? Do you want to have a night of wine and reading at mine?"

Adrenaline surged through me, making me desperate to tell her everything, but maybe talking on the phone about how I'd accidentally stolen state secrets or mining secrets or whatever was on the drive was probably not a good idea.

Telly was a tech genius. She owned Brinx Technologies and was a brilliant developer. She might be able to help me decipher what the hell I was carrying around. "Only you would offer a night of wine and reading."

"Well, to be fair, by reading I mean gossiping about very fit celebrities."

I laughed. "Yeah, we're overdue. I haven't seen you in a few weeks."

"We need to fix that. You think his royal highness will let you out?"

I sighed. "Telly, be fair." After the accident, Dex had struggled with post-traumatic stress. He'd also injured his hand and had to have some physical therapy. "Monday after work?" By then I would have figured out what to do. Maybe it would have resolved itself by then. *Like this is going to magically go poof.*

"I will put it in the books. So, tell me, how was it?"

I swallowed. What did I say exactly? "Fine. I was a bit anxious. But you know, nothing I couldn't handle."

She laughed, knowing me all too well. "So, how long before you ran off? And did you have your shoes in hand?"

I groaned. "One time I did that. *Once.* Why won't you ever let me live it down?"

"Because it was hilarious. You attempting to climb out the loo window with your Jimmy Choos in your fist."

"I don't like you." I'd begged her to go with me to the London Lords holiday party when I'd started as a temp six months ago. I'd had an anxiety spike and, erm, needed air. That was my story and I was sticking to it. Besides, I'd at least texted.

"So tell me, did you meet anyone even remotely cool? Or interesting?"

"Uhm, meet is the wrong word I think." I didn't actually get a name for the Viking.

"Dexter was supportive?"

I hesitated a moment too long, and she groaned. "Was he a twat?"

"He wasn't a twat, exactly. I just couldn't find him when I wanted to leave."

She sighed. "You're not home yet?"

"No. I took the tube."

"You're supposed to call me in those instances. I'll come and get you."

"What? All the way from Central London?" Her flat was located right above Vauxhall Station. Dexter and I lived on the edge of Chiswick.

"For my best friend, I will always turn up."

"I appreciate that, but I was fine. I mean after I broke the statue."

"What?" she gasped. "You were at the Van Linsted estate, right?"

"Yeah. Sure was. It was kind of humiliating. I didn't know what to do, so I hid... in the closet."

She choked out a cough. "Liv. Are you serious?"

"I know. Trust me I know. But then there was this guy, and he hid in the closet too."

"Oh, this is getting better. Please tell me. This is better than Pornhub."

"What? No. *Boyfriend*, remember?"

"Oh him…" Telly and Dex had never gotten along. She always said he didn't seem right for me. "Okay, fine. At least tell me he was fit."

"We hid in a closet. I was hardly focused on his looks."

"Lies."

"Okay fine, he was tall."

"How tall?"

Picturing him in my mind's eye was remarkably easy. "Maybe six foot three. Maybe a little taller. Blond hair that looks a little bit messy, like it was too long, a ridiculously chiseled jaw with one of those cleft chins, you know? Ice-blue eyes. And he's built like he's got one of those V-things pointing directly to the promised land. And he walks like it too. Lean, looks excellent in a tuxedo."

"I love how you say you barely got a look, but you're describing Eric Northman."

"What, from that show?"

"Yep, Alexander Skarsgård. Otherwise known as my secret baby daddy if I were into blokes. Basically, the perfect human specimen."

"I guess he did look a lot like that. But I'm thinking more like Brad Pitt from Troy."

"Okay, that works too. Wait, so you were hiding out from the party with a guy that looked like a cross between a hot Viking and a Greek god?"

"Basically, that's it."

"Please tell me you broke up with Dexter and had hot sexy times in your secret hiding place?"

"You have an overactive imagination. No, no such thing happened." I bit my lip. "I mean, he did do this thing."

I could almost feel Telly leaning into the phone. "What thing?"

"We were hiding, right?"

"Uh-huh." I could almost visualize her leaning forward as she listened.

"And he had one hand on my ass and the other on my mouth."

There was a beat of silence, then she whispered, "Oh my God, so hot."

"Then people came in the office and we pretended they'd caught us... you know, in the *middle* of things. He ordered me to moan."

"Jesus. Did you?"

I swallowed hard as I remembered that moment. "Yes, yes, I did. I did it so we wouldn't be caught." That sounded feasible... even to me.

"That is... Wow."

"He did this thing where he kind of growled in my ear. It was very unnerving."

"Look at you. You are the most frustrating human I've ever met in my life. This happens and you don't call me right away?"

"Sorry. It all happened so fast. Weird thing though, he got into a fight with Bram Van Linsted before I left. Security escorted him out and everything."

"I mean, not that I don't believe that twat would have an enemy, but an actual physical fight? It's so un-English."

"Yeah, I know, right? And then the craziest thing was, he handed me—"

I'd been so busy yammering away with Telly that I barely felt the inertia before the push from behind which made my next words lodge in my throat. I stumbled and crashed forward, my phone skittering away. And then my face was zooming ever so quickly toward the ground.

I knew not to put my hands straight out and instead

go forearms first and turn my head. But it was so hard to remember.

Down I went. When I rolled over onto my back, someone jumped on me, his weight pressing me into the wet pavement. Fear coiled in my gut, and my stomach churned from the little I'd eaten. Then he snatched my purse right out of my hand. "Hey. Stop that." I tried desperately to remember what I'd been told to yell. The only good thing was I managed to buck him off. Wrapping my ankles around his, I lifted my hips then listed to the side, and he rolled right off of me.

The bad news was he took off running with my clutch.

Jagged breaths tore out of my lungs, and my head simmered. My heart tried to break free of my ribcage. When I was alone again in the middle of wet pavement, it occurred to me that all he'd gotten was fifty quid, a credit card, and my favorite lipstick. Raspberry plum. It looked gorgeous on my brown skin.

Damn, and the shade was limited edition.

Plus side is you have your phone and the flash drive.

I patted my chest with trembling hands. It was still where I'd shoved it when I was on the bus. I didn't understand the sudden wash of relief. Except now, I still had a reason to go looking for the Viking. Somewhere to my right, I could hear Telly calling out. I winced when I picked up my now cracked phone. My hands were scraped and were going to require some cleaning. "Telly?"

"Jesus, what just happened?"

"Well, it would seem I've been mugged."

@

Ben

It could have been worse.

Really? How? How could it have been worse?

Sure, it smelled of piss and bad decisions, but if I was being honest, it was well worth it to hit Bram in his sorry face.

A guard appeared at my cell. "Mr. Covington?"

I looked up and grinned. "Mate?"

"Well, it appears that you are being bailed out."

"Did you have any doubt?"

He frowned at me as he shook his head.

That's it, fall for that nonsense. Just some rich kid here for kicks.

The role I had played was a perfect camouflage. I was led through processing and had to sign my name to collect my things. My watch. My phone.

Freedom. Now that I was out, I had to track her down. The woman in red.

Before I was out of the final gate, I caught a glimpse of East and Bridge waiting for me. East gave me a smirk as he spoke. "Did you have to hit him?"

I shrugged. "We needed time. It seemed like a good idea at that moment."

Bridge, however, looked well ticked off. "That was a fucking risk with the device on you."

I rubbed the back of my neck. "Yeah, that's the thing. I figured once I put my hands on him I was definitely going to the nick, so I ditched it."

Both of them gaped at me. "What?"

East's eyes bugged out. "Tell me you're kidding." He turned to Bridge. "Tell me he's fucking kidding."

Bridge stared at me. He dropped his voice to smooth ice. "Where the fuck is it?"

"The woman at the event, the one in red, if she's smart, she has it."

Bridge sputtered. "If she's smart? What the fuck, Ben? You realize you're risking all of us, right?"

"What the fuck was I supposed to do, mate? We needed more time. I got us some more time. You needed to download the information from both his phone and the device. I managed to do that. What would you have had me do? They were patting me down."

Bridge ran a hand over his face before scrubbing at his jaw. "Who is she?"

I winced. "I don't know."

East was generally an affable bloke. Easy-going. He'd give you the shirt off his back, but when he was pushed, he could be vicious. He stormed away, muttering curses that would make the most hardened prisoner blush. Bridge lifted a brow. "Mate, tell me you're not serious."

"I am. I had no choice. There was no way I would have been able to leave the building with it. So we just need to find her."

East came back after his mini tirade. "Do you think?"

I turned my gaze on him and pinned him with a hard glare. "The way I figure it, you can stand here carrying on or we can go back and start looking for her."

I could see East doing his deep breathing, trying to calm himself down and keep his temper at bay. After everything we'd found out about Toby, he'd been a mess. We'd all been in bad shape, but East had taken it the worst.

He'd internalized what had happened. And I could see him trying to work through his calming exercises before he lost his mind. "Think, mate. Was it a clean handoff?"

I closed my eyes and took a deep breath. "It was as clean as I could make it. Van Linsted hit me, and she came running over. We both went down with security, and I shoved it in her purse. She might not even know she has it."

East blinked at me. "Bloody perfect."

"That's all I've got right now. Are we going to yak on about it, or are we going to go do something?"

I watched him take several deep breaths. "Fuck."

"Do you have a guest list? She's probably on the security footage. We're going to need to ascertain who she was there with."

East muttered. "It's as good a place as any to start. In the meantime, we'll need to also comb the security footage to make sure that no one saw you make the handoff."

"I don't think they did."

"Thinking isn't certainty. If anyone finds that drive and puts two and two together, we're toast. Our lives are over."

"Like I was fucking around deliberately. I know why the drive was so important. I know what's at stake."

Bridge opened the driver's side door. "Then let's hope your mysterious woman in red has what we need. And you damn well better pray she's not going to sell us out."

I wasn't sure how I knew, but I did. "She won't."

East glowered at me as he climbed into the Range Rover at the curb. "You better be right about that."

I don't know what it was about her, but something told me that she wasn't the kind of woman who would dick us over.

But it wouldn't have been the first time I'd been wrong.

CHAPTER 4

Ben

3 Months Earlier

The pomp. The circumstance. Some would even say tradition.

I called it bullshit. My long-hidden tattoo itched and felt heavy under my ring. I often wondered what would have happened all those years ago if, when I'd been called to the Elite, I'd said no. What if I'd gotten the card that said *only a select few are to be Elite* and I'd burned the thing?

What if I'd encouraged Toby to burn his too? Would he still be alive?

The dim cavern of the initiation room made it difficult to see clearly. Or maybe I wished this was all a dream. The candles burning all around us sent an incense aroma into the air. And it was so thick I nearly choked with it. Sand-colored stone walls surrounded us in a massive circle, and above us, on the ceiling, was a tapestry depicting the first brothers of the Elite in their black robes and Bauta masks on a hunt.

The same robes and masks we wore now.

In the center of the room, the new initiates lay in their coffins.

I forced myself to stand still. Next to me, I could feel the glare of Bridge on my right. He hated this shit as much as I did, but he was better at hiding his disdain. Maybe because he'd been hiding it for so long.

To my left, East's jaw twitched. Because of the mask, I couldn't see his face, but God, I could feel his contempt. Drew, directly opposite of me, stood stoic. As if he bought into all the seriousness.

We were inducting a new class. None of whom had any idea what they were in for. That their lives would no longer be their own but would be dictated by a preset ledger of fate and destiny. If you were lucky enough to be chosen, you would thrive. If you were unlucky, well, no one ever wanted to talk about what happened to the unlucky.

To our left, Marcus Van Linsted, the current Director Prime, some would say the most powerful man in Britain, closed out the session. "To our newest brothers, lift your masks and know that now you are amongst the Elite. Your lives will never be the same."

Marcus had said the same words to us some time ago. We'd still all been reeling from Toby's death, still shell-shocked, unable to function. And we'd been forced to wear those masks and act as if we hadn't just lost one of our best friends.

We'd been told how powerful we would be, how we would be called upon to serve our brothers. I had brothers in the room, absolutely. East. Drew. Bridge. But those were the only ones I counted. To my far right, in the corner, I could feel the glare of my father. Almost like he could tell the direction of my thoughts.

I twirled my signet ring around my thumb, dying to get the bloody thing off. The moments when I wasn't in public were the best ones because it was the first thing I took off. Possibly like many women took off a bra. I could always feel the weight of it, digging into me.

The final sacred words were the signal that I was almost free.

When the ceremony was over, I tried to relax, but a scowl leaked as Bram Van Linsted clapped his hand on his father's back. The Van Linsteds had been in the Elite since the first class over two hundred years ago. Everyone liked to forget that those Dutch fuckers made their fortune on the backs of slaves and then increased it by pillaging a continent that had already lost so much for diamonds. Nope. Everyone likes to pretend they were on the up and up, but I knew the Van Linsteds. After all, I'd spent over a decade hating them.

As always, after the induction ceremony there was a reception, one the new recruits always looked forward to. Top shelf booze and women, carefully selected for them, of course. No one was allowed to bring their current girlfriend if they had one. All these women were escorts, discreet, and knew the game.

They were all compensated for their time and efforts. They'd been selected based on each new member's desires, predilections, and personal tastes. It was actually ingenious.

For the very few that had never known such wealth, it could be a heady experience. Every year, the selection committee chose one from an underprivileged background. Almost like their own sick *Trading Places* experiment. It didn't usually turn out well. Our year, that token recruit was Bridge. The joke was on the selection committee though. Bridge was as steady as they came, and he'd made not a single misstep. Now he was richer than half the membership combined.

Just when the recruits were out of their minds with whatever booze and drugs were on hand, they'd be taken away, separated into pairs, and pulled into their bonding ceremony. Then, to their bonded brother, they would make their confessions.

They'd leave their sins on the table in a process that would continue throughout the years. There was always an even number of recruits. In our class, there had been five pairs. Bridge and East had been paired. Drew had been paired with someone else. There had been two other pairs, and I had been paired with Toby. Since Toby had died, I'd had to make my confessions to my father. That awkward moment when my biggest confession was that I hated him was one I would never forget.

One by one, in a sea of black and gold, all the brothers filed into the vestibules to hang their cloaks and shelve their masks, then up the spiral staircase at the end of the darkened hall to the level that was comprised of elevator banks to the upper floor. There was no other way up to the estate.

The clipped sounds of our polished oxfords on the marble floor built like an orchestra crescendo while we loaded onto the elevators. I never felt I breathed more freely than when the stainless-steel elevators gave way to the white marble, chrome, and glass of the massive foyer.

I was free once again.

Above us, the enormous crystal chandelier gleamed. The cool forced air reminded me that I would not die in that tomb after all. Beyond the wide expanse of marble and the glass wall, I could see into the acres of garden, lit up with tea lights for the occasion. The miniature fountains lining either side of the double Olympic sized koi pond also had all the lights turned on. And the drawbridge leading from the house to the mini island in the middle, complete with seating and a Champagne bar, was drawn to allow guests use of the outdoors.

To the left was what the family used as their receiving

room. It was more intimate than their ballroom. The furniture was plush and designer. Many pieces were handcrafted. Every five years or so the décor would change to keep up with the times. The Van Linsteds couldn't be behind the times in any way.

I grabbed a scotch and headed for the balcony. Now that the ritual was done, senior brothers weren't required to stay. One more hour and I could head back to the city. I hated the fucking Van Linsted estate.

We'd been dragged there for workshops and to be inducted into the brotherhood of the Elite properly. I'd been tattooed there, lost my friend there, and I had also been tortured there. Induction was only the first step.

After you celebrated becoming a brother was when the real work began. They had trained us like we were military. Deprived us of food and sleep, preparing us for the harsh realities of the world outside. 'Molded us into gentlemen,' they said. Refined us to be strategists. Prepared us to be leaders. And I wanted to burn it all to the ground.

When I thought back to it, I thought it was absolutely insane some of the things they'd made us do. We'd only been kids.

It was hard to not wonder what would have happened if Toby had lived. I tried to shrug it off, but then the hairs on the back of my neck prickled, not so much for danger but with awareness, and I asked, "How long have you been standing there, mate?"

Bridge sauntered over. "I knew I'd find you out here."

"Where are the others?"

"East is involved in a tight conversation with his father. Drew is enjoying the ass kissing of the new recruits. Why does no one understand that when free booze is offered, you need to temper yourself because you don't know what's coming next?"

I shrugged. "Because everyone loves a party, and no one ever thinks they'll have to pay for it."

"I feel bad for them. They have no idea what they're in for."

"We certainly didn't."

He shook his head. "No, we didn't, did we?"

I turned to him, watching as he lit up his cigar. "Do you regret this?"

He shrugged. "Oh, I hate every single one of these fuckers, aside from you lot. But I'm not an idiot. I know that as much as we aimed to build London Lords without them, the skills that they taught us got us where we are now. So I can't say I regret it."

I turned back to stare over the expanse of grounds lit by the crystal lights to give atmosphere.

"Yeah, well, I think we would have made it on our own." I drained my scotch, letting the burn warm me from the inside as it hit my gut. "You ever think about him?"

He cleared his throat. "Every fucking day."

"Yeah. Me too." I put the glass down and turned to him. "I've had enough. I'm heading back to the city. Are you riding with me or with East?"

"I'll come with you. Let's tell him we're leaving."

I nodded. Starting a business with your best mates had its advantages. You become tighter than brothers. That was how both Bridge and I knew immediately that East needed a rescue.

It was in the tightness of his jaw, the stiffness of his shoulders as he spoke to what appeared to be an older version of him. Same face, but with salt and pepper hair and lines around his eyes. He hated his father. And he wasn't alone. The old man had never gotten over that East was more successful than he was. He'd never gotten over the fact that East hadn't needed a single dime from him. What was it like to be jealous of your own son?

Things were difficult with my father too. He'd never really acknowledged my existence or wanted me. Oh, and he liked my girlfriends a little too much. He wasn't the kind of father I needed, and I wasn't the kind of son he wanted. It was tit for tat.

But Bridge had it the worst. His father, even on days like this, refused to acknowledge him from across the room. Refused to say that Bridge Edgerton was his son. Lord Edgerton's bastard child. The blight on the Edgerton name. He'd lost it when back in school Bridge had decided to use his name. He'd even come to Eton and caused a stir.

He didn't bother speaking to Bridge though. Instead, he'd screamed at the headmaster for an hour about how lawyers couldn't be allowed on the campus to speak to his child without his permission.

Headmaster Tellerman had brilliantly said, "Well, sir, either he's your child or he's not." And he had been listed on Bridge's birth certificate, so Bridge could take his name.

I'd always thought it was the most brilliant 'fuck you' to a parent I'd ever seen, forcing him to do the one thing he didn't want to.

I marched over and forced a smile on my face to address Lord Hale. "Sir, it's been a long time."

He grinned at me. "Covington. You look more and more like your mother every day."

Inwardly, I winced.

I hated that all of those people had known my mother better than I had. After all, she'd been a fixture at my father's side until she passed. There were people there who knew her longer than I did, and it ate at me. "Thank you, sir. Ah, we're going to borrow East here for a minute."

"Yeah, of course. East, I'll have my secretary call you."

East rolled his eyes. "If you must." He turned to face us. "It took you lads long enough."

I shrugged. "Had to get a drink, sorry. I needed to burn out the taste of all this bullshit."

He snorted at that. "Are we leaving? Because I'm ready."

I nodded. "Yup. I'll drive."

We didn't even bother greeting anyone else or saying good-bye as we headed toward the door. I met Drew's gaze and inclined my head, and he put up a finger. He'd better hurry, because we were in no mood to wait.

Drew had a very different relationship with his father and the Elite. As much as he missed Toby too, he had leaned into this life. It was what he knew. He didn't hide from his family. And to be fair, they didn't treat him like shit. Lord Wilcox was actually decent. He gave to charities, with not only his money, but more importantly, his time. Every summer, he dragged Drew and his sister to different parts of the world that needed help and made them use their hands and get to know the people. I'd always liked him.

As we exited the estate with Drew bringing up the rear, I could feel myself starting to breathe again. The tension started to ease between my shoulder blades, the knots coming out. Once a month, I had to put up with this bullshit. Tonight was the initiation. The next would just be a meeting. I could deal with that. But the initiations were always the worst because there were too many memories associated with them.

We rounded the grounds, our feet making crunching sounds on the gravel as we chatted and headed toward the valet. To the left, moonlight glistened off the water in the pool and the soft trickle told me the infinity pool was cycling.

A shadow darted into my vision and I frowned, turning to get a better look as it vanished behind a wall of arborvitae. "What the hell? Did you see that?"

Bridge frowned. "Yep. Female, maybe a maid?"

East shifted on his feet, the gravel shifting with him. "She's running, so either she did something bad or something bad is about to be done to her."

Drew joined us then. "Lads. What are we doing?"

I sighed. "Apparently playing hero?"

The four of us headed into the maze. The Arborvitae were taller than I was and completely obscured us. Bridge called out. "Hello? Are you okay in here?"

When we were completely cocooned by hedges around the next bend, a slim figure dressed in all black stepped out.

I knew her. "Emma?"

©

Ben

Emma Varma dragged off her hoodie and her dark hair spilled out over her shoulders. "If it isn't the London Lords."

Bridge stared at her. "Jesus Christ, is that you?" His usually sure voice wavered.

She lifted her chin in greeting and tucked her raven hair behind her ears. She met his gaze for a long moment, before turning to give East a head nod.

East, not usually one to hide his emotions wrapped his arms around her and picked her up. "Oh my God. Little Tobes."

"You big oaf, put me down. I'm not here for a leisurely visit." East gave her one more big squeeze then released her.

Drew was uncharacteristically more reserved than usual. And well, *I* wanted to hug her. I wanted to hold her, but the fear and regret had me by the bollocks. There were too many memories. Emma had grown into a stunning woman with soulful big eyes, but there was something about her that reminded me too damn much of Toby.

I cleared my throat. "Ems, what are you doing here?"

She turned to glare back at the parapets. "You think I don't know it's initiation night? Ten bloody years. Of course I know the significance of today."

I rolled my shoulders, tension knotting between my shoulder blades. "Still doesn't explain what the hell you're doing here. You can't be seen here."

Her brows snapped down. "I'm walking into that party, and I'm going to confront all of those assholes."

Bridge stepped forward then. I was certain he was about to wrench me out of the way to get to her, but East stepped in. "Ems, we miss him too, but you can't go in there."

"Are you fucking mad? You put yourself in the crosshairs if you walk in there. You're going to risk that tight arse, for what, the satisfaction of yelling at them? Jesus, I knew you were a child, but this really takes the cake." Bridge's voice was barely more than a growl as he spoke to her. The two of them had never particularly gotten along, but this level of anger and tension was uncharacteristic for Bridge.

"Well, someone has to do something. You lot have clearly forgotten all about him. And I'm not an idiot. I'm not going there without a plan, and I'm not leaving empty handed."

Bridge started for her again, but this time I stepped between them. "Emma, not one of us has ever forgotten him."

"Bullshit. I mean, look at you. In ten years, you are the richest arseholes in London. You, like that lot in there, forgot him and trampled on his memory. Tell me, did they even say anything about him. Remember him in any way?"

Cold insidious dread wrapped around my spine. She was right. Not one of them had uttered a single word about Toby. It was like he was lost in the annals of forgotten brothers.

Bridge's voice was tight when he spoke. "So, what? You're

going to accuse them of forgetting him? Then what? It's a flimsy plan, Ems."

"God, you still think I'm some idiot kid?" She tapped the zipper of her hoodie. "It's a camera. What's the one thing a secret society doesn't want? Exposure. The whole lot of them. It's one thing to hear rumors of a society. It's another to have photo evidence."

Drew's voice was thin when he spoke. "You wouldn't. There's a reason it's secret, Ems."

"You think I give a damn? Those arseholes are responsible for my brother's death. I'm not going to let them get away with moving on like nothing happened. All of you have moved on like he was never fucking here. But I don't get to move on. Why do you?"

Those three words. *Why do you?* Wielded with the precision of a fiery sword. They mirrored my own thoughts for the last ten years. We'd all moved on. His friends. Those supposed to keep him safe. We got to move forward with our days. Build, grow, leave legacies. The kind of legacies Toby should have left behind.

Why do you?

I cleared my throat. "Emma, you know we can't let you walk in there. Those men, they're dangerous. And ruthless. Many of whom will think nothing of coming after you or your mother and ruining your lives."

Fire lit her gaze. "My life was ruined ten years ago. I'm a walking shell. I have nothing to lose. Those men in there, those titans of industry, masters of politics, they were supposed to keep my brother safe in the fold. Instead, they stood by and did nothing as he fought for his life. And you lot watched as he died. So I give absolutely zero fucks about *my* life."

The set of her jaw told me she was serious. She was going to implode her life. And I couldn't let her do that. "I'm sorry Ems, we can't let you go in there."

"You certainly can't stop me." She lifted her chin.

"Emma, we all loved Tobes. I know he would want us to protect you. If you think we're letting you walk in there, you're sorely mistaken. Now come with us, we'll get you out of here safely."

"The hell I —" She didn't get to finish because Bridge scooped her up and tossed her over his shoulder.

"Well that's one way of handling it," I muttered under my breath.

Emma wasn't inclined to go quietly though, and she kicked up a hell of a storm. He smacked a hand on her arse and growled something to her that made her shut up.

Running a hand through my hair, I tried to think. "Bridge, take East's car and get her the fuck out of here. Drew, see if you can get her car and drive it home for her. East, let's do a check and make sure she's not on any security cameras. We'll reconvene back at East's."

Just like that, everyone took their marching orders. After all, I'd been giving them for a damn long time. It was my fault we were all here. And Emma was right. We were all responsible.

When Bridge turned, Emma lifted her head and glowered at me. "You have Toby's blood on your hands, just like they do."

I knew, deep down in my bones, she wasn't wrong.

Ben

Two hours later we arrived at East's. One look at my mates and I knew they were feeling what I was feeling. Raw. Exhausted. Maybe a little ill.

East and I had arrived first and East had worked his magic wiping her from the feeds at the estate. Turns out someone had taught Emma how to work in the shadows. Only two cameras had caught her, and my guess was they only caught her because they didn't run on the main feed.

Where the fuck had she learned to do that?

It was after East rubbed the back of his neck and muttered, "I cleaned all the feeds," that Bridge and Drew walked through the doors.

My gaze flickered to Bridge, who sported a tight jaw and a scratch down his cheek. When I lifted a brow, he only shrugged.

Drew caught my gaze. "He wouldn't tell me how he got that either. My guess is Emma put up a hell of a fight."

I drained my glass of Lagavulin 16, the amber liquid burning all the way down. "Any of you seen her since?"

East answered first. "I used to go 'round the house regularly. But then Pamma Auntie moved them to America. What was that, five years ago? I haven't seen her since."

Drew shook his head. "No." He cleared his throat. "It was, uh, too painful."

I was going to be sick. The vomit threatened, and I had to ease down onto one of the leather chairs, dragging in long deep breaths.

Bridge's voice was low. "I check on them regularly. But since Emma told me to fuck right off, I haven't seen either of them."

I rubbed the back of my neck. We'd all failed her and her mother. Emma's words rattled around in my skull. *Why do you?*

"She was right. We all walked away. Toby died, and we all abandoned her." My gut knotted and bile threatened. "He was the best of us. He should have been by our sides. Instead, we all moved on."

Drew decided to forgo the glass and drank the scotch

straight from the bottle as he threw himself, still suited and boot-ed, across East's couch. "Hard to pretend all is right with the world with the evidence sitting in front of us," he muttered.

I swallowed around the lump in my throat. "Nothing has been right with the world since he died. Van Linsted was on over-watch that night. He should have protected him or something. Instead of facing repercussions for failing at his one job, he's in line to be fucking Director Prime. How is that for justice?"

"Fuck!" Bridge threw his glass, and it shattered against the wall.

East scowled. "Oi! What the fuck, mate?"

Bridge rounded on him. "Fucking Van Linsted. Bram always said if he had his way Toby and I would never have been Elite. And then he got his wish." For the first time since I'd known him, Bridge was well and truly shattered. Looked like I wasn't the only one gutted by seeing Emma again.

I scrubbed my hand down my face. "*We* failed him too. *I* pushed all of you to say yes. I was the one who saw family and power and legacy. Fucking bullshit. We're just as culpable as they were. And to make it worse, we all conveniently walked away from the Varmas."

"So what do we do now? Emma is going to keep trying to get to the Elite members. And she's going to get hurt in the pro-cess." East said.

He was right. Emma would keep going after them. And I could give two fucks if the Elite burned. They talked so much shit about brotherhood and family and bonds. But it was all lies. "We show her we're doing something about it."

Drew sat up. "What do you mean?"

"I mean, Bram Van Linsted has been living the charmed life. The life Toby should have had. If someone doesn't do some-thing, he'll be the next Director Prime. He stood there and did nothing to help Toby, and then our so-called brothers allowed Toby to be forgotten like he was nothing. So we're going to be the something that stops him."

East sat up straighter, the moonlight streaming through the floor-to-ceiling windows glinting off of his cufflinks. "So what are you saying?"

I met each of their gazes. "We're the something that's going to stop Bram Van Linsted. We're the something that's going to burn the Elite to the ground if we have to. For Toby."

CHAPTER 5

Livy
Present Day

I limped through the door with my shoes in my hand. Exhaustion permeated every cell as I forced one foot in front of the other. I'd taken off my shoes Britney Spears style. The good news was my feet were nice and cool. The bad news was they were now grimy. But at least I didn't have that dull, persistent ache going on.

At the curb, the police officer who had driven me home waited until I punched the code in for the front door before turning on his lights and pulling away.

When I shoved open the door, I found Dexter pacing. I didn't even make it past the foyer before he was on me. "Where the fuck have you been?" The scent of gin on his breath was strong.

"Hello to you too, Dexter."

"It's bloody nearly two o'clock in the morning."

"Believe me, I know. Perhaps you could hold your yelling for the morning."

His gaze skimmed over me. "Were you with someone?"

"Really, Dex?" Whenever he wanted to spin out, that was his favorite line of questioning. "We talked about this."

He sidestepped me, calling out, "Do you have my meds?"

I placed my shawl on the sideboard before turning to face him. "The chemist said the prescription doesn't renew until next week."

"You know I need them. My bloody hand hurts."

"You know how to resolve that. It's not my job to take care of you."

He frowned, lips parting like he wanted to argue. But he knew better. His therapist had been clear about drawing boundaries. It was a line not to cross.

"It's the least you can do. After all, *you* did this to me."

The guilt clawed at me, and I beat it back. I tilted my chin up. "No. *You* were too wasted to drive. So I drove and we had an *accident*. We agreed with Doctor Kaufman that you wouldn't throw that in my face if you wanted a second chance."

He stepped into my space, laying the stench of gin and sweat over me like a shroud. The guilt that accompanied it was the heaviest to maneuver under. He was right. He was in pain because of me. I *had* been driving that night. The night that had changed everything. But he couldn't talk to me any way he liked and get away with it.

He'd never put his hands on me. He must have known that would be my limit. But he *did* like to wield the guilt like a weapon.

My mother had really liked Dex. He liked to invoke her name when I was on the verge of giving up on him. But she'd often told me how happy she was that I had him so I wouldn't be alone when she died.

In the last six months, there had been moments daily that I'd considered walking out. But her last words to me haunted me. *We all need love. Don't throw it away.*

She was right. We all did need love. And I tended to

self-isolate. Without Dex and Telly, I'd go ages without socializing. So I tried. Relationship work was a lot of effort, but this was Dex. We loved each other. And thankfully, therapy was working… mostly.

"I do want that. I'm sorry. But I need you to do this. I have work."

"So do I, Dex. Not to mention I'm working on the book."

He rolled his eyes. "But my job is *important*. Actual high stakes. No one is going to lose their life savings if you don't get Kennedy's coffee. And you need to be realistic. You're not going to win a Pulitzer with that book."

The double whammy made my hands twitch to throw something. If I'd had the energy, I'd have screamed. I'd have let the rage nestled behind my sternum explode and consume everything in my path.

But I had nothing left to give. "Nice, Dex."

Before my mother died, she'd been working on a true crime book about the disappearance of one of her friends. When she'd died, I'd taken on the book. It helped me feel closer to her and acted as excellent grief therapy. And I'd come to find I actually loved the story telling. I felt *alive* when I was writing. I could see the pieces fit together in my mind, like a movie. Dex didn't understand why I needed to finish the book so badly. He saw it as another thing that dragged focus away from him and us.

He frowned as if suddenly seeing me for the first time. "Where were you? And why are you so disheveled?"

"Gee, thanks, Dexter. I'm all right, thanks for asking. Nothing that a hot bath and a soak won't fix. After all it was only a light mugging."

His face fell. "You were mugged?"

"Yep. A stellar end to a stellar evening."

He recoiled. "Oh, so this is my fault?"

"You vanished on me."

"Well, I needed to unwind, so I went up to the balcony for a smoke. And for the record, I didn't *abandon* you. I was talking to Mills and lost track of time."

I frowned at his lie. Doubt crept up my spine like a huntsman spider stalking its prey. He could well have been embroiled in a conversation with Mrs. Mills when I'd been looking for him, but he'd clearly tried to imply he'd been caught up with his boss.

In the morning. You can deal with this in the morning.

I was halfway up the stairs when I paused, remembering we were meant to go out on Thursday. "Don't forget, Thursday night is the thing for my mother to spread her ashes."

He sighed as if I was asking the world of him. "You sure you don't want to take Telly? It's not really my thing. I think I have physical therapy that night anyway."

For fuck's sake, was he really doing this? "Can't you move it?"

"Not really. I want to get better as quickly as possible. You want that too, right?"

I did want him to get better as quickly as possible, but this was for my mother. She'd been his biggest champion. "You're serious?"

"Look, let's chat about it later. Head on up for a bath. You look a wreck."

As I trudged up the stairs, I couldn't help but wonder if my mother was wrong about relationships. Surely, I was better off on my own.

@

Ben

The three of us convened in East's suite at the hotel. He'd taken one of the penthouse units as his own. At one time, we'd all lived in the hotels.

Eventually, Bridge had left bachelorhood for Belgravia Square. And when I'd become engaged to Lila, I'd bought two townhouses down the road from his and spent a million quid to renovate them into Covington House. But then my life with Lila had blown up, and I'd come back to the anonymity of bachelor life. I still had a staff to keep up that place, and every now and again I got it in my mind that I needed to make it a home... but then I didn't. What was the point with no one to share it with?

I didn't occupy a penthouse though. I had one of the corner loft units. Besides, it was more convenient to stay at the hotel. East's penthouse was fully lived in, unlike my loft. There were flashes of color everywhere. Art on the walls. Photographs by Xander Chase and Z Con. We'd actually gone to a Z Con exhibit in New York two years ago.

East was the sort of bloke who had colored pillows and candles and things. I'd never understood how he even knew or cared about that shit. On the shelves, he had photographs. So many of us, Drew, and Toby that I couldn't count them all. There were several of his mother and sister but none of this father. His place looked lived in.

My place was where I slept. His place was where I came to watch a football match or to hang out. It never even occurred to me to host football viewing parties at my place. I knew it was sterile, but I liked it that way. Minimal. Less to get attached to.

When we walked in, East tossed his keys onto the mantle and we all took up our usual positions. East grabbed his laptop and plopped himself dead center on the couch. I always picked the massive oversized leather chair, and Bridge always seemed to like the chair by the fireplace. But this time, he stood at the floor-to-ceiling windows, staring out over London.

East tapped away at the keys. "Okay. Let's see about the security cameras."

From the window, Bridge said, "I remember a woman in a red dress. There were a few people wearing red, but she was noticeable. Bloody thing was backless. Sexy as hell. Great arse."

I glowered at him. I didn't want him thinking about her arse.

Why not? You did.

And it was true. She had a phenomenal ass. Like a peach. I wanted to take a bite— *No. No. No. No. No. Get the drive and move on.*

Likely easier said than done. The chances that she wouldn't get nosy were slim, and it was going to get dangerous. The guilt ate at me, knowing she'd ask a good deal of questions and I wouldn't be able to give her answers.

East tapped away. "She didn't give you anything to go on?"

I shook my head. "Not a thing."

"Okay, there, I see her. She is talking to Fenton Mills and someone else. One sec… let facial rec do its thing. She's linked arms with Dexter Ford. He works for Mills at Mills and Crawford Investments."

I snorted at that. "What kind of name is Dexter Ford? Sounds like a git we might have gone to school with."

And then Bridge reminded me why we'd been mates all these years. He turned to me and nodded his head. "That's a knob's name if I ever heard one."

I gave him a nod of solidarity.

East chuckled. "Ah, okay, there we go. We have her. Her name is Olivia Ashong. Her mother was the Ghanaian ambassador to the United States for most of her youth, then she was eventually assigned to the UK. She was a diplomat for twenty years. Her father was English and died when she was nine. Her mother passed away six months ago."

I forced my face into neutrality. "Rough go." I kept staring at the photo with her and Ford and his hand dangerously close to her ass. Where *my* hand had been earlier that night.

My hands fisted and I forced them to unfurl. Didn't matter that I didn't know her. She felt like mine.

East scanned her information. "Oh, she's been with Ford for two years. As far as I can tell, they're not engaged."

My chest loosened. As if all of a sudden I could breathe. *Game on.* If he wasn't going to put a ring on it, she was mine for the taking.

East whistled low. "Well, what do you know?"

I sat up straighter.

He grinned. "It seems that we will have no problem finding Olivia Ashong."

Bridge frowned before heading over to the bar and pouring himself a whiskey. "Why is that?"

"Because she works for us. She's an admin to Kennedy Bright."

She had been under my nose all this time? "How long has she worked there?"

East held up a finger. "Looks like she started as a temp right around the time her mother died. And then Kennedy hired her on as a full-time executive assistant three months ago."

"Okay, great. I'll make the approach and get back the data." I was going to approach her about a whole lot more too, like why I was in a perpetual state of semi arousal just thinking about her.

East pursed his lips as he slid a glance over his laptop. "I think I should make the approach. You already fucked it up, mate."

My brows rose as I took the drink Bridge handed me

"Say what?" The hell I was going to allow him anywhere near her. Not with him looking like he could be the next Becks. No way, no how was that going to happen.

He didn't seem to get the memo from my death-glare eyes. "Mate, you fucked it up by letting her see you in Van Linsted's office. You flubbed the pass. I think you're done."

He was the one who was going to be done if he didn't back off. "Now, just wait a minute. I made the best decision I could in the moment. And as for letting her see me, she was in the fucking closet. There wasn't much to be done."

We both glanced at Bridge, and he shook his head. "I'm not in this one. You two sort it out."

I pushed out of my chair to see what East was staring at. And then I saw it. There was a photo from the event when she was turning and looking over her shoulder at someone. Her dark skin glowed under the golden light. Even in the photo, her eyes spoke to me. She was absolutely stunning.

Her hair had been pulled back up her neck, with a few tendrils escaping. Skin the color of a fawn, high cheekbones, enormous almond-shaped eyes with lashes that fanned her cheeks. Fuck, she was beautiful.

East sat back and crossed his arms. "It makes more sense for me to approach her."

I laughed. "Over my dead body. She doesn't know you. She'll recognize me."

East pointed a finger at me. "You see the look on your face right there? You're already distracted by her. We made a pact, for Emma, for Toby... No more distractions by this side shit. We owe it to them."

"I'm not distracted by *anybody*, ever. I will make the approach. We had a connection." Total bollocks. I was ready and willing to kill East if he thought he was getting anywhere near Olivia Ashong.

I could see Bridge's smug smirk behind his whiskey glass as he chuckled. East didn't even bother to hide his laugh. "Oh yeah, sure. If you think you can make it work, Casanova, make it work. We need that drive. And we need to figure out if we can trust her or not. Right now, she's an unknown factor that could be dangerous to us. To this whole plan."

"Yeah, yeah. I hear you. We'll get it back."

We didn't have any other choice.

CHAPTER 6

Ben

Finding Olivia Ashong had been easy enough. After all, she worked in my bloody building.

And somehow you missed her all this time?

How many times had I passed her in the hallways or ridden with her in the elevator and just never noticed her before? Missed those eyes on me. Missed the catch in her breath.

No. You would have noticed her.

Those eyes would've locked me in place even if she hadn't been wearing that devil of an eye-catching dress. East was right. I had other reasons for wanting to be the one to make the approach. I certainly didn't want *him* to be the one. I didn't usually get attached to women. There was a very good reason for that and a hell of a reason to be wary of this one.

Alas, all the rationality in the world couldn't calm the buzzing in my brain at the thought of possibly seeing her again. It hadn't stopped the dreams of her scent as I tossed and turned all night. And my rational functioning brain had apparently zero control over my body that morning when I'd managed to drag my arse out of bed.

Do this and get it over with.

I needed that drive back, and I was prepared to give her whatever she wanted to make that happen. Thanks to East, I knew enough about her background to know she was overqualified for her job, so I'd start there and stop somewhere short of the bloody moon.

The scent hit me first, crawling under my skin. Making me remember her little moan. Her office was meticulous. Overly so. Everything had its place, and nothing was out of it. She has this row of pens lined up so perfectly that I couldn't resist the urge to nudge one askew.

She had an interior office, so no massive wall of windows, but she did have one window letting in the light. And on her desk, the only personal item was a photo of her and a woman who looked like the older version of her with a complexion several shades darker. They both wore bathing suits and life vests and held paddles over their heads while laughing like loons.

It was an image of pure unadulterated joy.

When was the last time you felt like that?

Clearly, whatever they'd been doing, probably paddle boarding, had been a hell of an adventure because they'd ended up soaking wet but triumphant.

I had to grin at that. She looked so happy. And I could tell from the photo that she laughed with her whole body. Was it throaty like her raspy voice suggested?

There was nothing else personal in the office. It was almost too sterile. As though if she chose to leave her office tomorrow, all she would take was that picture and be done with it. Always ready to run.

And that was how she found me, examining the one personal item in her office as I tried to glean as many important details as I could from that one image. That woman, whoever she was, meant the world to her. That much I knew.

"Excuse me, what are you doing in my office?"

Ah, that voice, grabbing me by the balls, forcing me to pay attention.

I'd woken up that morning with a raging hard-on just thinking about approaching her, what I was going to say and how I was going to say it. I could walk in and demand that she give me what I needed, or I could ask her nicely. Or I could try and coax it out of her, make it good for the both of us. Would she make that same keening moan she'd made in the closet?

Except for the small problem of her boyfriend.

Instead, she'd caught me unaware, so all I could do was turn slowly at the sound of her voice. When our gazes locked, I found her standing, one hand on her hip, one wrapped around a laptop. Her hair that had been straightened and sleek for the fundraiser was now pinned neatly back into a bun. She wore simple studs in her ears, minimal makeup, a charcoal gray pencil skirt paired with a prim silk top, and the look was totally buttoned-down. The vamp of the other night was tucked away neatly.

I almost liked this version of her better. I could make this version dirty.

There was something about her direct stare that hit me straight in the sternum, and it took longer than I liked to force my brain to work.

Nope. Focus. Get the drive.

I took several steps toward her and watched with respect and a little pride as she held her ground and even lifted her chin a little. "Just the woman I was hoping to find. You know, your scent has been lingering in my mind."

That's it, pour on the charm.

Her dark eyes went wide at that. But she quickly schooled her response into one of indifferent composure. The only thing that hinted to any fun in her personality were the buttons on her blouse. Looking closely, I noticed each one was a different emoji. But you would have to be super close to notice. I probably should've taken a step back, but I didn't budge.

"You still haven't told me what you're doing in my office?"

I lifted a brow. "Oh, this is how you're playing it. I have to say I'm surprised. You're going to pretend you don't recognize me. And I thought I'd made a memorable impression." I leaned forward to make my point. Rookie mistake, because once I was that close, I needed to be closer. Still though, I doubled down. "I was the one with my hand on your arse. My lips and your skin are very well acquainted."

Her little sharp intake of breath gave her away at the moment of recognition. Then she squinted and slid her glasses on. Once they were settled on the bridge of her nose, her eyes flared wide. "Oh, I remember. I've been trying to forget."

Then she swallowed hard and blinked several times before directly meeting my gaze.

Holy shit. That penetrative gaze stirred something deep inside me. Something I'd buried long ago. I quickly pushed down the unknown yet somehow familiar emotion.

"You sure? Because the way your pupils have dilated, I'm fairly certain you've been remembering... a lot." I gave her a sly grin. "Does remembering make your knickers wet?"

Her lips parted like maybe she might tell me they were indeed wet right now. Oh, fuck me, even better if she didn't have any on. But instead, she pursed her lips and lifted her chin. "I'm sure you would love to know, but I, it seems, unlike you, have work to do. So can you get the hell out?"

I lifted a brow. So she was going to make me work for it.

Fine by me. I liked a good challenge. "I suppose you thought you'd never see me again."

"Well, I had thought that you would be in jail. And I didn't know why I would need to see you again. At least not at first."

So she had it. "At least you're aware of why I'm here then?"

She frowned, a light crease forming between her brows, and her lips pursed. "I had originally wanted to see if you were okay. Security didn't look too gentle. But then I realized you'd used me to smuggle something out of the estate, so my feelings turned less charitable and I'd hoped not to see you again."

The spark of fire in her eyes had me grinning. "There you are. The mouthy little imp from Saturday night. I will admit to liking you being concerned about me."

"Don't get too excited. What do you want?"

Charm, be charming. "I'd like back what you have of mine."

She laughed then. "So you tracked me down. And how did you do that anyway? Was there a tracking chip in that drive?"

No, but that was a hell of an idea. "I need the flash drive, and I'm prepared to give you something in exchange."

"Let me get this straight, you used me, and yet I'm supposed to be thrilled you found me? What's on the drive?"

"Nothing you need to worry about. You hand it over and we're done."

"Or what?"

I frowned. "What do you mean 'or what'?"

"I hand it over, or what?"

"Why wouldn't you hand it over?"

"Because I don't know what's on it. And I don't know why you were stealing it. I mean, what kind of thief are you that you would hand off something valuable, unless you thought I could be manipulated after the fact?"

What? No. "I'm not a thief, and it's complicated. And I'm

certainly not telling you what's on it. But thanks for telling me you haven't already tried to look at it."

Her brow furrowed, and I wanted to smooth the worry from her expression. *What the fuck is wrong with you mate? Head in the game.*

"I don't think I can help you. The kind of help you probably want is not something that I can provide. I'm not the kind of woman that sneaks into off-limits, top-secret locations and hides in the closet with a stranger. Saturday night was an anomaly. I don't know how you found me, but you can be on your merry way. I'm handing that drive off to the police."

I gritted my teeth but forced my lips into a semblance of a smile. "Well, you're pretty easy to find. Your face was all over CCTV of the event."

She swallowed hard. "Am I in trouble? How much was that statue worth? Oh God, tell me. I need to know so I can figure out how I'm going to pay it back."

"The statue? What are you talking about?"

She blinked at me. "This isn't about the statue?"

I folded my arms. "No, but now I feel like I need the whole story."

"Oh, you're not going to get it. You can go." She tried to sidestep me, but I blocked her. "I'm sorry, you need something from me and yet you still haven't told me exactly who you are."

I lifted a brow. "Sorry, I'm Ben. You're Olivia. Now, about that flash drive, love…"

"You slipped it to me on purpose. You didn't want anyone to find it. So, until you tell me who you are, what you want with it, or what's on it, I'm not giving it back."

"Right." It was probably time to pull out the big guns. "Okay, I said my name is Ben. Maybe I should finish that for you. Ben Covington."

She frowned. "Why do I know that name?"

I couldn't help but chuckle. "Well, you should know it because I own the building we're standing in."

If there was a picture of a cartoon character with eyes going wide in total shock and disbelief, mouth going agape, that would be Olivia. "You're *that* Ben? Ben Covington."

I nodded slowly. "Yup, that's me."

"But what were you doing at the fundraiser? And why were you hiding? What is on that flash drive?"

The questions came out in rapid-fire, staccato sentences. "Jesus, you talk a lot. Look, all that doesn't matter right now. What does matter is that I need it back. I'm even willing to give you something for the drive. I took a look at your resume. I don't know why you're hiding out here as Kennedy's executive assistant, but you need to be in operations. Your resume warrants it. You're good at what you do, and I've looked at your employee evaluations. Kennedy has nothing but amazing things to say about you, so how would you like a job working for me? I need a new operations director, a right hand. Not to worry, there will be no hint of impropriety. You'll report directly to Jessa Ainsley, so you don't have to worry about all your fantasies about where you would have let me touch you."

She stared at me. I would have expected most people to jump up and down, be thrilled, be excited. Not Olivia Ashong. She stared with a gaze so intense I started to shift in my discomfort. "I hate to be the one to break it to you, but you're not that good. I've already forgotten the whole thing. But I am curious, why would you give me this job?"

Oh, but I was that good. "Because until Saturday night, I didn't even know you worked here, which means that you're invisible. You can't get promoted if you're invisible. I don't know exactly why you took this job with Kennedy, but you are capable of doing so much more, and I can offer you that opportunity."

"So, just like that, without a proper interview or anything, you would give me the kind of job that pays a ridiculous amount of money to get that thing back?"

"Whatever you want, yeah. How about it?"

"I say until you can tell me what it is, or why it's so critical, or even better, why I shouldn't turn it into the police, my answer is no."

@

Livy

Ben had been right in my office that morning when he'd talked about my wet panties. They'd been soaked. He'd been so damn smug. No way I was letting him know he affected me. And besides, I was with Dex. Ben Covington was merely a little harmless fantasy.

Right. So that's why you're running to Telly's for a second opinion?

To be fair, it wasn't the *only* reason, even though I knew what I was doing was a mistake.

Well, I'd made a series of them starting with turning down flipping Ben Covington for a job. I was out of my mind. The series of decisions I'd made since going to that stupid fundraiser had sent me on this path, and I wasn't sure I could course correct.

What the hell was wrong with me?

Of all the stupid things you've ever done, Liv, this takes the cake. But like my mother always said, some mistakes had to be made.

It wasn't like I didn't know I was making one. I knew the moment I made a copy of the flash drive. Even when I'd brazenly told him he couldn't have it, I'd known I was going to give it to him. But he'd used me, and I needed to know why and how much trouble I was in.

When I saw him in my office, some primal, feminine part of me had wanted to preen. He was dangerous with a capital D. And I was going to need to stay the hell away. But boy had I wanted to lean into his sandalwood scent.

I'd wanted to do other things to his towering frame too. I was pretty sure I needed a grappling hook to climb that mountain, and there was a part of me that was totally into that.

Nope. Stop it.

I had to stop thinking about him. Those ice-blue eyes. The charcoal vest over the crisp white shirt. The swatch of cerulean silk in his tie that accentuated the color of his eyes. God, I had problems. *One,* I had a boyfriend. *Two,* Ben Covington was possibly the most handsome man I'd ever seen on the planet. *Three,* he'd used me.

There was a reason he'd done it, and I needed to know why. I couldn't explain it, but I hoped knowing would buy me some assurances. He was willing to give me a triple-pay upgrade. He owned the place, but no one did that unless they were desperate.

As I furtively glanced over my shoulder, I skipped up the stairs of the waterfront flats toward Telly's place. She basically lived above Vauxhall tube station. After work, I'd taken the tube from Soho and headed straight to her place, knowing with every step that I was making a grave error.

But if I was making a mistake, I knew Telly was the friend to go with me. I was about to do something that was probably going to get me into trouble, but I couldn't let it go. He was hiding something. Something that might be important for me to know. Like a scab, I couldn't stop picking at it. I had to know if this was going to blow up in my face. I had to have answers.

At Telly's, the closed entryway with keypad access didn't

stop me. I pulled out my set of keys and opened the door. There were several people on the lift with me as I headed up to the third floor. With each step toward Telly's flat, I wondered what had gotten into me.

I knocked at Telly's door, and it took a minute before I heard her footsteps on the other side. When she yanked it open, she was out of breath. "Hey, you gorgeous slag. Give me a minute."

"Hey, Telly."

She laughed. "Come right in. The look on your face clearly says, 'This calls for wine.' Tell me, is this a breakup surprise? Don't tease me."

I groaned. "Telly."

"Okay. Sorry," she grumbled. She stepped back to let me in and then closed the door behind me before she ran into her room. "Let me hit save on what I'm working on."

"I'll get the wine." I practically lived there, so I knew exactly where to find it.

In her kitchen, I reached into the fridge. I knew I'd find a Moscato in there, because Telly, like me, didn't actually like real wine. She liked the sweet stuff that tasted more like fruit juice than anything. I uncorked it and poured two hefty glasses. It was our shared joke all through Uni. We'd never be sophisticated enough for the real stuff. She'd always said it kept her real and then proceeded to laugh at all the wine snobs who insisted they could taste every single flavor and flower. She claimed that in her bartending days she often served cheap wine and no one could tell the difference.

I was inclined to believe her.

When she jogged back into the living area, she gave me a smile. "I love you. And I'm so glad you're here. Sorry about the break-up comment. But what the hell? Is this about the mugging Saturday night?"

I laughed because only Telly could say that to me. Since Uni, we'd vowed to only tell each other the truth. The side effect of that promise was that now she could read me like a book.

I reached into the pocket of my trench. I hadn't even bothered to take it off. The chill from the misty rain outside was still running through me. That was London in the early spring for you. I pulled out the drive and laid it on the kitchen counter. "No, this isn't about the mugging. I cancelled my credit card. The police are not hopeful it'll ever be found. But that's not what this is about. This flash drive, can you find out what's on it for me?"

Her gaze slid to the flash drive, to my face, then back to the flash drive. "Where did you get this mysterious drive?"

"Uhm.., it's a long story. But I couldn't read it. I figure you can do some hackery magic or something."

She laughed then. "You recognize I can't hack everything, right?"

"I know that. But I need you to hack into that." I drank two large gulps of my wine. "It's important."

I stared at the flash drive, wondering what the hell I was doing. In the last two days, I had been afraid, worried, curious... and free. These were feelings I had been searching for half my life. And that energy had fueled my writing. It was like the adrenaline I still carried from that night had unlocked my creative center.

Ever since my mother died, there had been this empty part of me, and it tasted like dissatisfaction. It was eating at me. It ate away the carefully constructed life that I'd told myself I wanted and what I understood as living.

There had been an edge of danger, a spike of adrenaline, the fear of getting caught. God, I sounded insane even to myself. But I'd felt a little more... *alive*. And I'd certainly felt that when I found Ben in my office. Like suddenly something had turned on all my machinery.

It was terrifying but also exhilarating. I wasn't a complete idiot. I knew my therapist would tell me that I was displaying risky behavior. While I was exhilarated, I was putting myself in danger. And before I took things even further, I needed to know what the hell I was dealing with.

Telly crossed her arms. "Is it going to require more *wine-ing*?"

I nodded. "Yeah. I'll grab the bottle and turn on the heat lamp."

She met me a minute later with some chocolates and cheese. "Well, you know, we have to pretend that we're not just having wine for dinner."

I nodded solemnly. "That's a good point."

Once we were settled in with the heater blasting and our gazes trained on the flames, she spoke. "So, what the hell have you gotten yourself into, Liv? You don't come to me with random flash drives. Something is happening."

I chewed my bottom lip, worried about how much to say. "Remember the thing with the Viking in the closet? And how I felt alive, and you know... generally, all the shenanigans?" She nodded slowly. "Well, the part I left out before, you know, I got mugged... he passed me something."

"He passed you what? Like chlamydia?"

I snorted wine up my nose. That was my fault for taking a sip while she was talking. I knew Telly was prone to outrageousness.

It felt good to laugh and release some of the tension coiling between my shoulders. "No, I told you I didn't *bang* him in the closet."

"Hey, no judgment here. Not like you don't deserve a good bang in a closet, to be fair."

I opened my mouth to defend Dexter, but then, well, she was right. I did deserve it. Since Mom died, he hadn't laid a hand on me. And when I initiated, he'd make some kind of an excuse not to do it. But that was another problem for another day. "So anyway, I told you we hid in the closet, and then he went his way and I went mine and returned to the party. Then he was in a scuffle with security after he was in some kind of altercation with Bram Van Linsted."

"So, he was having an altercation with Van Linsted and security came. How did you get involved?"

"Well, I stopped the security guys as they were dragging him off Van Linsted, trying to tell them to let him go. They were trying to pin him down, he fought their hold, I went too close, and then all of us took a tumble."

She frowned. "You left that out on Saturday."

"I know. It was something out of like a hilarious blooper-reel from some movie. Like something Anne Hathaway would act in."

"You know what? You could easily be the brown version of Anne Hathaway."

I grinned. "You think? I guess my boobs are good enough. I'll take it."

She nodded. "Okay, so you fell. What's the big deal?"

"The big deal is *that* flash drive. He slid it into my purse, as if he didn't want anyone to find it in his possession."

She leaned forward, her glass of wine cradled between both palms. "Are you sure *he* did it?"

"Yes. I went to work this morning, and there he was, in my office."

Her mouth fell open. "What?"

"I know. He was standing there like he owned the place. Gorgeous. And he was wearing a vest and a white shirt with the sleeves rolled up, showcasing some discreet ink. And his forearms were thick and strong, and it was just…"

"Right. Yes. So you told me how he was in your office, and his forearms were exposed. Did he bend you over the desk, because… yes. I've been looking for a romance too, you know, but I'll use your life as a substitute for now."

"Stop it. You have Carmen. He didn't bend me over the desk, but he offered me a job."

"Okay, back up. This is the same bloke who hid with you in a closet, whispered sexy nothings in your ear like, 'stop moving, be quiet, stay here,' while you were grinding against his very big dick. And then he slips you something, nothing inappropriate, of course, just, you know, a flash drive that could be virtually anything. And then on Monday, two days later, he's in your office."

"Yes."

"Is there more?"

It all sounded ridiculous when she said it out loud. "Um, yes. As it turns out, he's my boss, Ben Covington."

Telly's head snapped back, and then she eased herself to the back of her chair. "Jesus fucking Christ, the *billionaire*?"

"Yeah, apparently. London Lords, it's him and two friends."

"I know that. They're in the business papers all the time. And they go through women like they're candy."

"I suppose I need to catch up on my reading. How do you know this?"

"Look, I have no need for cock, but that doesn't mean I can't admire the gorgeousness it's attached to. And game recognizes game."

I shook my head and licked my lips. I sounded like an idiot. How could I not know? I'd been lucky to get this job. I'd said yes without knowing much about the company. And between the accident and loosing Mom, I'd been… well, complacent.

Telly, ever my bestie, was maybe a little too kind. "Well, you've had a lot to deal with lately. I could imagine you not paying attention to who your employers are."

"Yeah, well anyway, there he was, wanting the flash drive back. And in exchange, he offered me a better job."

"Ah jeez, this is a slippery slope. Do you want to take the job?"

Hell yes. "I think I do. Look, the job is right up my alley. I can stop being an executive assistant. But I can't shake the feeling of being used. What if I'd been arrested getting that thing out of there? And what if it's some kind of corporate espionage?"

Telly chewed her bottom lip. "Look, I'll have a look at it and see if I can decipher what's on it. But you be careful with a man like that. He's a billionaire. What's on that flash drive could be billionaire things."

"Billionaire things?"

"Sure. You know what I mean. It could be about some corporate espionage, political intrigue, money, women, drugs, jewels."

"Yeah, I know. He had it at the Van Linsted fundraiser, and he was doing something in that room. But I don't know what."

"I hear you. But be careful. I'm worried that he found you."

"He said he checked CCTV. Maybe taking the job *is* a good idea. I can keep an eye on the situation."

"Hon, I'm not sure that's wise. Why run *to* danger?"

She had a point. Why was I pushing this? "I have to know, Telly. I just... I need to."

She sighed. "Okay. So, this new job... Will you be working directly with him?"

"Yeah."

Telly drained her glass. "Liv, you need to be careful. We don't know what the hell we're dealing with."

"That sounds like you're with me."

"Honey, I'm always with you. Even if it means women's prison. Who knows, I might meet the love of my life."

CHAPTER 7

Ben

"**W**here are we on the drive?"

I glowered at Bridge as I stared up at him from East's couch. The sun had long set. And we could see St. James Park and Westminster lit like twinkle lights as cars and buses darted around and tourists cavorted and enjoyed London nightlife.

"Working on it." I knew they weren't going to be happy. Hell, *I* wasn't happy. I still couldn't believe she had said no to me. No one said no to me. I usually charmed them into compliance. But not her. What burned the most was how wrong I'd read her. Going by the closet, she'd felt that instant hum and buzz between us, like you could hear the electricity.

But in her office, she'd been much more reserved. Cool and distant. Like the woman who'd moaned and molded herself to me had never existed.

I'd been so out of sorts after striking out with Miss ass-so sweet-I-want-to-take-a-bite-out-of-it, that I'd asked for lunch with my father. Clearly, I hadn't been in my right mind. But at least I wouldn't be coming to the damn meeting completely empty handed. So finally, something the old man was good for. I only hoped what he had told me would bear fruit.

East lifted a brow. "Mate, working on it? Everything hinges on you getting that drive. Do I need to remind you that Van Linsted already has a head start with whatever is on that drive?"

"I know, and I'm *working* on it."

Drew came in from the kitchen holding a bacon butty. "What he means is he struck out."

I scowled at my mate. "With the best restaurants just downstairs that will deliver, you're eating a bacon butty? And what it means is that there's work to be done. I'll make it happen."

Drew took a bite of his sandwich as he flipped me off.

East ran a hand through his hair. "We're not playing around here. You want me to do this?"

I dragged my feet off the coffee table and sat up, leaning forward on my elbows and pinning him with a direct glare. "Do you really think I'll give up? Even if I have to steal it from her, I'll do it. I was the one who walked into that fundraiser and made it happen. So when I tell you I will get it back, what does that mean?" I wasn't used to being questioned. They knew me. They knew how single minded and determined I could be. Not to mention if East went near Olivia, I might consider hurting him. But I kept that to myself.

Bridge, uncharacteristically, acted as peacemaker. "East, mate, he'll get it. I know he will. No one wants to get payback for Toby more than Ben does."

I ground my teeth. I knew East wanted revenge. So did Bridge, and so did Drew. There was no one-upmanship when it came to our pain. "Sorry. Things didn't go well the first time. But I have this. Don't worry. But even more pressing, I had lunch with my father today."

Bridge and East exchanged glances. Ever since the Lila

situation, my father and I hadn't exactly been on speaking terms, so likely they were wondering if I was pretending he wasn't still alive. I had been, but I needed information, so I'd swallowed my pride.

"I asked for a little background and got more than I bargained for. He didn't really tell me anything we didn't already know about the Van Linsteds, but what he did bring to light is how much of an uphill battle we have. For starters we'll need to make friends and influence people. With two hundred members of the Elite, it will take too much time to talk to them all. We need the Five to assist and sway opinion in the preliminary member votes for Director Prime."

The Five were the most influential members of the Elite. They were hand selected by the senior council. Terms were for life once selected. The Five each had ten votes, so physically, they could change the outcome of a Director Prime vote. But also, their job was to sway and influence *within* the Elite. They were never supposed to reveal their identities, and if they were compromised, they were to step down and allow the senior council to select another. Each member of the Five was an expert in politics and negotiation, and in their early days, each would have excelled at all aspects of Elite training.

There were procedures for stepping down because of being compromised and in the case of death. But since the terms were for life and there was such secrecy, members of senior council having to select a new member was a rarity. And as members of senior council served ten-year terms, it was rare for any member to know the identity of more than two members of the Five at a time.

Rumor was that there were provisions in case all five members died in a freak accident. But as that had never happened, there was no one who could know who they all were.

"Not news, I know. Here's something that is. We need to put forth a candidate to run against Bram. It's not enough to make sure he's not elected. We must suggest a suitable replacement. That's how the Elite works. The Five need someone to point the membership to. Bram's running unopposed at the moment."

East said, "So we're fucked."

"I wouldn't say that exactly. Dear old Dad might have finally done one thing for me after all these years. He let it slip that Rowan Downs is one of the Five."

Bridge's mouth fell open. "Holy shit."

East just gave me a satisfied nod and then pressed a button so that a massive screen descended from the ceiling, covering the TV. Another couple of taps on his keyboard, and our plan projected on screen so we could all see it. "Okay, so Benny boy has just given us all some hope. As you know, the name of the game is vengeance. Phase one, Ben getting the download from Bram's hard drive and phone is in progress. The next step is to identify the Five. Thanks to Ben, we have one name. But likely, so does Bram. If not more."

The drive Olivia was holding hostage had everything, the history of council votes, meeting notes, and travel schedules. Vital information that would at least help us narrow down who the other members of the Five might be. The Five were supposed to be a method of checks and balances on the Elite, just in case power was corrupted. If we could find out who the rest were before Bram did, we could find leverage to get them to block a vote for Bram as Director Prime and loosen the Van Linsted stranglehold on power.

Easy now, who is your viable candidate?

One problem at a time. We'd figure something out.

Blocking Bram was just the first step. I intended to destroy the family.

East continued. "We have to assume that since his father is currently Director Prime and the senior council has inducted a new member into the Five in recent years, Bram Van Linsted already has at least one of the names. So we're starting on our back feet."

Bridge nodded. "Yeah, but Marcus is an old-timer, and as much as he wants Bram in power, wouldn't he just work the back channels for him? I find it hard to believe he'd give up the name. You remember Marcus's training exercises. A gentleman above all, private matters stay private, and secrets whispered are never revealed. He's a bloody true believer. No way he'd give Bram a name."

Drew took a sip of his scotch as he rattled the keys in his pocket with his hand. "He might not have given him a name, but I'll bet Bram still has it. Remember, Bram's specialty is politics. He had the same clandestine training as us, and he knows how to play the game. As much as we would like him to be, he's not a complete idiot. So he might have found another way to get the other names."

East nodded and turned back to the monitor. "Okay, so assume we get the drive and the names. We're going to need leverage. As much as possible. The Five should be above reproach, but that doesn't mean they haven't buried some secrets and skeletons somewhere. No one's going to do something for nothing."

I rolled my shoulders. "It's entirely possible that no one else wants another twenty-year reign of the Van Linsteds. Let's not forget Bram's got a brother, Miles. He's younger, but I imagine he's around to take up a term right after his brother. Then we'll never be free. And there are others who see the writing on the wall. We're not entirely alone."

East nodded. "No, but let's not assume that the Van Linsteds don't have something to offer. Because they do."

He was right. At the core of it, most people were greedy and would do anything to have their names associated with the most powerful families in the world, including sell their souls. "All right, so we get the drive back and get the names. What next?"

East nodded. "We also need to assume we're being watched. I checked surveillance. We've got Ilya Tosca outside the Soho Branch. Bridge, Drew, I've spotted Joseph Link and Terrence Randolph, both known fixers, outside your homes. Maybe the Elite is always watching. Maybe they are paying attention because of the anniversary of Toby's death. They are in fact watching our every move, so we need to be aware of the moves we make and how they'll be perceived. We don't want to clue anyone in on what we're doing."

Bridge had started to pace as he tried to walk through the issue. "Downs is going to be a problem too. He's notoriously reclusive. Only turns up for the major votes. If any of us take a trip to Oz to speak to him, they'll know."

East nodded. "Let me work on that. He's an art lover. We might be able to lure him to us."

"Okay, in the meantime, one of us needs to run interference with Bram now. If we can get any insight into what he's doing next, that'll help," I said.

Bridge stepped forward. "I'll do it."

The pit fell out of my stomach. No way I could ask Bridge to do that. "You hate him. He knows you hate him."

He shrugged. "Maybe, but we need to keep an eye on him."

Drew agreed with him. "I hate to say it, but we do need someone watching him. I could, but any of my dealings with him jeopardizes my father, which I don't think we want to do because it would upset the balance of the voting seats before we have time to establish who the Five are."

I threw up my hands. "Bridge is my best mate. How is anyone going to believe we've fractured now?"

Everyone was silent for a moment. Then East shrugged. "Well, actually, that's not hard to do. We just make sure that footage of you two arguing outside of the nick is circulated. A few strategic placements where we lay some breadcrumbs of discontent and a fracturing of your relationship. We make them think that he is on their side."

Bridge had clearly given this some thought. "If it gets us close enough to provide you some shield and cover, then I'll do it. We need as much time as possible before the Van Linsteds figure out what the fuck we're doing." Bridge said.

I shook my head. "Bridge, mate, this isn't you. You're going to hate every moment of it."

He met my gaze darkly. "I've hated every moment without Toby. For him, I can do this."

"But you're going to be in the viper's nest. You're going to have to pretend you want to be there."

"Let me do it." His silvery gray eyes were intense, focused. He wanted to do this. It was how he was going to make the Van Linsteds pay. I couldn't begrudge him that, so I nodded. "Yeah, all right. But we'll have to come up with a plan to make sure everyone believes that there's a rift between us."

East nodded. "Like I said, easy peasy. We'll also have Bridge feed some strategic information to them about Ben's movements, what he's doing. We'll set the narrative instead of them setting it."

I glanced around at my friends. "So we're for real doing this?"

East nodded. "Looks that way. We just have to make sure to get that drive back."

"All right, as soon as we have it back, we'll hit the ground running. Let's start getting justice for Toby."

©

ℓLivy

"Kennedy Bright's office, how may I assist you?"

I didn't know what in the world had happened, but everyone was on a tear and had questions for Kennedy this morning. She was the Global Head of New Business and Corporate Affairs. It seemed that there were new client issues left and right.

When she called me into her office, I smiled and gave her a stack of messages, my notebook up and ready. "Hey, Kennedy, what do you need?"

"It's wild today, isn't it? It's like they can sense when I'm off the phone then the next person calls."

I puffed out a breath as I took a seat, tucking one of my wayward curls behind my ear, but all it did was spring free again. "I was just going to say it's like Mercury in retrograde or something."

She chuckled then got straight to business. I'd always admired her. When I'd started at London Lords six months ago, she was very clear with me that I was overqualified to be her executive assistant, but that if I stuck with her for a year, she'd help me get hired in Operations, which is what I'd been doing before.

"I got a call from one of our CEOs, Ben Covington."

I groaned then pursed my lips. Unfortunately, my body also clenched, remembering the timbre of his voice. "I wondered when he'd reach out to you."

She smiled. "He seems to think that you would make a fantastic operations director."

What was I supposed to say? I wanted to move up, but I wanted it to be on my merit. "Would I now?"

"Oh, but I think you would. Why didn't you tell me you applied for a position on his team? Jessa Ainsley is terrific. You'll learn a lot from her."

My mouth fell open as I tried to process her words. "What? I didn't apply."

She blinked in surprise. "Well, that's the impression he gave." She narrowed her eyes, her gaze more shrewdly assessing now. "Do you know him personally?"

I saw where she was going with this. "No, I do not." Sniffing me and having his hand on my ass notwithstanding.

"Oh god, he's good. He made it seem like you'd gone looking, knowing full well I'd be more inclined to give you up that way than if he just poached you."

"I always keep the resume fresh like you suggested, and it is on the company server, but I absolutely did not go looking for another opportunity. I promised you a year."

"Oh, you're not in any trouble. I know how he works. He'll get what he wants by any means necessary."

"Determined, isn't he?"

"That he is, but I think this is great. Honestly, in the last few months you've shown exemplary organizational skills. I gave you the same spiel I give everyone at the beginning. You know how it is... some twenty-year-old intern walks in here and thinks that she should be wearing her power suits and be in charge within a month. Meanwhile, she knows nothing about the business except 'Oh my god. My socials.'" Somehow, despite being British, she pulled off a perfect Kardashians impression.

I couldn't help but snort a laugh. "I know. That's not me though."

"And I see that. I think it's a great opportunity for you."

I ground my teeth at that. "I appreciate that, but I'm not sure what I want to do yet."

"Well, give it sincere thought. Working on Ben's team is a huge coup. Jessa is fantastic. I think you'll report directly to her."

He was trying to force my hand, the jackass. Fine, if he wanted to play hardball, then so could I. "Well, it's nice to have your support. Thank you."

"Of course. You are far too smart to be sitting in my front office for any length of time."

"Thank you. I admire you a lot."

"Same here. Now, if we could just fix my dating life, then the world would be perfect."

I laughed. "Are you still trying the apps?"

"You know what, don't write me any more profiles. The last one you wrote me was so good I got all these guys who were trying to have intellectual conversations with me but didn't seem to want me for my body at all."

"What happened to the perfect man right in the middle? Where is he?"

She laughed. "Not anywhere I can see. Feels like I was jinxed a long time ago in love. Doesn't matter though. What matters today is we have good news for you. I'm really proud. I've loved having you on my team, and I'm sure it'll work out. Whatever you decide, just let me know and then I'll work out a transition with Ben."

"Thank you. I appreciate that."

There was nothing else to say. Looked like Ben was going to get his way.

CHAPTER 8

Ben

We had a plan. We just had to execute. But no one could execute a damn thing until I had the drive, and so far, I was coming up empty.

I threw my stress ball up in the air as I leaned back in my seat. I needed to figure out a secondary approach and fast, because if she took it to someone who could figure out what she had, it was risky for everyone. Especially her. I had to find a way to get the advantage.

So, what? Be her friend?

When was the last time I had been friends with a woman? It wasn't even an option. She was in my system.

Never.

I loved women. Women were beautiful. Certainly engaging. But having some kind of a long-term relationship with someone I wasn't sleeping with would be complicated and not on my top ten list of things to do.

Ever since Lila, I'd kept a healthy emotional distance from the fairer sex.

Not that a woman from five years ago should be clouding

my judgment at all. She just informed so many of my interactions with women. So being friends with a woman I wanted wasn't going to work. I wasn't capable.

A knock sounded on my office door, and I assumed I'd find East or Bridge jamming their big frame inside my doorway, but instead I found oh-so-delicate Olivia. Her dark eyes met mine levelly, and my fucking dick twitched. Traitor. "Had a change of mind, love?"

She just scowled at me. From behind her back, she produced the flash drive. "You want this?"

I blinked as I sat up straighter. "Yes, I do." I wanted so much more too. Like her pretty mouth around my cock. I kept that to myself though.

She wagged her finger back and forth at me. "Easy does it. Possession and all that."

I crossed my arms. "Fine. What do you want?"

"Well, I want you to tell me why this is so important."

"I can't."

"Is it something illegal?"

"All that's on that disk is information. You are just going to have to trust me."

"Trust you? I don't even know you."

My skin hummed. Didn't she feel that? Was I the only one suffering? I took a sip of coffee from my mug. "Yes you do. Your body was molded against mine a few days ago. I know exactly how you fit against me. I know your scent. You know mine too. You can feel the electricity, can't you?"

She watched me intently. "Did you know your mug says world's biggest dick?"

I grinned. "Yep. It was a gift from Jessa. Not sure how she knew, but I'm happy to announce it loudly."

"I don't think that mug means what you think it does."

I frowned at the thing. "What else could it mean?"

She snorted and rolled her eyes. "If you don't know I won't tell you. Look, I don't like to put faith in things I can't see or touch."

Smart. But she could touch the electrical charge between us. She just didn't want to yet. "Then that makes you a very smart woman. What do you want in trade?"

She stepped into my office and then eased the door closed behind her. The look she gave me was one of calculation. "Well, the job you offered, I'll take it."

My heart tried to punch its way out of my chest. She was saying yes? I arched my brow. "I thought you felt like I was buying you."

"You are. And I accept."

Bloody brilliant. "All right then. I see your sense of morals took a quick dip."

"Sometimes I can be stubborn. But if the job is legit and I'm not like your personal naked assistant or something, then I would like to accept."

Too bad. I liked the idea of her as my personal naked assistant though. *Why didn't I think of that job title?* "Fine, what else?"

She smoothed her hands over her blouse and then cleared her throat before tucking her hand behind her back. "I have some tasks I need to perform, and I would like you to accompany me."

I blinked slowly as I considered the tasks. "Excuse me? What kind of tasks?"

She lifted her chin. "Do you want this drive or not?"

"Oh, I do. But I didn't get to be a shrewd businessman by blankly agreeing to things. I like to know what I'm getting into." Especially if it involved me with my tongue between her thighs. *Stay focused.*

"I won't be asking you to do anything illegal, immoral or otherwise. I just have to get some things done and it will be a lot easier if someone is there. And I am not going to tell you what I have to do. I just want to be able to call you, and you'll have to turn up."

I shook my head. "No deal."

Her brow lifted. "Okay then. Guess I'll just call the *Guardian* and give them the drive. Apparently, you don't want this so badly after all."

Hardball? She had to be fucking with me. *You can show her hard balls.*

I forced myself not to laugh at my internal joke. I couldn't let her walk out of here with the drive.

Bollocks. "Fine. Call when you need me to accompany you to something, and I'll turn up. But I have a few limitations. I'm not going to shave your dog's balls or something."

Her face scrunched up. "Don't be so dramatic."

"Hard not to be when you're blackmailing me."

"Well, you brought this on yourself. And it's not blackmail since you offered me the job."

My fingers itched to get my hands on the drive and her skin. "Anything else you'd like to ask me for?"

She shifted on her feet and her gaze scanned over me. Did she stop on my lips?

"No, that's it for now."

She stepped forward, her palm outstretched with the flash drive on it. When she was close enough, I pushed myself to my feet. I realized how small she was then. Even in her heels, I loomed over her. "Think about it, princess. This is your last chance to ask for something else." *Like my tongue on her clit.*

Her gaze flickered to mine and held. "I don't need anything else."

"Okay." I took the disk from her warm palm. "Glad to hear it. I guess we're in bed together."

She stunned me with a brilliant smile before she hit me where it hurt. "I don't think you're that lucky." And then she turned on her heel, sashaying out, the red soles of her shoes mocking me as she clicked away. I'd just been outplayed by a player. And I couldn't even be mad about it.

©

Ben

I waited until the day was over and let myself into East's flat without even thinking about it. He didn't usually bring women back to the penthouse. Anyone who was temporary he took to a room downstairs. He often told them that he was spoiling them with room service and all that jazz, but mostly, he just didn't want them in his place. He looked up from his laptop. "You never knock, do you?"

"What's the point?"

"Yeah, yeah."

"Bridge was held up in his meeting."

"Tell me you have good news."

I held up the flash drive. "I have good news."

East jumped up. "Thank fucking Christ. What did you have to give her?" He smiled at me lasciviously. "Did you show her Big Ben? Is that why she gave this to us?"

"Shut it. I mean, it's not like I didn't offer. But she wasn't interested. Boyfriend and all that."

"Ugh, what does it feel like to have a deflated ego?"

I tossed the drive at him, and he caught it one-handed. "Nothing deflated about my ego. It's perfectly intact, just like always."

He rolled his eyes then. "So what did you have to give her?"

I poured a scotch and eased back on my usual spot, staring at the muted game of football on the telly. "I gave her a job."

He laughed. "Seriously? You really did give her a job?"

"Yeah. And she's actually qualified for it too. I don't know why she's been working as an admin."

"Okay, if you say so."

I winced. "There's something else."

He lifted a brow. "What?"

"She wants me to do some things for her."

He grinned then. "See, I knew you'd get to the good part eventually. Tell me more."

"There's nothing to tell. I don't know what these things are, but she assured me it would be nothing illegal or immoral."

"Wait, she got you to agree to do something and you don't know what it is?"

"I had to agree, or we wouldn't have that." I inclined my head toward his palm. "I did what I had to do."

He grinned. "Well, if you'd shagged her, I would also be okay with that. You know, taking one for the team."

Bridge opened the door a minute later. "Hey, losers. Ah, the prodigal son. Tell me you got it."

I lifted my arms wide and said, "Have I ever failed you? Who's your daddy?"

"If I were you, I wouldn't lead with that question. I hate my father."

I sighed. "Good point."

East held up the drive. "We've got it. I'll start the decryption tonight."

Bridge laughed. "Well, golden boy delivers. What did you have to do to get it?"

I shrugged. "You know... Why do you have to ask such questions? The point is I got it. Just like I said I would."

Bridge just turned his attention to East. "He shagged her, huh?"

East shook his head. "He claims he didn't. But considering how well fit she is, I'm surprised. Watch. Give it a week. He'll be begging her to shag."

"Dream on." I took a sip of my scotch. "I beg to no one."

Bridge and East just exchanged glances, and then Bridge laughed. "How much?"

East sized me up with a long glance. "A hundred grand. I say before all of this is over, he'll beg her and shag her."

Bridge whistled low. "That's your opening salvo? Okay, I'll bite. I know my mate. She's pussy. He can get that anywhere."

I nodded. "Yes, I can get that anywhere. Olivia Ashong isn't anything special." Even as I said the words, something within the very core of my cells rebelled against them, shying away from that statement and wanting to expel it from my body. But I wasn't saying a damn thing. Neither one of them needed to know. Mostly because they'd give me shit for the rest of my life, and I wasn't in the mood for that.

"So what's the plan?" Bridge asked.

East nodded at his laptop. "Now we wait. We decrypt this and find out what information we have. It's two months until the next voting meeting, one month until the next members' meeting where Van Linsted will likely start calling in all his chips, so we have to be ready. We'll reach out a hand to every member we can get on our side. He'll be doing the same. We need to figure out who's got the most weight and how to sway them. Emma is counting on us."

Just those words, 'Emma is counting on us,' reminded us who else had counted on us and who we'd failed. We wouldn't fail again. We owed that much and more to Toby.

Ben

"Toby. Toby!" Cold hands ripped me from my friend as I kicked and fought. I awoke from my recurring nightmare with sweat coating my skin and my breath coming in sharp, rugged pants. I glanced around, expecting to see my new brothers holding me back from the scene of Toby's death, but they weren't. I was in my room in my massive bed. The view of London open to me on three sides. I was safe.

Unlike Toby.

I scrubbed a hand over my face, scratching at the stubble on my jaw. "Fuck."

I threw off the covers and then stripped the bed. I had soaked the sheets. Quickly, I dropped them on the hamper before grabbing a fresh set from the closet and remaking the bed. I dragged my ass into the bathroom and turned on the hot water. I stripped out of my boxers and climbed in, not caring that I was basically searing my skin. As I scrubbed off the sweat and tried to shake the vestiges of the dream that clung to me like slime, it didn't matter how much soap I used. There was a smudge of dirt on my soul that I couldn't get at.

I had failed him. We all had. And now it was time to fix it. Emma was right. We were the ones in the position to do something about it.

After I turned off the water, I grabbed my towel and quickly ran it through my hair and over my body. I grabbed a pair of boxers and a t-shirt. I knew there was no way I'd get back to sleep. I checked the time and groaned. It was only 1:30. If it was closer to five, it would make sense to get up and go on my run, get some exercise, and start the day early, but this was ridiculous.

I climbed back in bed and grabbed my laptop.

I knew what I shouldn't do. What I shouldn't do was think about Olivia Ashong or the way she'd outmaneuvered me. I wasn't supposed to think about those dark eyes and the way she looked when she smiled or about the curve of her ass fitting against my palm.

Stop thinking about her.

There were rules to this. Rules I was breaking. But I couldn't help myself. For some reason, she was like a tether to this world that I didn't know I needed. I had no idea why the fuck I felt that way. I didn't know her. She didn't know me. But still, everything about her made me feel solidly planted, which was ridiculous because she had me by the balls.

I still had a favor, or favors, to do for her, and I had no idea what they were. I just knew they were coming. And she knew about the flash drive. Not necessarily what was on it but that I was implying its importance, and that was dangerous enough. I opened the images that East had pulled off CCTV from the fundraiser.

She looked regal. Elegant. But I almost liked her dirty secretary look better. The bun, the glasses, the buttoned-up vibe with a spark of mischief in her eyes and the hint of anger. I zoomed in on the photo and frowned when I saw her pin. Was that what she'd been looking for? Like the dick that I was, I hadn't stopped to think about it or to help her. When I zoomed in, I frowned. Was that a Batman pin? That's what she'd been looking for in the closet?

She must really like the caped crusader. And then I had another flash of memory. The photo on her desk. In it, her mother had worn a pin just like it.

Jesus. You are a wanker.

I absolutely *was* a wanker. What the fuck had I done? I had broken it and then left her to pick up the pieces.

I'd broken it, so I needed to replace it.

Looked like I had more than a few debts to pay.

CHAPTER 9

Livy

"**H**appy first day of work!" Telly's voice carried through the restaurant and several people turned to look. She blew in like a storm, her dark hair fanning out behind her like she travelled with a personal wind machine.

I grinned as I stood. "Hey, Tell."

She gave me a tight hug. "We need wine, immediately."

I laughed. "I already ordered. And remember, I still have to go back to work."

"Ugh. God, killjoy. It's five o'clock somewhere."

"Well, in that case, I'll drink to that." The waiter arrived then with the wine, and Telly sagged in her seat. "Oh my God, yes, pour."

"What's wrong with you? Everything okay with Carmen?" The two of them had been dating for several months, and they were coming up to the six-month is-this-moving-forward term. I could practically see Telly's feet turning into blocks of ice.

"She's good actually. She's coming down from Bristol at the weekend."

"I have to say, Tells, I'm proud of you for stepping into rela-tionshiphood. I, for one, think she's good for you."

"I like her a lot. But how are you supposed to know if someone is right for you?"

"I don't know. Faith in fate, I guess." Since when did *I* believe in faith *or* fate?

She took a big sip. "Do you really think Dexter is *it* for you? I mean, it's been two years."

"Oh no, you're not deflecting with me. This is not about me. Besides, part of those years were long distance before he moved us to the States and back again. Lots of transition. Our situation is different." Even Telly didn't know how far things had disintegrated.

I dragged my attention back to Telly. "I mean I *like* her; I just don't know if it's a *love* thing."

"Wouldn't it be so helpful if there were a sign people could wear that said, *Yes, great love potential. I'm not an asshole.*"

"Yes! Where is this invention in my life?" Telly said as she snorted a laugh.

"You just gotta build it, Tell."

"Speaking of my complete badassery, that flash drive you gave me, it's heavily encrypted."

"You mean you can't do it?"

She lifted a brow. "Oh, I can do it, but I might need some help. I've got a call out to this bloke called Matthias. He lives in New York, but he has more experience with stuff like this. I have to wonder… If it has this level of encryption, should we be messing with it?"

I chewed my bottom lip. I wasn't ready to let it go yet. "I need to know."

"Okay, then rest easy. I'm on the case. Enough about my boring hacking attempts. How did Dexter take the news about the big job?"

I wrinkled my nose, remembering the thirty-second

conversation in passing. "Okay, I guess. He was worried about my time commitment."

She sighed. "Honey, I love you; you know that. I have loved you since you came here for Uni. But let me be really, really clear when I say your boyfriend is a dud. He's more worried about how you might not be around to wait on him hand and foot than he is thrilled for you."

She wasn't entirely wrong. "Enough about Dex."

"Okay, fine. So, just how fit is your hot new boss?"

I laughed. "I thought you would have looked him up by now."

"Oh, I have." She pulled out her phone from her purse, typed on it quickly, and then pulled up a picture of none other than the gorgeous Viking god himself. His hair was shorter, and he had some scruff on his jaw. God, that scruff did something for him.

"Yes, he is pretty, but it doesn't matter. You know guys like that are bad news. Trouble with a capital T. I'm not looking for trouble."

"Love, if you don't want him, I will take him off your hands."

"Except you're not exactly a fan of dick."

"Sweetheart, for that face, I could figure out how to make it work. I mean it's a dick, how hard can it be?"

I snorted a laugh, nearly taking some of my wine on the ride.

The rest of lunch went well. As always, we ate more bread than we should have, making it nearly impossible to finish the rest of our meals. But still, it was delicious. And the one glass of wine I had allowed myself in the middle of the day had somewhat eased that tension that had developed in my shoulders. Until somewhere around dessert, as I moaned around a spoonful of tiramisu, I could have sworn I saw Fenton Mills at the bar.

No. There was no way that could be him. What the fuck was he doing there?

Telly handed the waiter her credit card when he stopped by at with the card machine. "What are you looking at?"

I slunk into my seat. "Don't look now. I think that's Fenton Mills."

Her brows lifted. "Dexter's boss?"

"Yeah."

"Maybe it's not him." She tried to turn around, and I grabbed her hand.

"Do not look. He'll see you. Let's just go."

"Well, hurry away. The front door is that way."

The waiter passed our way, and I signalled him. When he came over, he had a wide smile on his face. "Is there anything else I can get you?"

I shook my head. "No, thank you. But I wanted to know, is there a back door?"

He shook his head. "Nope, the only way in and out is through the front there."

"No staff exit?"

"There is, but it's just the garbage bins out there."

I scowled. "Fine. Thank you." I was going to have to go out the front, which meant I was going to have to be stealthy.

"Telly?"

She raised a brow. "Let me guess, interference?"

I nodded. "I don't want to deal with him. I don't want to talk to him. I just want him to leave me alone."

"You really need to talk to Dexter about this. Or maybe the police or something, because he always seems to be where you are."

"I've tried. Dex is sure I'm overreacting. Says he's harmless." *Also creepy. Don't forget creepy.* But I was pretty sure I couldn't get him arrested for being creepy. "Come on."

"Of course. Anything for my bestie."

I grabbed my purse. There wasn't a direct path to the front, but there were some columns that I could possibly duck between if Telly pulled him to the far left of the restaurant and chatted. Then, I could be free and pretend I hadn't even seen him.

I waited until Telly was out of her seat and approaching the bar. The sashay in her hips was designed to draw the attention of any man.

The problem was I could practically feel Fenton staring at me. And thanks to the mirrored candle on the table, I could see the image of him at the bar looking in my direction. Well, maybe he wasn't watching me. Maybe he was trying to look for someone he knew?

Oh God, stop making excuses for him. He is creeptastic.

I could hear Telly's voice above the din of the restaurant. "Oh my God, Mr. Mills, is that you?"

I waited until she was facing my way and his back was to me, then I bolted out of my seat. I hightailed it past several tables, walking with a purpose, and then I ducked between the pillars. There was one large plant on the way to the front. If I could just pause there, I'd be home free.

But as I started walking, I heard a familiar voice. "What do you think you're doing?"

I whipped around. It was none other than Ben Covington.

"What the hell are you doing here?"

His brows rose. "You are the one hiding between two pillars, and you want to know what *I'm* doing here?"

"I'm not hiding. I'm strategically placed as I exit the premises."

He laughed. "You know, I pay you enough now that you can afford lunch here. You don't need to run out on the bill."

My jaw unhinged. "I would never. And that is so arrogant and classist of you to even think that."

He frowned. "Relax, I was just making a joke. It was just kind of funny."

"Well then, you missed the mark."

"All right. Sorry. But what are you doing, anyway? Why do you look like you're hiding?"

"I'm not hiding."

I heard Telly still talking, which meant Fenton was still looking for me. "Sorry, I've got to go. See you at the office." And then I darted. Brisk walk, almost there. Almost there. *Almost there.* At the plant, I realized I hadn't shaken the Viking. "Okay, you're definitely hiding. Who don't you want to see?"

God, he was annoying. "Mind your own business."

And then it happened.

Fenton. "Ah, Olivia, I thought that was you."

I went stiff. "Mr. Mills. What are you doing here?"

"You know, I was in the mood for Italian today."

I frowned. "All the way across town from the office? Surely, there must be Italian places nearby on the South Bank."

"Yes, but Emily and I, we eat here often. Remember, we used to live around here."

"Oh, did you?" I knew what bullshit smelled like and this was a grade A variety.

I'd make it a point to never eat here again. Ben's gaze ping-ponged between me and Fenton, and then Telly, and back again to me. There was no way I was going to get around this. "Mr. Covington, this is Fenton Mills, my boyfriend Dexter's boss. And this is my best friend, Telly."

He shook hands with her, but his eyes stayed on me and I

couldn't help but shift under the scrutiny. He completely ignored Mills. "Yes well, if you will excuse us, Olivia and I have a meeting back at the office. Telly, I'm sure she'd like to give you a tour, but we need to get back to prep for Peterman."

I turned and stared at him. *Peterman?*

He was giving me an out. "Oh yes, the Peterman meeting. I still have some files I want to go over with you. But Telly, I think I have time for a quick tour if you're up to it."

The muscle in Fenton's jaw ticked. "I was hoping to buy you a drink or lunch. I didn't know you were busy."

Ben smiled. "Yeah, Olivia here is one of our brightest new talents. I plan to keep her busy for a while." Then he escorted us out of the restaurant.

The sun tried to peek out from behind the cloud cover as tourists packed the streets of Westchester Square.

At the tube closer to the office, Telly grinned up at him. "Oh, I can see why she took the job with you."

My face flamed. I was going to kill her. Best friend or not, this calls for a debt. She winked and then went off to the tube station.

I turned and he grinned at me. "I like her."

"Don't get used to her. She's going to die later."

"Don't murder a mate on my account. She seems to be looking out for you."

"She's the best."

"Then why aren't you asking *her* for those favors you mentioned?"

I sighed. "Because she would try to fix things for me. I need someone neutral. Since we're on the topic. I need your help for a thing if you're up for it."

He lifted a brow. "Great, let's get it over with then. Where are we going?"

I took a deep breath, sighed, and released it slowly. "On a Jack the Ripper tour."

He blinked. "Are you serious?"

"Yes. I am."

"What's to keep me from going back on my word?"

"Well, my research on you tells me you tend to keep your word. You don't make any bargains that you don't intend to keep. That's your reputation anyway."

He nodded slowly. "So, you finally decided to look up who the hell you were working for."

"Well, if I was going to make a devil's bargain, I wanted to know who I was getting in bed with."

He shook his head. "You're stubborn. I like that."

"Can you come, or can't you?"

His gaze narrowed as it swept over me. "I wonder what it is about you. You're a complete mystery, yet somehow you have me by the blue balls."

I blinked. "I do not have you by the balls. Besides, they wouldn't be blue. I haven't done anything to you yet."

"That, my dear, is debatable. What time?"

"Eight. We'll meet at Traitor's Gate."

"Why can't we just go together after work?"

"Well, I need to go home and change."

There it was again, that slow perusal of my body that made my skin feel tight and too hot. As if he'd just put his nose all over every inch of my skin like he had in the closet. His nostrils flared as he if he was inhaling deep.

I swallowed hard.

No. Fantasies about this man are not on the menu. Dexter. Remember him?

He chuckled. "You know what? I'm curious. So, I'll come."

"Really?" I was surprised. I had expected him to put me off

with some kind of plans until I had to browbeat him. I never actually expected him to comply.

"And here is a piece of advice, sweetheart. When you have the upper hand, act like you know it. Don't ever show weakness. Don't ever back down. Don't ever be surprised that someone is willing to do what you demanded. Act like you knew it was going to be that way all along.

"That's excellent business advice."

"It's excellent life advice. Follow it, or you'll get eaten alive."

@

Ben

"Okay, gentlemen. What we have here are proposed candidates for the Five. There is a list of ten names, so we'll need to vet each one. We don't want to waste time chasing our tails."

I stared up at those ten men on the screen in front of me. Men I'd known since I was in secondary school.

East continued. "We know that Rowan Downs is in fact one of the Five." East moved his image down into our roster.

Bridge walked over. "That's Adam Hilton. He's been a senior member of Intelligence for the last fifteen years. He's my vote."

Drew nodded. "We should put him down on the list. Even if he isn't one of the Five, he's still influential in the Elite."

I considered the list. We didn't have time to approach them all. "How do we narrow this down?" I glanced at Bridge. "We've got to make our best educated guesses. Bridge, you're on Van Lindsted. You're our eyes in the street. East you're our background and tech guy, so your job is finding us some leverage we can use. Drew and I will handle the approaches. Does that make sense?"

Bridge rubbed his jaw. "Yeah, divide and conquer. That way we don't have to do everything."

I nodded. "East, how quickly do you think you can find us some information?"

He grinned. "Please, what am I, some kind of amateur?"

"Yeah, yeah, don't be a show-off cunt."

He grinned at me, and I realized I hadn't seen a smile like that from him in years. Somewhere in the last decade, we'd all grown a little shrewder, a little less open. Each of us more reserved. But the change had been most notable in East.

I didn't even notice the changes in myself, but I was sure they were there.

A few quick taps on his keyboard, and we were looking at just a photo of Adam Hilton. "All right, so Adam Hilton. He likes the ladies. Frequents several escort agencies. But primarily, he has a dominatrix called Trix Lagrange. She's been in business fifteen years. She's very unlikely to roll on a client, but I might be able to hack her system unless she's analog."

"I guess everyone has their thing, don't they?" I muttered.

East shrugged. "True. Hilton is married. Old English money. While he and his family were already wealthy, it was his wife's family fortune that really made him. What few people know is that he has *another wife.*"

I sat up straighter. "What?"

East grinned and nodded. He pulled up another photo of a woman who could have been Spanish or Italian. Long, dark hair, olive skin, beautiful dark eyes, and looks that hinted at a smile on the way.

"Well, he has decent taste, at least."

Bridge chuckled. "What, is your plan to seduce his wife?"

"I mean, is she actually his wife? Because that's bigamy."

East tapped again. "Yes, it is. Another note. Elia, his Spanish wife, has a ten-year-old son. *Hilton's* ten-year-old son. His wife in the UK was unable to conceive. They adopted three children. But Elia's son is Hilton's only biological heir."

"Okay, that's good. I can use that."

"Now, here is the really interesting part. Elia, beautiful though she is, is 26 years old."

I frowned as I did the math. "What?"

Drew shook his head. "Ugh, God. Perverted little shit."

"That he is. He met Elia on the beach in Spain when she was sixteen years old and knocked her up. Her family insisted on a quickie marriage, and he neglected to tell them that he was *already* married."

I nodded. "Okay. Adam Hilton is our first. We have to make it work."

Bridge nodded. "While you are working on that, I'm working on setting up a meeting to have Van Linsted come to London Lords. A show of good faith that if I'm willing to meet with him openly, then I'm not afraid of you, or whatever."

I grinned. "Now, we both know that's bullshit."

Bridge just chuckled. "Please, I could take you."

"You know I've still got half an inch on you."

He started to push to his feet, and East silenced us both. "Oi. Behave. You're not breaking anything else in my flat today."

Bridge just gave me a smirk and a lifted chin, and I grinned at him. "And so it begins."

Bridge, East, and Drew nodded along with me then muttered in unison, "And so it begins."

CHAPTER 10

Ben

I pulled up my collar as I shuffled from foot to foot, the wind chapping my ass. If I was being honest, I had no idea why I was freezing my balls off on a spring night in front of the Traitors' Gate souvenir shop, but there I was, waiting on a woman I wasn't sure I could trust.

I'd considered not coming. I had enough going on with the Elite, and I could have made an excuse. I could have gone back on our bargain. *As if.* But that wasn't me. Mostly, I was curious because she'd made such a point of having me agree to do this with her.

Why did she want a perfect stranger accompanying her? From what I'd seen, she had at least one really good friend. Where was the woman with the wild black hair?

There were a few other people milling about, and I could only assume that they were there for the same reason we were. They too liked creepy things.

Olivia didn't seem like the sort who would enjoy this, but what the fuck did I know about her? Other than the fact that she was a shrewd negotiator.

I looked up to find her approaching. "Sorry, sorry, sorry, I'm late. It's kind of a disaster. Trains were late, and apparently there is no signage to the Jack the Ripper tour."

Her hair was down, and curls were blowing in her face. She'd opted for black leggings with some kind of leather embellishments and a black top that was not quite a turtleneck but close. She also wore a black leather jacket. Basically, she looked like she'd asked for cat burglar chic at the store. "I see you didn't dress for the occasion."

I shrugged. "Well, what does one wear on a Jack the Ripper excursion?"

One by one, the other people who'd been milling about, not approaching me, were happy to come talk to us when Olivia was there, which I found fascinating. Eventually, a gentleman with a close-cropped beard, hawkish features and a wool hat, strolled up. "Ladies and gentlemen, I assume you are all here for the Jack the Ripper tour?"

One of the other women nodded. "Yeah, that's us." As she spoke, you could see the condensation of her breath in the brisk night air. The tube station and souvenir shop provided artificial light, but most of the street was only lit by pubs.

"Well, glad to see you all." He did a quick headcount. "I'm Jack." He chuckled. "Yes, I know. It's a little on the nose for me to do my own tour, but I think it's great for comedic effect."

There was some tittering, but then we got underway. Much to my surprise, he was actually quite knowledgeable. As the tour went along, we found out that he was a professor. Which made sense for why he loved doing the tour so much.

The whole time, Olivia was mostly quiet and introspective. I had expected her to continue chatting, but she seemed to retreat more and more into herself. I still didn't understand why she'd wanted me to come.

As nights out went, it wasn't bad, but I expected her to en-gage more.

We stopped along the river for a moment, and Jack was giv-ing us more history about the brutality of the murders and the speculation about who Jack was, but my gaze was on her lithe form as she crossed the street to the river, took something from her pocket, and then seemed to pour it out. Then she put some-thing back in her pocket and came back to the group.

"Olivia, are you okay?"

She sniffed, wiping away a tear with a knuckle before giv-ing me a tremulous smile, her eyes a little misty. "Yeah, I'm fine. And it's Liv or Livy. I figure if you can join me on this, then you might as well call me that. I had to spread my Mom's ashes. It was one of her requests."

Jesus. I'd stepped in it, but I couldn't help but ask, "Isn't it a little odd doing something that important with a stranger? What about the woman with the black hair? Wendy?"

She laughed, and the sound hit me right in the dick. Christ, she needed to warn someone before she did that. "Telly. She would have come, but I guess it's sometimes easier to do things with strangers."

"Less judgmental?"

"Something like that." She shrugged. "Well, you can judge, but I don't have to listen to you. And your opinion isn't weighted that much."

"That's good to know."

She chuckled then. "Sorry. I just didn't want to do it alone."

"I make a good stand-in."

"Yeah, you do."

"Right. Anything else you need me to stand-in for?"

"Actually, now that you mentioned—"

We both glanced around then realized that, somehow, we'd

lost the rest of the tour. We'd kept walking across the Thames, and they must have ducked in somewhere. "Ah, it looks like they're probably back there."

She frowned. "Yeah, let's go."

"I have to say, this wasn't terrible. It's actually informative. And kind of fun."

We turned around at the sidewalk, and two men approached. One was a big guy, taller than me. Broader too. The other was shorter, average height, but also broad-shouldered.

"You can always count on Jack the Ripper for a barrel of—" She froze. "Shit. Not again."

I frowned. "What are you talking about?"

When she planted her feet and her hands balled into fists, her body went rigid. "Olivia, what's wrong?"

The two men were several feet closer now, and one of them had a knife. I could handle them, but would Olivia be a liability? I needed to keep her safe. On my own, I'd have taken them on. But with her there, I needed to play it safe, play it cool.

I turned my head at them. "Mates, I guarantee you don't want to do this."

The large one pulled out a gun, and I frowned.

"Come with us, beautiful." His voice was all cockney.

My brows snapped down. "She's not going anywhere with you. What the fuck do you want?"

They both angled their heads toward the alleyway to our right. With a gun and knife in play, we didn't really have much choice. I raised my hands, but Olivia stayed frozen. "No. No way is this happening twice in a week. I'm not letting this happen again."

I finally had to grab her by the upper shoulders and move her along. I said, "Look, you can have my wallet. Anything you want in there." Why did she have a death wish?

I started to take off my watch and he laughed at me. "We're not here for you, Ritchie Rich. We're here for her."

I frowned. "Her? Why?"

"She knows why."

The one with the gun loomed over her, and she backed up against the alley wall. I stepped between them. "That's enough. I've already said I'll give you what you want, but she's not going anywhere with you. Back off."

The short, stocky git smirked. "And we've told you, we want her."

Okay, so we weren't doing this the easy way then. I shoved her behind me and squared my shoulders. "In that case, you can fuck right off."

"Don't want you, rich boy."

"I'm the one you've got."

Livy did a completely unexpected thing. A screech tore from her throat, and she lunged herself at the short one, going straight for his eyes, pressing her thumbs in his sockets and screaming, "You will not ruin this for me." And then she proceeded kicking at his shins.

I had milliseconds to assess what was going on in front of me before I sprang into action on his friend with the gun.

Remembering all my anti-kidnap self-defense training, I reached for the gun as if I meant to grab it from him. But instead, I put one hand on his thumb, the other on his wrist. *Bend back, crunch. Bend forward, crunch. Turn toward him, more crunching, and ease the gun off the finger.*

The metal clattered to the pavement, and I kicked it into the dark shadows. He howled, cradling his hand. While he was doing that, I delivered a jab to his nose and his head snapped back. Body hits were going to be useless against the guy. So, like my tiny honey-badger, I went for his face. More jabs, more crunching. I grabbed his ears and pulled down, and then delivered a knee straight to his face. More crunching. That put him down easy enough.

Meanwhile, Olivia wasn't letting up. She was doing damage to the bastard's shin. The idiot's head was thrown back. She used both her hands and went to grab his throat, inadvertently hitting his trachea. He immediately doubled over, coughing. She lunged for him again, but I was quicker. Two quick taps to his face with my fist and he was down, groaning.

I took her hand and dragged her running behind me. "Come on." Through the alley and back out again, I didn't stop pulling her until we were just outside the pub and I caught sight of Jack and the others inside.

I dragged her into the shadows before running my hands over her, checking her for injuries. I told myself I was being methodical, simply making sure she was okay. Her eyes went wide as my fingertips traced over her head, temples, and cheekbones. Then the smooth lines of her neck and clavicle. For the rest, I had to keep it perfunctory, or I'd notice how full her breasts were, remember the feel of her ass in my palms. Worse, I'd inhale deep and she would hold me captive.

So it was a good thing I knew how to make it quick and professional. *Is that why your dick is hard?* I released her and stepped back. I told myself it was the smart thing to do so I could identify if she needed to go to the doctor.

"We're going to go in there. You're going to go to the restroom and clean up. When you come back out, we are leaving the tour and then you're going to tell me what the fuck is going on. Do you understand?" She glanced up at me and her eyes were glassy. Not all there. Clearly out of it and wavering on her feet a little. "Do you understand?"

She nodded slowly, her lips trembling. "Why would anybody

want me? I'm nobody. Up until a couple of days ago, I was a perfectly boring admin."

"I don't have any idea, but we're going to find out."

@

Livy

My hands were still shaking.

I'd never been violent a day in my life.

Okay, if we were counting that time when Elena Fitzgerald pulled on one of my Afro puffs and told me my hair was a Brillo pad before I punched her in the nose, there had been *one* time. But since then, after my mother had given me a very stern talking to, I had never hit anybody again. It probably showed.

The others hadn't really noticed we'd been missing at all. They'd all started having a pint, so when Ben casually sidled up to them, they just handed him a beer.

I'd excused myself to the bathroom to try and pull myself together, because what the actual fuck? My first inclination was to call Telly, but I didn't want her to worry. She'd go into full smother mode. It never even occurred to me to tell Dex, which probably said more than I wanted.

Who were they? Why did they want me? I was nobody. I already hadn't slept much since Saturday. Now there was no way I was ever closing my eyes. I couldn't even have one night to say goodbye to my mother. I took a deep breath and then another.

I splashed one more round of cold water on my face before leaving the dark, dank loo and returning to the bar. I found an empty high table to the side and went about pretending everything was just peachy. I finally thought I had my breathing under control, and then Ben leaned over. "Everyone's getting ready to go. You and I, we're going to stay and have a little chat."

"But I wanted to finish the tour." I glowered at him mutinously.

"They only have one more stop left anyway, and it's not important. I think you and I can stay here. You did what you needed to do for your mom, didn't you?"

He was right. I *had* done what I needed to do. Before she died, she'd made me promise to spread her ashes doing the things that she loved. I'd made arrangements to do this tour since it was her favorite. She also loved riding a helicopter over the Thames and Kew Gardens where she and Dad had their first date, so I had the idea to spread her ashes along every one of her favorite routes. And then, of course, Paris. Paris had been her favorite city. It would take me a while, but I figured if I could do the first few with someone, I wouldn't feel nearly so alone.

You were supposed to do them with Dexter.

I swallowed that down. I didn't really have time to deal with my Dexter bullshit at the moment. Not when someone had tried to kill us on the street.

Everyone said goodbye. Some phone numbers were exchanged among people who wanted to hang out and do crime types of things together, which was really an odd hobby when I thought about it. But these were my mother's people. So if I ever wanted to remember her, or needed to feel the essence of her, talking to them would be good for me.

Once everyone was gone, Ben turned to me. "Now would be a damn good time to start talking."

"There is no need to swear at me."

"Coming from the same woman who just shouted 'not fucking today' at a would-be attacker?"

I flushed. "Well, it was appropriate at the time."

"Hell yeah, it was appropriate. I'm not mad about it. I'm just saying now is a hell of a time to become a pussy."

"I'm just feeling a little high-strung at the moment."

He sighed. "Okay, breathe. Just relax. But we do need to talk about what's going on. Like who you really are."

I frowned at him. "What? Who *I* am? This all has to do with you. I never knew a single moment of adventure, or craziness, or hell, even whimsy until you turned up."

"Says the woman who drags me on a Jack the Ripper tour."

"For my mother!"

His gaze narrowed at me as his eyes searched mine. "You see, that's the thing. You seem believable, but are you?"

"Why am I still here?"

I managed to stand up, but then one of his big palms totally encapsulated my hand. "Stay put. First of all, I don't know who they were. And we're still far too close to that alley for me to let you out of my sight. I will see that you get home in one piece."

"Thank you very much, but I don't need your help." I tugged my hand free.

"Were you going to tell me that you were mugged?"

I sputtered, "Why is that even relevant?"

"Well, in and of itself, it wouldn't have been relevant, but considering armed men wanted something from you today, I'd say it's probably related."

My voice shook. "It probably is related… to *you and that flash drive*. I'm not exciting. Up until a couple of days ago, I was an executive assistant for Kennedy. I have a perfectly normal, boring boyfriend. A night out for me involves one glass of wine. If I'm really feeling crazy, maybe two. Hell, I haven't even had that many sexual partners. Really. There was the guy before Dex, and then there was Dex. Other than that, I'm as boring as they come. I pay my taxes on time. I meditate because I'm told it's good for me. I work out for the same reason. I have one really good best friend and a boyfriend who mostly doesn't even know I exist."

His brows lifted. "We're going to talk about that boyfriend but later. Right now, walk me through it. When your purse was stolen, did they say anything? Did they do anything?"

"No. I was walking home from the tube the night of the fundraiser. I had taken the tube from King's Cross then home like I normally would."

"You took the tube in that dress?"

"Well, I had my shawl on by then, thank you. And yes, in that dress. I didn't really want to take an Uber. Dexter would have been on me about the cost, saying I was wasting money and I hadn't waited for him."

"A real charmer that one. Why were you even alone?"

"Well, he didn't want to leave just yet. And to be honest, I couldn't find him."

His brows lifted. "You couldn't find your date?"

"He was probably chatting or something, and honestly, I was quite a bit fried from what we'd already experienced, you know, in the closet and what not?"

The corner of his lips tipped up at that. *Asshole.*

"I just wanted to get out of there."

He frowned. "So much so that you didn't find the person you came with?"

I bit my lower lip, and then he frowned. "What am I missing?"

My top row of teeth worked on my bottom lip. "I have social anxiety. Sometimes I really can't do crowds. Sometimes, I manage okay. I might go to a concert and never even feel a twinge of adrenaline. But at other times, there could be five people and I'm sweating buckets. I was pretty pumped tonight. I was able to do a tour and had no sweats or anything. And I felt pretty comfortable talking to everyone. Anyway, Dexter was upset with me at the fundraiser. He said that I was making too much of everything and that I was faking it in some way, I guess."

"Why are you with this bloke?"

"I have my reasons." *Not really.*

"You have to admit, this looks bad. I run into you when I'm in the midst of liberating critical information that I need. The next thing I know, you're at the right place at the right time, and I had no option but to slip you the drive, otherwise, I'd have been found out."

"That wasn't my fault. I was coming to yell at you for breaking my pin. Last thing I wanted to do was help you."

"Or you were trying to steal the drive from me, which makes me wonder who the hell you are and what you want with it? How would that information benefit you at all? Unless you mean to blackmail everyone."

My eyes went wide. "I would never blackmail anyone. How dare you even suggest—"

He shook his head. "You see how I'm here with you right now on a Jack the Ripper tour? Isn't that blackmail?"

My jaw unhinged. "That is *not* blackmail. We had an arrangement."

"Blackmail."

"No, you're twisting what happened."

"Am I?"

"Oh my God, yes. You came in and offered me a bribe to not ask any questions."

It was his turn to sputter. "You weren't handing over what I needed."

"And now you're shouting."

He quickly lowered his voice. "Come on, let's get you home."

"I'm not going anywhere with you. And for the record, you joined *me* in that closet. I was minding my own business."

He sighed. "Oh my God, you are the most infuriating woman on this planet. I swear to God, if you would just once do what you were asked or told..."

"Why?"

He frowned. "What do you mean, why?"

"Well, I mean, why? Why should I do what I'm asked or told? What, because I'm a woman? Because I work for you? Because you know better and I know nothing?"

He opened his mouth to speak but then shut it promptly. "You know that's not what I mean."

"Isn't it though, Mr. Arrogant? Why should I just do what you tell me?"

"Jesus Christ. Because I'm concerned about your safety."

"Well, you weren't concerned about my safety when you handed me whatever the fuck was on that drive."

"I didn't hand it to you. I needed it tucked away for safekeeping."

"And you slipped it to me. How is that safekeeping? Because I am not safe."

"I don't know if the two events are related, but I don't see any possible way that they couldn't be. I'm sorry about that, but who the fuck would have seen you? That slip was clean. No one should have noticed. And even if they did, why would they be after you, not me?"

I should tell him the truth. Tell him how I had made a copy, but I didn't.

"Okay, let's get you the hell out of here, and then we'll figure out what to do in the morning."

"What do you mean?"

"Well, for starters, you're going to need security."

" I do *not* need security. That is ridiculous."

He stood, sliding off his stool with a feline grace. "Are you going to tell me that you don't need anyone and that you're perfectly safe all on your own, notwithstanding the mugging on Saturday and the attempted mugging tonight? Because how did anyone know that you were doing the Jack the Ripper tour?"

I opened my mouth to answer him, but I couldn't, because that was a very good question.

"Hell."

"Yes, my sentiments exactly. So, for the time being, let me get you home where it's safe and then we can figure this out later."

"Jesus, what is on that drive?"

"I promise you, it's nothing that would be of any interest to anyone else."

There was a level of sincerity in his gaze, but still, there was a shadow, as if he was holding something back from me.

Before I knew what was happening, I was ushered outside, and there was a black car at the curb. He held the door open for me and gestured that I should slide inside.

I frowned. "Is this your Uber?"

He laughed. "I don't take Uber. This is my private car." He slid in the seat next to me then leaned forward. "Evening Jason. Can you please take us to..." His voice trailed, and he slid his gaze at me expectantly.

I told them my address and then sat back. "You didn't have to do this."

"Well, it seems that I did."

When we reached the flat, he stepped out first, held the door open for me, and then walked me to the front door. "When you get inside, lock the door behind you. Set the alarm if you have one."

I frowned. "Am I really in danger?"

"That remains to be seen. But it's certainly a lot more

helpful if you're not walking around the streets by yourself. You know, basic safety."

I sulked, feeling petulant. I should be allowed to walk home at night. "I'm not an idiot. "

"Prove it. Stay inside."

I don't know what it was about him, but every time he opened his mouth, I felt the overwhelming urge to hit something. "How dare you—"

He didn't let me finish though. Instead, he turned around and was already walking toward his car. "Get in the house."

He left me very little choice but to unlock the door and step through. Tomorrow. Tomorrow, I would give him a piece of my mind.

CHAPTER 11

Ben

I told my driver to go to Bridge's after dropping off Olivia. I'd stayed to make sure she got inside okay. When he opened the door, he was in sweats and a T-shirt.

His dark brows lifted. "Ben? What are you doing here, mate? Any idea what time it is?"

I shook my head. "I don't know. Somewhere around midnight, I guess."

Bridge might not say much, but he had an intuitive knowledge about people. He stepped aside and let me in. "What's wrong?"

How did I even fucking start to explain? "I need to run something by you."

I went straight for the study to the right, while he veered toward the kitchen. "Fancy a pint?"

I shook my head. "No. I don't need anything even temporarily dampening my senses after the night I've had."

He preceded me to the study instead, the soft shuffling of his feet in contrast to the muffled squeak of my trainers on the wood. "Where were you tonight?"

"With a friend. Let me ask you something. Do we have exposure on this Toby thing?"

He frowned. "Does this have something to do with the same woman who was supposed to *be easy to handle?*"

"Something like that."

"Fucking Christ, Ben."

"I know." Quickly, I recounted what had happened.

Bridge pinched his nose. "Mate? Any way you were seen?"

I'd been racking my brain since it happened. "I have no idea. Maybe someone saw me leave then saw her leave. I don't know what she was doing in that office that night. She said she was there just to be alone for few minutes then hid in the closet to keep from getting caught, but I don't know."

He rolled his shoulders. "No such thing as a coincidence. So the question now is what the hell are we going to do with her?"

"Devil's advocate. Maybe she was there for another reason. Trying to get information on the Van Linsteds. We need to look into her." *You know who she is.* But what if I didn't?

He sighed. "We're sitting on a powder keg. We need to know who she is. If we got it wrong and she made a copy of the file, or worse, if she was able to decrypt it, she's going to have blackmail information on Elite members, men who would do anything to hold on to power. We need to find out what she knows, and in the meantime, get her some protection. If she's innocent, we just put the target on her. If something about the pass wasn't clean, we're obligated to look after her, but there's no way she won't ask questions."

I swallowed hard. He was right. But it was my responsibility. "I got her into this."

He sighed as he crossed his arms. "We're a team, mate. *We'll* take care of this." His silvery gaze bore into me. "Is she a problem for you? Can you stay detached? Unemotional?"

I ground my teeth. I knew what he was asking. "She's not Lila."

"That's not what I asked. We'll protect her. But if we find out she's not who she claims to be, can you keep your shit together? The stakes are higher now."

"I'm tight." *Total bollocks.* I was already fucked in the head over her.

"I was giving you shit the other day, but if you're spinning, you can tell me, mate. You know that."

I swallowed hard, trying to fight through the wall of emotion. Olivia wasn't Lila. She wouldn't shag me, pretend to love me, then try to upgrade to my bloody father. And I would not go off the rails like before. We couldn't afford for me to.

There was a shuffling near the door, and I lifted my gaze. Dark eyes met mine. "I should have known it was you, arsehole."

I inclined my head. "Mina, always nice to see you." And by nice, I meant I had the inexplicable urge to do murder. Just kidding. It was explicable. She was a conniving bitch. I could see right through her.

She pursed her lips. "It's late, Bridge."

"I know, babe. We're just having a quick drink and catching up."

She glowered at me but turned and sauntered off.

"Nice to see she still adores me."

"I don't know what it is with you two." He shook his head.

I knew what it was, but I wasn't telling him. Mina was a class-A viper. She'd gotten her hooks into him early, and there was nothing about her I trusted. She didn't love him, at least not that way he really should be loved. Bridge needed someone that would warm up his life. Mina wasn't it. But it wasn't my choice, so I kept my mouth shut. "Not sure. But hey, she's not mine to shag. She's all yours."

Bridge snorted. "One day, I'll find out why you two don't get on."

If it was left to me, he would never find out. I wouldn't be the one to break my best mate's heart.

I shoved my hands in my pocket to ask my next question. "We haven't had a chance to talk about all of this. But you okay after seeing Emma?"

Bridge was usually so good at masking his emotions, but his eyes narrowed imperceptibly. "Why wouldn't I be?"

I lifted a brow. "C'mon mate. I remember your face the first time you ever saw her. I don't think I've ever seen you look like that since."

He shook his head. "That was kid's stuff. Been a long time since we were kids."

I searched his gaze, but he was too hard to read. Running my hand through my hair, I muttered, "Right. A long fucking time." He wouldn't say shit until he was damn well good and ready.

He frowned down at my hand. "Mate, your ring?"

I knew what he meant right away. I'd taken it off before my Olivia outing. "Would you believe it itched?" I absolutely rubbed the tattoo on my thumb, the one that was usually covered by my signet ring.

He pressed his lips together. "Mate, however much you hate them, it's your job to play the part."

He was right. I *knew* he was right. "Yeah, fine. I hear you."

"Put it on, Ben. Appearances are everything."

He wasn't wrong about that.

@

Livy

After our adventures with Jack the Ripper, I'd expected Ben to act different in some way, but he was mostly normal. He'd been out of the office on Friday but had emailed to let me know the police would be by to take a statement.

And that had been all he'd said on the matter. He mostly let me get on with it as if nothing had happened.

Which was handy because there was a lot to learn about the running of the business. I had my work cut out for me.

As annoying as Ben was sometimes, with his deep voice and strutting around here like he owned the place, which he did, I really, really liked the job. It was challenging. I had to bring up all my organizational skills and put them to good use.

But however the hell they'd organized things before didn't make any sense. The folders were difficult to find, I could not locate our clients, and half of the department didn't really communicate very well, requiring everyone's bosses to get involved to make any sort of decision.

Things would be so much better if they just organized cross-functionally. So I put together a report outlining a better way to work. If there were project teams and everyone had a stake in it, then resources would be sorted across teams as well. And for every project, it would be a renegotiation of what team it would end on. Why didn't they know this?

I also learned that everything was pretty much siloed under each of the CEOs, which was ridiculous, considering they managed one company. And as resources went, that meant if someone was being underused on one side, it was almost impossible to reallocate them.

I'd already started implementing some of those changes. I

was pretty sure Ben hadn't even noticed. Which was fine. I got to do my job and be left alone. I really didn't want his input anyway, nor did I need his ire. It wasn't my fault I'd been mugged twice in one week.

After a series of three meetings back to back, I was relieved to finally reach my office again. All I needed was a good couple of hours of uninterrupted work. I'd been digging in so hard in my new role, that I'd been getting home later and later each night.

Granted, Dexter hadn't exactly been home to notice. Most of the time he texted me to say he was working late. And to be fair, I didn't even notice that he had texted until I got home and he wasn't there. Which probably said something.

Like how long are you going to put up with this? It had been going on too long. We needed to have a sit down because really, we were just glorified roommates. My mother hadn't wanted me to be alone, but I was certain she didn't want me to be unhappy either.

We would talk at dinner next week. It would be fine. We'd either work this out or realize that we couldn't. It made my heart squeeze a little. This was Dexter. He'd been there for the toughest parts of my life. I didn't want to just give up.

And the guilt still ate at me. Everything had changed because of me. And that was a hard pill to swallow.

Looking forward to getting off my feet, I gasped when I saw the bright bouquet of pink roses, complete with baby's breath. *What in the world?* They were beautiful. They looked velvety soft, and their aroma already filled my office. But I wasn't really a *roses* girl. I was more into interesting flowers like orchids or lilies. But there was no denying how gorgeous they were.

I placed my laptop on my desk and then I hunted for a card. I found one nestled deep in the nest of thorns. All it said was *I'm so proud of you.*

The instant welling of tears was unexpected.

Dexter.

God, just when I was on the verge of giving up, he came through. I didn't even stop to think when I grabbed my jacket. It was close enough to lunch that I could leave early and go say a surprise thank you.

It was a straight shot to South Bank from Soho on the tube, so within fifteen minutes I was walking into the sleek glass and chrome of Mills and Crawford Investments. I knew where Fenton's office was and managed to deftly avoid it. It was 11:45, so the office was nearly a ghost town with everyone off to lunch.

Good old Dexter, though, was at his desk. "Hey there handsome, are you accepting blow jobs as recompense?"

His head snapped up and his eyes went wide before he shoved up out of his chair. "Olivia. Wh-what are you doing here?"

I smiled up at him as he came around his desk. "Silly, I'm here to say thank you."

He frowned then looked around me to his door, which I'd closed behind me. "Thank you for what?"

Laughing, I looped my arms around his neck. "For my flowers, silly. They're beautiful. I was so surprised. I love them though. I know we've been disconnected for a while, but—"

He pulled back from me, unlooping my arms and holding them between us, effectively forming a barrier. "What are you talking about? I didn't send you flowers, Olivia."

I blinked, my arms going lax as he released me. "Are you sure?"

"Seriously? I would know if I sent you flowers." A frown creased his brow. "Who the hell is sending you flowers?" His voice rose.

"Well, clearly I thought it was you."

"What did the card say?"

"Just that you, or I guess *someone,* was proud of me."

"You're serious. Someone sent you flowers *masquerading* as me?"

I sighed, then shifted on my feet, not really sure of what to do with myself now. This was hardly how I'd pictured my surprise visit. "I'm not sure they were masquerading as you. I *assumed* it was you. I mean who else would send me flowers?"

He pursed his lips and crossed his arms. "Have you checked with your boss? From what I've been reading, he does like the ladies."

Clearly, coming here had been a bad idea. "Dex, c'mon. You can support me getting promoted." I cleared my throat. "Well, since I'm here, do you want to go to lunch? You know that offer for a blow—"

His office door opened, cutting me off. "Hey Dex, you ready—" The beautiful red head in leggings, booties, and a fitted top froze when she saw us. "Oh, sorry. I thought we had an appointment."

Dexter shoved his hands in his pockets, then quickly dragged them out. He always did that when he was nervous. But *why* was he nervous? I watched him closely as his gaze just darted back and forth between us.

What the hell was wrong with him? When he didn't introduce us, I stepped forward and extended a hand. "Hi, I'm Olivia."

She stared at my hand for a long moment, then shook it. "I'm Andrea. I'm Dexter's—"

"Physical therapist," he quickly finished for her.

He's into her.

I wasn't proud of my first thought. I wasn't the kind of woman who felt threatened at every new beautiful woman my boyfriend encountered. After all, I'd end up angry a lot then.

Dex was always entertaining for work. I also wasn't the kind of woman who thought I could keep tabs on him or wanted to control who he was. He was a grown man.

You're better than this.

I was better than this. Dexter was with me. Had been for years. We might have been working some things out, but we were committed to that.

I dragged in a deep breath to force my calm then ran through what he'd said. Physical Therapist. The subject of his hand was a red-hot button with us.

Was that why he was so cagey? He hated it when I asked about him doing his PT exercises. "Oh. It's nice to finally meet you. Dexter has gone on and on about how he loves PT with you." I frowned at her lack of equipment. "You guys going to work out here? In those shoes?"

Again, it was Dexter who answered. "She's just going to walk me through a few things for my hand. I've been having those flare ups of pain."

He had? Why didn't I know he was in more pain than usual? "Oh, right. I guess I'll get going and leave you to it." I forced a smile. "The video games you suggested, have really helped with his dexterity." That sounded encouraging right? Not at all jealous girlfriendy? *If you need to believe that.*

I reached for Dexter to kiss him, and what I got was an air kiss on the cheek. Oh yeah, we were bringing all the sexy back.

His voice was firm and cool when he said, "Call the florist. Find out who sent the flowers. I'm curious."

"I guess I will. Sorry I bothered you at work."

His response was a terse nod. "It's fine."

"I'll see you at home, yeah?"

"Yeah, yeah." His attention was already on the redhead.

I forced myself to swallow the sting of jealousy. I would not let someone else eat at me. Dexter and I were in a relationship. He wouldn't betray that.

You sure of that?

When I returned to the office, I rearranged the flowers to the corner of my desk so I could have an unfettered view of my door in case someone came in.

It was only after I moved the vase that I saw, next to it was a small black box. I frowned as I picked it up. This was beyond weird now. I tugged on the ribbon and tried to calm my breathing. I just prayed I didn't find something like a finger inside.

I squeezed my eyes shut, but then exhaled and peered one eye open as I lifted the lid.

Nestled in the black velvet was a batman pin with the Ghana flag on it. Just like the one Ben had broken the night of the fundraiser.

Ben. He was responsible for the flowers and he'd replaced my pin. My eyes suddenly stung, and I blinked away the mist forming in my eyes. Someone must have brought onions for lunch. *Or, your boss isn't a complete dick.* Just when I'd started to solidify my opinion on him, he did something so thoughtful.

There was a knock behind me and I widened my eyes, willing the mist of tears to evaporate. I turned slowly with an impassive gaze. "Yes?"

Ben was in my doorway. Just seeing him made everything inside go all warm and fluttery. "I'm sorry it took so long to replace it. I guess you can't just buy the pin anywhere, so I custom ordered it."

My stupid tears were so close to the surface. If I wasn't careful, I was going to become a blubbery mess. "You didn't have to do this."

He stepped inside. "Yes, I did. I felt bad the night of the fundraiser, and I was a bit of a wanker. I'm sorry. After I learned how much it meant to you, I knew I had to replace it."

I blinked rapidly. "Thank you. Getting the pin back is a big deal, and it's much appreciated." I chewed my lip and gathered courage for this next part. "Mr. Covington, I just wanted to say that—"

He shook his head. "*Ben.* Or Bennet if you must. Mr. Covington is the former Prime Minister. I'm not him."

I sighed. "Okay, fine, *Ben,* while I appreciate the pin, the flowers are going just a bit too far."

His brow lifted. "What?"

Be firm. Be direct. It was the only way I was going to be able to contain the runaway butterflies in my lower belly. I couldn't indulge any kind of crush or whatever this was. I approached him as I spoke. "Obviously, you are very, uh, *attractive*, and *kind* as well, but you are my boss. And while I do need someone to accompany me on the things for my mother, I was not *propositioning* you."

He frowned and nodded slowly. "*Propositioning?*"

Why was he repeating the words I was using? "Exactly. I wasn't in any way saying that I was going to shag you or anything like that." Though I'd maybe, just maybe, fantasized about it. But that was not something I needed to clue him in on.

"Shag me?"

"Yes. I mean, I don't exactly know you, but I'd hoped maybe we'd started to be friends, except for the part where you yelled at me last night when we almost got mugged."

"There you go again, saying I yelled. I spoke firmly to get your attention."

"That was clearly yelling."

"I was not yelling." His voice rose.

My tone matched his. "Oh, I think that was yelling. And you can't send me flowers. I have a boyfriend." *Oh yeah, way to trot that one out.*

He shook his head. "I appreciate your directness, but I didn't send you these. And let's face it. Pink roses are boring and unimaginative. You're clearly an orchid kind of woman."

My face flamed. "Th—they're not from you?"

He shook his head. "No. Nor were they here when I dropped off the pin for you earlier this morning. But now I'm concerned because you don't seem to know who would send you flowers."

He was serious. I could see it in his eyes. He hadn't sent them. "I went to thank Dexter, but they're not from him either."

"How mad was he that someone had sent you flowers?" He asked with a smirk.

"Um, let's go with mildly annoyed."

His brows really scrunched up then. "Another man sent you flowers, and your boyfriend is only mildly annoyed?"

"He trusts me. But if he didn't send them to me and they're not from you, then who the hell sent me flowers?"

"That, Miss Ashong, is a very good question." He searched for wrapping or packaging and found nothing. "Sorry, there are no hints. Maybe Amy removed the packaging before she put them in here?"

"I'm not sure. I'll ask. I guess it's a mystery for now."

"A mystery you're okay with?"

I shook my head. "Not really, but I have work to do. Maybe they were delivered to me by mistake. Maybe there is some poor woman in here whose birthday or anniversary it is, and she thinks her boyfriend forgot."

He frowned at that. "It's a possibility, but who knows?"

I was still standing in the middle of my office when he moved to pass, and it was like being hit in the face with a heat lamp as he walked by. *Geez.*

The scent of sandalwood teased me enough that I wanted

to lean in. I wanted to sniff him. Why did he smell so good? It wasn't fair. He was supposed to be a troll, completely unattractive. It would have helped a lot.

But you can handle one man.

I could. Besides, I had work to do. Ogling my boss wasn't on my to-do list.

CHAPTER 12

Livy

Perched in the corner of the couch in the living room with the light dimmed, I tapped away. I wanted to at least finish this chapter of the book. Dexter had gone to bed an hour earlier, claiming he needed his beauty rest. Mostly I thought he was trying to avoid me because I was asking to talk to him specifically about our next appointment with Dr. Kaufman.

But I preferred him going to bed rather than getting in another fight.

Or you wanted your peace so you can think about Ben without feeling guilty.

No. No more thinking about Ben. I could accept that the man was sexy. He was. He was full of power and arrogance, and he was more than a little bit naughty. But that was the kind of problem I didn't need, and I was merely a curiosity to him. Someone like him was not going to be into someone like me. Not for the long haul anyway. He dated models and heiresses. Not real people.

Not that I cared. But our worlds were not the same. I was merely a fascination for him.

I rubbed the back of my neck as I searched through my research notes for a name. My mother had been extremely organized with her outline, her sources, her research. Everyone had their own little dossier. I couldn't believe how much work she'd done and how in depth she'd been.

Her friend, Caroline Ritter, had worked at the embassy with her in London some years ago. In more recent years, she had started doing more human aid work, trying to work with The Hague for better anti-trafficking laws and penalties. She was a real crusader. But then one day, five years ago, she'd called her mother, told her she was going on a holiday, and then she hadn't come back.

The paper trail showed that she'd gone to Barbados as planned. But upon digging further, there was no evidence of her ever checking into the Grand Bajan Hotel, no evidence that she'd actually ever landed in Barbados. But flight manifests showed that she had indeed boarded a flight from Heathrow.

And that was just the start of the mystery. Her life, the people she met, who she talked to, was endlessly fascinating. But what made it even more rewarding was just knowing that my mother had been on this path, chasing down a mystery. She'd always been a true crime junkie. If the show had *Law and Order* in the title, she was definitely watching it despite it not being quite so true. Anything Interpol was her kind of jam. And I found that I loved it too.

As I typed the last line, my phone buzzed next to me. I smiled when I saw it was Telly. "Hey, love," I said in greeting. "Does Carmen know you're up past your bedtime?"

Telly groaned. "Do you know she shoved a smoothie in my hand today? It had kale. You've lived in America. What is that country's obsession with kale?"

I laughed. "It's good for you, I guess."

"Ugh, I'm British. I want a bacon butty and sausage rolls any day."

"You can have that too. But you should probably eat some green things."

"She's a leafy green Gestapo."

"Oh my God, you're so dramatic. What's up? Why are you up this late if there isn't wine involved?"

Telly immediately sobered. "Okay, listen. This flash drive, it's harder to crack than I thought. I made my own copies, just in case, and I'm glad I did. My first attempt to crack it immediately erased the drive."

"What?" My heart hammered. Had I done all that just to lose it?

"Yeah. You trip the wrong wire on that thing, and data starts running away from you like someone's literally doused it in gasoline and set it on fire."

"Jesus." I scrubbed a hand down my face. "How many copies did you make?"

"I have at least three more. But now I wonder if making copies also corrupts the data."

I frowned. I hadn't even thought of such a thing. " Were you able to get any information at all?"

"A little. I'm not going to be able to make much sense of most of it though. It's like a giant dump of data, some of it seemingly inconsequential. It could also be some kind of code. I don't know. And loverboy wanted this really bad? Enough to have you smuggle it out?"

"I guess. I mean maybe it's some kind of corporate sabotage, but last I checked the Van Linsteds weren't into property development. Or hotels."

"No, they're not, at least not as far as we know. If it doesn't shine and glitter and they can't steal from impoverished indigenous peoples, they're not interested," Telly muttered. "Okay, I want to keep trying. But I need you to be careful. Some of the data I am seeing points at Eton College."

I frowned. "The secondary school for boys?"

"Yeah. I know that Ben and his mates went to Eton. Other than that, it just looks like bullshit data. I'm going to keep digging, but I might need another set of eyes."

"What do you mean another set of eyes?" I clearly was no coder.

"Well, you know there are people better than me out there, people who actually black hat hack and white hat hack. I happen to know someone who rides the line. I'm going to fire off this data to him and see if he can come back with anything. Because it is bizarre."

"Telly, if you think it's at all dangerous, then maybe we should stop."

"Oh no, Neo, we've gone down this white rabbit hole, we're going to continue to take the damn blue pill."

I chewed my nail. "Okay."

"I'll send it to my friend. He'll be discreet. But in the meantime, I want you to be careful. Anybody with data who is this desperate to hide it is likely dangerous."

"I'm not really in anyone's target. No one knows I was there. But I have questions. So many questions."

"I hear you. But just do me a favor and keep an eye on that Viking. Whatever he's dragged you into, it stinks of bad news."

"Okay, I hear you. And Telly, thanks."

"Of course, love. Ride or die. Though I'd really like to know where we're going and why one of us must die when we get there."

With a chuckle I hung up the phone. I had no idea what I'd tripped into, but there was no way I could pull back now.

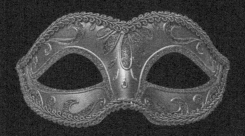

CHAPTER 13

Ben
Two weeks later...

I was fucking distracted.

How was it one woman, in the span of two weeks, could have turned my entire world upside down?

I was a bloody disaster. Between fighting with my mates about how best to handle this fucking situation and waiting on East who was still working on leverage, I was twisting in the fucking wind. And now, I was sitting next to her and she smelled fucking insane.

Her perfume should be named Tease. Just a hint of coconut and lime. Just when you thought you had figured out what it was, where it might be coming from, it morphed and changed into something else. It was something both familiar and unknown. God, I was a mess. It was bad enough after our little adventure with the attempted mugging and my detour to Bridge's that she'd been all I'd been able to see in my dreams. That fucking smile, her goddamn voice... And let me just say, in my dreams she was a hell of a dirty talker. Willing to beg, practically purring... *Jesus.*

I'd tried to be nice by replacing that stupid pin. I just wanted her to have something good, since I'd broken hers the night we met. I wasn't sure how I knew that it was so important to her, I just did. But even that gesture had taken a wrong turn. Nothing about the woman was ever straightforward. And she was sitting there with a soft smile, smelling like temptation and every bad decision I'd ever made.

I dragged my attention back to the meeting, and next to me, Olivia shifted in her seat. Her skirt migrated and inched higher, and holy hell, was that the end of a stocking? I bit back a groan and dragged my gaze away.

Do not look. I didn't need any more fodder for the goddamn wank bank. It was already too easy to think about her, to dream about her... She was already fucking torturing me. I didn't need any more.

She cleared her throat and stood up. What was she doing?

"Hello, everyone. I've met most of you in meetings over the last couple of weeks. Glad to be on board. Before going on vacation this week, Jessa asked me to present today, so I'd like all of you to turn your attention to..."

I could hear the words she was saying. I understood that she was directing people to the PowerPoint on the board, and she had the clicker. Why did she have the clicker?

Clearly, she's giving a presentation you wanker.

I frowned. But it was my job to present the priority projects.

My frown deepened, and I interrupted. "Ms. Ashong, what are you doing?"

She blinked at me. "Mr. Covington, I'm giving the presentation on the direction we'll be moving, what's currently on everyone's plate right now, and suggestions for how to streamline."

I gave her a brittle smile. I was pissed off that she thought she could take over my meeting.

Well, it is her job.

That spike of rationality got smothered quickly. This was *mine*. It had always been mine.

Then why did you hire her?

I had no fucking idea. I was pissed off and annoyed. For someone who had me all twisted up, she didn't look at all perturbed.

"Oh, sorry sir. I thought that you would want me to. But go ahead."

I took the remote from her and stood. That's right, my meeting. She gave me a soft smile. Why the fuck was she smiling at me?

You're losing it. Calm down. Focus on what you need to do.

"All right, as you know we've got the Paris property going. We're waiting on final bids from Wes and then we'll finalize. Also, I went over the Peterman file and what we'll do is have Max Peterman and his crew take over on the 20th for that site. We'll get their estimate and—"

Olivia raised her hand. "I'm so sorry to interrupt sir, but Max Peterman can't lead on that project."

I frowned. "What? Why the hell not?"

"Because his wife is having a baby the week before. He sent notification via email. He's got his foreman ready and willing to go, but you weren't happy with the results the last time his foreman ran a project for us. What I am suggesting is an alternative. We'll have a crew work on the luxury villas. It was a separate crew anyway, because that was going to require special permits. We'll keep that moving and on track instead of waiting. And then after Peterman's paternity leave, he and his team can resume in two months."

I could only stare at her and try to decipher her words. She'd clearly asked me something because she was waiting for a response. I shook my head. "What?"

She spoke more slowly, and I was well aware of everyone around the table staring at us. She stood and took the remote out of my hand and clicked. "You see, on this file, I circled when he would be ready to start. That means that the luxury villas would be built, mostly fitted, except for plumbing, and we have a separate team to do that and the electrical, which will be wired into the main system, so we can have Peterman's team do that as normal while he's on leave. He would start here,"—she clicked the calendar—"eight weeks from now, and the whole team will be able to function while he's gone. There will be no starts and stops. This will be more efficient and means we can actually finish ahead of schedule."

She clicked again, showing what that did to the calendar on the project.

I blinked at her. "Right." Why hadn't I known about Peterman?

I handed the rest of the meeting over to her. After all, she had all the slides, and well, I felt fucking obsolete at my own company. This was my meeting. My team.

It's her job now.

God, I was losing it. After just a hint of this woman's perfume, I couldn't think right. *Jesus.* I was no better than a goddamn teenager.

When the meeting was over, I scowled. "Miss Ashong, please stay behind." She has just stood but eased herself back into her seat and turned around slightly so she could face me.

When everyone was gone, she crossed her arms. I didn't know if it was a protection of herself against me or if she was irritated. Either way, it made my anger simmer to life. "What the hell was that?"

"That was you trying to take over my meeting."

I blinked hard. "*Your* meeting? Whose name is on the building?"

She grinned. "London Lords."

I narrowed my eyes at her. "You know what I mean."

"Do I? You hired me to do a job. Let me do that job."

"Why didn't I know about Peterman?"

"When I asked you to hand over the file the other day, you must have known I was going through it. I wanted to double-check dates. That's when he mentioned to me that he was going on paternity leave, so I adjusted the calendar accordingly. I did some juggling and moved things along. I sent it in the prospectus two days ago."

I frowned. She *had* sent me some emails. I hadn't had a chance to go to through them all yet. "I didn't see them."

"I marked them as urgent."

I'd had my hands a little fucking full. "You didn't deem it necessary to sit me down face to face?"

"Sir, when you gave me this job, we didn't exactly set any parameters, so Jessa and I discussed them. If you need me to sit you down and discuss every little thing with you as part of this job, I can do that, but you need to make yourself available. It's also redundant to do that with Jessa and with you. Are you who I directly report to, or is she? Or maybe you should realize that you hired someone qualified and let me deal with the job you've hired me to do. If I run everything by you, I'm nothing more than your glorified assistant."

I scowled at that. "You are going to be a pain in the arse, aren't you?"

"Yes, I am. Is that a problem?"

I opened my mouth to yell, but instead, my stupid lips twitched. I liked that she had spunk. I liked that she stood her ground and was smart enough and didn't need me to make every little decision. *Shit.*

I was going to regret this. I could feel it. Working this closely with her, being this close to her, not touching her, was going to be a problem.

"We can work together. You don't have to fight me. I just want to do my job, and I am grateful for the opportunity because I would have been stuck as Kennedy's assistant for far too long. So please, let me show you what I can do."

"You already have. It's not bad."

She laughed, pushed back her seat, and stood. "Not bad? Please, I'm the best operations director you've ever had. You'll see."

And then I could only stare at that delectable ass as she sashayed out of the damn room.

I was so utterly fucked.

CHAPTER 14

Ben

Music thumped inside the club, and I had to blink rapidly to let my eyes adjust to the dark. SKIN was one of the most exclusive strip clubs in London. The girls were high-end escorts and dancers. The owner, Cassia, a former Russian ballerina, made sure her girls were clean, safe, and drug free.

This was where I found Adam Hilton, getting a lap dance from a dancer called Candy. I slid into the booth with him, and he frowned at me. "Oi, mate, this is a private booth."

I grinned at him. "No, Adam, it's not."

His frown deepened, and then he squinted. "Covington? Is that you?"

"In the flesh."

Candy glanced back and forth between us. "I'm sorry, but if you would like a friend to join in, you'll have to pay extra."

I took several hundred-pound notes out of my billfold and handed them over. "I'm so sorry to cut this short. But I need to speak to him."

She gave me a smile and her gaze perused my body. "Shame. We could have had fun."

Not that I was one to judge, but very likely I'd want to disinfect myself after leaving here. We definitely would not have had fun. "Yeah, next time, love."

"I'm going to hold you to that."

I made a mental note to never step foot in there again.

Hilton glared at me. "What is it you want? Why are you ruining my perfectly good evening?"

"Well, I needed your attention."

"Out with it."

"There's a certain rumor going around the Elite that you are one of the Five."

He laughed. "Is that why you're here? I already told Van Linsted I'm not. So you're wasting your fucking time."

Fuck. He'd beaten us to Hilton?

I didn't know how far the Five would go to protect their identities. I only knew that I still had to try and get his vote. And if not his vote, then I needed to at least try and get his thoughts on who might be in the Five.

"Look, I'm not trying to jam you up. But this is vital. I don't know what Van Linsted said to you, but if you're like me and several other members of the Elite, the idea of another Van Linsted having control of our future for years to come is, at best, concerning."

He sniffed and drained his glass. "You're barking up the wrong tree lad. I can't help you."

I nodded. "I understand. And honestly, I get it. You have a life to protect. But we are at an impasse. We simply cannot allow the Van Linsteds to gain more power, so we need to do what we can to remove them."

He frowned at me. "You don't seem to understand, Covington. Why did you never learn the lesson that your father did? You can't just be unhappy about the scenario. You have to provide an alternative solution. One everyone would support."

"And get the Five to endorse him?"

"Exactly. No one can back a horse they don't know."

I took out the envelope that was in my pocket and handed it over. "What I want is your support against Bram Van Linsted regardless of the candidate." I could see now that we'd have to offer up an alternative.

He laughed. "Again, I hear you saying things that *you* want. But what do I get?" He looked inside the envelope. There was one photo... of his son. He sputtered. "Where the hell did you find this?"

"Doesn't matter *where* I found it. The point is that you have a child. A child with a woman who *supposedly* is your wife. Funny thing is this wife is young... so young."

Even in the dim light of the club, I could tell he'd gone ashen. "Why are you doing this?"

I blinked at him. "None of this information needs to come to light. Your wife, the one with the money, need not know about your other wife in Spain who actually has a child. She doesn't need all that pain."

He sighed. "You don't know what you're playing at, boy."

"I think I have an idea."

He frowned. "I can't give you blanket approval on a candidate."

"Yes, you can. You just know that it's not going to be Van Linsted. Adam, this is what we need. Either you're with us or you're not. And if you're not, well, I'm sure you can guess what will happen."

He stared at me and then back at the envelope.

"It's not what it looks like."

I placed my hand on my chest. "I swear I'm not judging. I'm sure there's a very good reason you shagged a sixteen-year-old girl and knocked her up. I'm sure there's a reason her family doesn't seem to know that you're already married. I'm sure there are reasons for *all* of this, but I don't care about any them. I just want your support. Do I have it?"

He swallowed, glowering at me. "Fine."

I nodded. "One more question. When Van Linsted came asking for your support, what did you tell him?"

"He hasn't asked yet. He called for an appointment."

"Excellent. So what *will* you tell him?"

"I'll tell him that I can't be bribed. I'll tell him what I've already told him, and you, that I'm not one of the Five."

"Excellent. It's a pleasure doing business with you, Hilton."

"And I have your word? The word of a gentleman, that you won't expose me?"

The man made me ill. Those poor women, both his wives... I didn't know them personally, but they didn't deserve his deception.

"On my honor as a gentleman, I will not be the one to share these details. But if my team found it, it's entirely possible someone else will."

He drained his glass. "It's a risk I'm willing to take."

I didn't bother looking at him as I left. I was pretty sure I would never wash the taste out of my mouth. But at least we had won his support, and that was all that mattered.

Ben

Knowing what had to happen and actually *making* it happen are two very different things. Bridge had finally managed to secure a Van Linsted meeting. I didn't particularly think he was one for an academy award, but we were all counting on him to sell it.

East was in my office as we listened. Bridge's listening device was loud and clear.

He'd greeted Van Linsted in the lobby, buttered him up, and said it was great that they were really talking after all these years.

Van Linsted wasted no time with a personal jibe at me. "Well, I figure we would have forged a stronger relationship a lot sooner if you had chosen your friends more wisely."

Bridge's response was immediate. "I hope you don't hold Ben's actions against me. Ben and I aren't as close as we used to be. His recklessness has become a problem, as has his lack of foresight." His lies rolled off his tongue smoothly, and I could only be proud of him. He was good, better than I had given him credit for.

He managed to pull off that cool air of disdain and indifference, which was exactly what we wanted. We wanted it to seem like he gave two fucks and that he was willing to do whatever was called for.

Bram's voice was smooth as they rode in the elevator. "You know, I will admit, I was unsure of you for the Elite. But you have proved yourself more than capable of being the right kind of man."

"Well, I certainly worked to get here."

My gut churned. Once a wanker always a wanker. I forced myself to listen as Van Linsted both stroked Bridge's ego and simultaneously put him down.

Ten minutes in, even East had grown weary of the bullshit as Van Linsted made his pitch for why he was a fit for Director Prime. "Do you feel sick too?"

I slid him a glance. "Yeah, it doesn't feel brilliant."

Finally, when their phones had been in close proximity a few minutes, East hit Compile to see if the program he'd put on Bridge's phone had done its job. We'd hopefully be able to get more valuable information from Bram's phone.

"It's going to take a minute. After it's copied, I'll still need to decrypt it. Don't you have to get ready for the Blake Boynton meeting?"

"I'm meeting him a few blocks from here at six."

"I can't believe he actually took a meeting."

"I was surprised too. I have a feeling he's not one of the Five, but we need to be sure."

"We do. You're caught up on the file?"

"Yeah. Basic embezzlement from the family trust. But leverage is leverage."

He nodded and I stared back. Finally, he just kicked me out. "Mate, get off my tits. I'll call you if I get anything."

I took a left out of East's office and was surprised to find Olivia barreling down the hall toward me. "Good, there you are. I have been looking for you."

My brows lifted. I had to make a visible effort to calm the erratic uptick in my heart rate and kill any interest from my dick. "You have? Is there a problem?"

"I wanted to talk more about Peterman, you know, the meeting and how it went."

I frowned. "Okay, why?" I planted my feet and it seemed like she was trying to back me up. "What's going on? Do you want to discuss it in your office?"

Her eyes went wide. "Um, my office?"

Her body language said she wanted me to back up, like she was trying to herd me in the direction she wanted. "Yes, your office. Or is there somewhere else you'd rather talk? Does my office work better?"

She glanced behind her. "Yep, why don't we do that." She physically tried to turn me, and I had to laugh because she wasn't getting very far.

I lifted a brow. "What's going on?"

She gesticulated as she spoke. "You know, just... let's go this way. There's something I wanted to show you. It's at the other end of the hallway."

It took another moment before I realized she was trying to steer me away from Bridge's office. She knew who was in there and didn't want me to blow up.

"But I wanted to go this way. I wanted to ask Bridge something." I was a prick. I knew I was, but I couldn't help having a laugh with her.

"No. Honestly, you're the smartest of the London Lords. I'm sure you don't need his input."

Now I knew she was shitting with me. "Oh, yeah?"

"Oh, absolutely. I have always said so."

I finally allowed her to turn me around so that we were walking toward my office.

I couldn't help laughing at her antics. She was a badass in the board room and a complete spaz out of it. Also, I wanted to kiss her.

What? No. No kissing. The fuck was wrong with me? We were in a mountain of shit. I should be focused on keeping her away from this mess.

Yeah, there was that. Also, she worked for me, and likely, the Elite knew about her, so kissing her was a big fat no-no. It would just set the target on her directly, and I wasn't going to be responsible for that.

I leaned close, letting her tease of perfume dull my rational senses. "Hey, Olivia?"

"Yeah?"

"Is there a reason you don't want me going down to Bridge's office?"

She swallowed hard. "Yes. Bram Van Linsted is in there with him. I think they have an appointment. Given how you two reacted the last time you saw each other, I figured it would be ugly. And you don't want your employees seeing you get into a fistfight, so I'm trying to take you away. Anywhere but there basically."

I grinned down at her. She really was very cute. "Fine. Where are you taking me?"

She blinked in confusion. "What?"

"You said you were going to take me away so I don't lose my shit over Van Linsted. Take me somewhere."

"Oh, right." Her brow furrowed slightly as she tried to think. And then away went the worry lines and that brilliant smile appeared. "Follow me."

It scared the shit out of me that my immediate response was to follow her anywhere.

CHAPTER 15

Livy

Why wasn't he mad?

I would be mad. I would be so livid if Telly started having secret meetings with my arch nemesis. Amy Sorensen from the second grade who told everyone my hair was like a Brillo pad. But no, Ben seemed cool as a cucumber. Not fussed at all. Why not?

He waited until we passed the square that sat kitty corner to the hotel before he leaned over. "So, you were worried about me?"

Jackass. I frowned. "No. Just so happens that I like my new job, pain-in-the-ass boss notwithstanding. It would be a shame if he got put in jail and then I lost my new gig. I'm being self-serving, really."

His low chuckle was like warm whiskey by the fireplace on a winter's night. Warm and crackling, sending a chaser of heat through my core. "So, you're enjoying the new gig?"

"Jessa is amazing. She's a powerhouse. I mean, she lives on two different continents and handles it with a husband and royal duties. I dig her so much. Can you explain to me how it is you know a princess?"

His smile was quick. "Starting to believe in my magical abilities, aren't you?"

"No. Never that."

"Of course not." His gaze searched mine, leaving tracks of heat everywhere it touched. "How are you doing?"

That was a good question. Was his question about the job or about my emotional state after our night out? It was such a loaded question. It had been a couple of weeks since the attempted mugging, and I was mostly normal if normal meant that sleep was a distant memory, but I was sure that would come back at some point. "I'm fine."

He shook his head. "Don't lie. You don't look fine. You look tired."

I narrowed my eyes at him. "You are the worst. How is it someone hasn't told you yet that you can't tell a woman she looks tired?"

I watched with rapt attention as his big shoulders moved up and down in a shrug. Even though he had a lean frame, his shoulders were set wide. I had never noticed anyone's shoulders before, but I certainly noticed his.

"I have a thing about honesty. I didn't say you still weren't absolutely stunning, but you do look tired."

"I'm fine. Everything is just peachy."

So far from peachy.

Dexter had his own bad couple of nights. He'd been so drunk last night he hadn't made it to the toilet... or the bedroom.

I'd found him asleep on the bathroom floor, so I'd had to wake him, toss him in the shower, and then clean up the bathroom. Not like I was sleeping anyway, but it would have been great to have pretended.

At least we'd finally been able to pick up a new prescription for him last night, so he didn't complain of pain this morning.

Sooner or later, I was going to have to have a huge come-to-Jesus talk with him.

But it was easier to be at work, easier to deal with challenging new responsibilities. *Coward.*

Easier to run.

I didn't want to run. Hell, I wanted to stay and make it work, which is why I'd done it for so long. But God, it was hard. Too hard. I was getting to that point that I was losing so much of myself and had no idea where the old me had gone.

"Penny for your thoughts?"

I didn't realize I'd sunk into a reverie. "No, it's all good."

"So, you are having fun?"

"Yes, and you know, in case I didn't say it the other night, thank you."

"I wish you'd told me about the earlier incident."

"What was I supposed to say? You'd just become my boss. I didn't want to share with you that I'd been mugged. You know the deal; don't be a problem child."

"You're not a *problem* child. I take offense to someone trying to hurt you." He spoke through gritted teeth.

"Yeah? Why is that?" He didn't even really know me.

"Well, considering you blackmailed yourself into the job, I want to protect my investment."

"I did *not* blackmail you." How could he still think that? It was only after I caught the corner of his lips turning up that I realized he was kidding. "Are you just trying to get a rise out of me?"

"It's so easy, honestly, you have got to work on your poker face." We walked past a bustling boutique of women fighting over bargain-bin clothing. "Can you tell me more about the thing with the ashes? What were you doing?"

"My mom passed away six months ago. Cancer."

"You were saying. I'm sorry."

"It's fine. I mean, not fine, but anyway, I haven't been able to spread her ashes yet. Every time I even think about it, I get locked up. She was so full of life. And I've been trying to finish her book by the one-year anniversary of her death. In Ghana the one year mark is a huge celebration of someone's life. I'd love to have it done by then."

He stopped right in front of the La Perla store, and it was all I could do *not* to stare at the display behind him. "You're writing a book?"

"Well, she was. I'm just trying to finish it for her. It's kind of a fictionalized true crime."

He blinked at me several times as if only just now seeing me. "That's incredible."

I shrugged. "Yeah well. According to my therapist, it's also helping me cope with the grief. But sometimes I wonder when I'll *feel* better, you know?" It was far too easy to talk to him.

"Well, that's... I'm pretty sure that's absolutely normal. I think it took me years before I came to terms with my mother's death."

My heart cracked in two for him. "How old were you?"

"I was eight. The worst part was watching my father, who had never been overly affectionate, completely shut down. She was the bridge, you know. Between us. And it's like without her there, we had no idea how to talk. We grew further and further apart, and our relationship deteriorated. And let's just say lots of mistakes have been made along the way."

"Families are complicated. Mom was always working. My dad died when I was a kid. A car accident. And from that point on, she was always on the move. I needed to have a bag packed and ready to go for whenever a quick move would happen."

"That must have been rough on you."

"It was. But I thought, you know, she needed me. I think she threw herself into work. She would take any assignment. I spent a lot of time in embassies around the world, never really getting to explore or see the countries we lived in. It wasn't until she was much older and she retired that she decided she was going to live life a different way, you know? Enjoy it. That's when she and I got really close."

"I'm glad you got that time with her when you were older, when you could really talk. That must have been really special."

I nodded and tried to blink away the tears at the same time. "Yeah, it was."

"So, since I didn't actually get to interview you, tell me, who is Olivia Ashong?"

I laughed then. "Well, my friends call me Livy, and there's not that much to tell. Like I said, I was a diplomatic brat. Went to Uni, partially in the States, then when Mom retired and opted to settle in the UK, I transferred here to be with her and finished school at LSE. It was the best thing I've ever done in my life. I fell in love with London. I fell in love with travel and food and, I don't know, it was just a very impressionable time for me."

"Well, for a Yank, you fit in decently."

I took offense to that. "What? I'm almost more a Londoner than you are. I doubt you know the London I know."

He laughed. "I grew up in Downing Street. You don't get more London than that."

I wrinkled my nose. "Snooty posh London. Not the same."

"What? You think I haven't run around in South London in dodgy clubs and partied in East London so drunk off my arse I couldn't see straight?"

"Yeah, still snotty rich London. You've got to see the really grimy bits. The markets, the people. I'll take you to this Ghanaian restaurant which is so incredibly delicious. But you might want to leave the fancy threads at home."

"You're on. Is that where your mom was from?"

"She was the Ghanaian ambassador to the UK for years. And then to the United States, Japan, France for a bit, and Italy. All over, really. Dad was British, but I happen to have been born in the States while she was stationed there. And then I just went to international schools most of the time."

"And you're talking to me about being snooty?" His laugh was more conspiratorial than teasing.

"I'm not snooty. I hated all of that stuff. So wherever we moved, I quickly found the nicest local I could and hung out with them as often as they'd allow. It was the only way I really learned about a place. It kept me grounded. So, I'm very down to earth. I watch all the best down-to-earth shows," I joked.

He laughed then. "God, something tells me I'm going to be scared of your telly viewing."

I rolled my eyes at that. "I'm sure you consider footie on ITV to be the end all-be all of what's on television?"

He laughed. "Well, I don't really have a lot of time for TV."

"God, don't you ever just veg on Sunday? Take a walk, do something that isn't putting oodles of money in your bank?"

To my surprise, he laughed. "No, I guess I don't."

"I want to make you a viewing playlist immediately."

He brushed a blond hair out of his face. "Oh, yeah? What's going to be on it?"

"First thing that's going to be on there is *Turn Up Charlie*. Idris Elba's in it. He's British and part Ghanaian. It's excellent and hilarious."

"It's a comedy?"

I smoothed my hand down over my hair as a quick wind gusted through the square. "I can't believe you've never heard about it."

"I guess I've been living under a rock."

"You have been. We'll fix that don't worry." He was easy to talk to. Too easy. I could forget that he was my boss. Or rather my boss's boss. I could almost forget how we'd met and that I'd blackmailed him into helping me.

Not blackmail when he bribed you.

"You are an odd one."

"I think I'll take that as a compliment."

"You should. You can come off as so buttoned up. Almost sterile. Like in your office. Why don't you have any pictures or plants or something?"

"I was taught you might need to be able to move quickly. Best not to unpack too much."

"Yeah, I kind of guessed that. Always ready to run."

"Something like that. Granted, running isn't by choice most of the time."

"If you say so."

We rounded a corner and strolled through cafés and boutiques. As we were headed back to the hotel, I heard a screech. A lorry was coming around the square, honking its horn. It jumped the curb, and I squealed. "Oh, Jesus, he's going to hurt someone."

Before the words could even finish tumbling out of my mouth, the driver lost control of the lorry with a trajectory directly toward us.

I don't know what possessed me. Ben was busy looking in the window of a cigar store, and he was turning a moment too late.

"Look out." I shoved him hard, toward an alley. He didn't budge much, but he did trip over the lip of the curb into what looked like a trough of water of the nearby florist.

"What the fuck?"

The lorry skidded again and then managed to right itself before careening off.

"Hey!" I shouted. "Come back."

Ben blinked up at me. "What are you doing?"

"I'm sorry. The lorry—"

"Yeah, I saw it. But why did you jump in front of it and push me away?"

Was he serious? "I was trying to save your life."

Several people had come over at that point to try and assist us. Someone had gotten the driver's license plate. As we were relatively unharmed, there was no point in waiting for the police, really. With slippery hands, a couple of people helped me get Ben up out of the trough.

When he was free, he glowered down at himself. His shirt, vest, and trousers molded to every muscle on him, and I stared.

Focus. You just shoved your boss into a trough of water. He's not going to be thrilled. "So, is this the moment when you realize I saved your life?"

His glare told me everything. This was not a life-saving event to him. I was so totally screwed.

@

Ben

I was soaking wet. And it was all thanks to Olivia Ashong, who was currently chattering a mile a minute as she followed me into my office.

"It's fine. It's just a little water."

I kept a change of clothes in the office for such an occasion that I stained my shirt or something. I just hadn't planned on doing a full change.

"I'm really sorry. I was just trying to get you out of the way.

"I'm just going to grab a change of clothes."

"But oh my God. I'm so sorry. I was trying to help. And honestly the lorry was so close, and we could have been killed."

"We weren't going to be killed. And I like the idea of you jumping in front of danger to try and save me."

"If I hadn't, you'd be flat as a pancake right now."

"I tripped."

Her eyes sparked with fire. "I saved you."

She was holding a towel and blotting me dry. And standing far too fucking close. Her coconut lime shampoo was wreaking havoc on me. I couldn't really think properly. I wanted to lean into her, to take a good whiff, to wrap myself in her scent and do all kinds of dirty things with it.

Jesus, you need help. "You are a magnet for trouble, did you know that?"

"I have never been a magnet for trouble until I met you. In a *closet,* mind you."

"*You* were there before I got there."

"But if you hadn't ever come in, I never would have gotten that drive in my purse, or gotten mugged the first time, or almost gotten mugged the next time."

"You're blaming me?"

"Yeah, I'm blaming you. Before I met you, I was completely boring. No one paid me any attention."

"You think this is my fault."

"I'm just saying."

"You're the one who needs to be careful. You're small and delicate, and you traipse around jumping into messes like you can't get hurt. When someone tries to mug you, you try to fight back."

"I just couldn't let it happen again. Besides, they wanted to take me somewhere, and even I know that's not a good idea."

"At least you know that much."

She jabbed me in the chest, her finger leaving an invisible, searing burn on my skin. And I wanted more.

"You need to be more careful."

"Careful, Mr. Covington, someone might actually accuse you of caring."

I squared my shoulders. "Hardly." My gaze fell on her lips, and my gut tightened. *No. Stop looking at her mouth.*

Olivia swallowed hard. "I am... uh..." The spark of lightning between us danced. I could physically *feel* the tension in the room. I needed to get changed. I needed her to get out for me to do that. But goddamn, her hands were on me as she patted me dry. "Look, it's fine. I'm just going to help you, and then we'll get back to our day, okay? God, I'm such an idiot. I was really trying to help."

She continued to pat me with the towel as she spoke rapidly, hardly taking a breath. Each press of her palm was stoking the flame, playing with fire. "Um, Livy?"

She kept on talking though. About how I needed to be more careful. That I should have better situational awareness. Have a clue as to what was happening around me.

All the while, she had zero idea what was going on in my head. The war I was having with myself about touching her, about what was appropriate. All the blood rushed south, and I clenched my teeth, trying to fight against my growing erection. She chose that moment to glance down.

Fucking brilliant.

Her voice went throaty when she mumbled, "Um, I think you're mostly dry. You can handle this yourself. I'm going to go."

I cleared my throat in a desperate attempt to regain control. "You probably should."

But she didn't move, just stared at me with those wide dark eyes. Daring me.

"Olivia?" It sounded like a plea.

Her wide dark gaze met mine. "Yeah?"

"I'm going to kiss you now."

Her mouth opened as if she meant to gasp, and I didn't waste any time.

Yes. I knew it was wrong.

Yes. I knew it was a bad idea.

Yes. I knew I had zero business kissing her when I didn't know if she could be trusted. *She has a boyfriend you wanker.*

Well, fuck him.

Deep down inside, she belonged to me. And yes, I knew that once I had broken the seal, it would be nearly impossible to put that genie back in the bottle.

But the kiss happened so fast that I didn't even have time to register my own movements.

My lips slid over hers, and electric heat struck like a stick of dynamite. She gasped, and I slid my tongue against hers, while hers teased mine in a slow, seductive caress, making me momentarily lose track of time and space, of who I was and what we were doing. There was so much I wanted to take. So much I wanted to have. So much I wanted to communicate in the kiss.

My hand caressed her face before sliding into her coily curls. I pulled the pins free, letting her curls spring apart and cascade down her back and over her shoulder.

I liked her like this. Hair out and free, a coiffure better matching her personality. Sliding my hand into the springy softness, I tugged gently, angling her head just enough so I could deepen the kiss and chase the taste of sweet berry on my tongue.

I couldn't think. Hell, I couldn't fucking breathe. All I knew was the blood flowing thick through my veins had drummed out all rational thought. I slid my other hand down her back to just over her ass, itching to cup her like I had before.

I wanted to claim her. Mark her. Make her mine so she wouldn't run again… so she wouldn't want to.

Kissing her felt like time stood absolutely still. We stood locked in time for what could've been a second. A minute. Or it could very well have been three hours.

My skin was too tight, too hot and flushed, and my cock was convinced it absolutely needed to reside inside Livy. He was working on his escape plan from my pants, and he wasn't taking no for an answer.

I kissed her until she made this little mewling sound at the back of her throat. Part whimper, part demand. Then we were moving.

A flat fucking surface.

That's what I needed. But this, whatever this was, wasn't going to be some hurried rush job on the desk. Not that I could stop kissing her.

I wanted her melting on my tongue and wrapped around me. Desperate as I was, I backed her up against the wall and angled my body so I could kiss her just the way I wanted. Desperate. Demanding.

Her hips ground against mine. There was no way she could mistake the hard press of my length against her.

Another whimpered plea and something shifted in the air. Instead of her fists grabbing into my shirt like they had been before, they were flat, and pressing against me.

I frowned, dragging my lips from hers, trying to make sense of the input I was getting. She sucked in deep breaths of air and pushed me away as she shook her head.

I released her easily and backed away. Even if it felt like I was cutting away a piece of me.

The severance of bodily contact enabled my brain to come back online. What. The. Fuck. Was. That.

"Fuck. That was not supposed to happen."

Her eyes darted around and looked anywhere but at me. Her lips trembled when she spoke. "I—I have a boyfriend," she stammered. Her cheeks were flushed and her lips swollen from my kiss.

I knew about her boyfriend. I just had stopped caring for a minute. All I cared about was tasting her again. Already like a junkie in need of another hit. "Livy, wait." I reached for her, but she evaded my touch.

"I have to go."

She darted around me, making her escape out of the office before I could stop her.

@

Livy

Two truths.

One, Ben Covington kissed like they were giving out Olympic medals for it.

Two, I'd kissed him back.

And not just kissed him back. I'd enjoyed every damn moment of it like I was never going to get another opportunity to kiss again.

And you're not. At least not him.

I leaned my back against the bathroom stall and tried to catch my breath, but it was nearly impossible. Hell, I could barely stay upright my knees were so weak. My stomach knotted. I'd kissed him back. Who the hell was I? The old me wouldn't have kissed her boss. No amount of crackly tension and heat would have made me do that.

I needed to find Dexter.

I had to talk to him. Apologize. *Something.* If I was going to be with him, I needed to be *with* him. I couldn't have one foot out the door and ready to leave. It was either all in or all out, and I'd ridden that fence for too long.

I checked my phone to see where he would be tonight and recognized the swank pub where they often had their work happy hours. I needed to go talk to him. I had to tell him and apologize. Hell, what was I going to say, it'll never happen again? He had no reason to believe me.

But I had to try.

From the bathroom, where I had every intention of hiding until it was time to leave, I used my phone to text a message to Jessa that I would be out of the office and on my phone if she needed anything.

Now all that was left to do was to remedy the guilt on my face.

CHAPTER 16

Livy

Finding Dexter and his team wasn't difficult.

They'd taken over the whole upstairs portion of the pub. It wasn't even really a pub. It was more bar turned pseudo nightclub. They had dart games and billiards, loud music and a dance floor.

When I climbed up the stairs, I spotted Dexter in the corner playing billiards. He expertly sunk a ball in the corner, and I couldn't help but think his hand seemed fine.

Fantastic.

I swallowed my annoyance. I needed to do this. I'd messed up. Our whole relationship had gone off the rails. And if I wanted to get it back, I needed to fix this. To undo the harm that I'd done.

Assuage your guilt you mean.

This wasn't me. I wasn't the kind of person who cheated. I wasn't the kind of person who kissed and made out with her boss. I wasn't that person. And Dexter needed to know.

I waved him down. His eyes went wide, and he faltered a moment.

He drank his drink before coming over to me. "Liv, what are you doing here?"

"Well, I checked the calendar, saw where you were going to be, and thought I would join you."

"No, we're entertaining clients. I can't really have my girlfriend turning up for that."

My heart sank. "Oh, I didn't realize. I'm sorry, I just wanted to see you. We've been sort of missing each other like ships in the night."

"Yeah, I know. We've just been busy, I guess. You've got your new job."

I swallowed down the annoyance, the anger, the fear that he might not be helpable. I swallowed all of it because he was Dexter. *My* Dexter. He loved me, and I loved him.

He doesn't act like he loves you. I ignored that twinge of reality.

"I just need five minutes, and then I'll leave you to enjoy your clients."

He sighed, leading me down the stairs. "Liv, this is really inconvenient."

"Sorry. I can go, I just really needed to see you."

He rolled his eyes. "Is this about your mum again? Look, I get that you're sad, but I thought you had a therapist for all this stuff."

"I do. I see her and it's good. But I need to see *you*. Look…" I shifted on my feet. This was not the way I wanted to have this conversation. "Can we go outside?"

He pressed his lips together into a firm line. "Christ, you're so fucking needy right now. I need to get back to my client."

Why was I here, begging him to love me? "It will just take a second, Dexter."

We finally went outside where I could hear myself think. Whispered kisses of an impending drizzle brushed my face. I glanced up at him. His eyes were bloodshot, his pupils dilated.

Come to think of it, he'd been using his hand just fine upstairs. I'd watched him angle a billiards cue. *Expertly*. His grip steady.

Stop it.

"Something happened today, and it made me realize that I want to work on us." *The hell you do. You're running scared.* "Really work things out. I know things have been a bit shaky, but I just want us to get back on track, you know?" *You're only here because you are desperate to know how else Ben can use his expert tongue, and it terrifies you.* "I didn't realize tonight was a client thing. I thought it was just a bunch of mates from work." *You did realize, but you need to cling onto this reality so you don't slip your boss your wet panties.*

He rubbed at the back of his neck. "Can't we just talk about this at home?"

"Yeah, I guess." I wasn't sure what I'd thought. That he'd magically turn into the old Dexter who would have been happy to see me on a night like tonight?

"Everything okay out here?"

The hairs on the back of my neck stood at attention, and a cold chill crept in through a crack I'd left unguarded. Dexter turned with a smile. "Fenton. There you are. Look, Olivia came by. She wanted to hang out. Why don't you and her chit chat. Get to know each other better. Liv, Fenton and the missus have been saying we need to go over there for dinner. Why don't you two sort it out? And be nice."

I forced myself to smile at Fenton. More of a gritting of teeth really. "Just one moment please." I pulled Dexter aside. "Dexter, I told you he makes me uncomfortable. Please don't leave me with him."

"Oh, just stop being such a fucking cunt. That's my boss. The least you can do is help me grease the political office wheels a little bit, yeah?"

My stomach turned. "What the fuck do you mean grease the wheels?"

"He's going to notice you're always rude. You never want to do dinner, you won't even talk to him at events, and you won't dance with him."

"I didn't realize it was my job to *dance* with your boss. And I do all those other things. To support *you*. But you're going to go back inside and *leave* me with him? That makes me really uncomfortable."

"Well it's not my problem. Leave if you want. It's not like you ever gave a shit about my career anyway."

I winced as if I'd been slapped. "Are you being serious? Or are you taking the piss?"

"I don't even know what you're doing here."

I straightened my back. "You know what, neither do I."

I couldn't even watch him walk inside. But when I turned, and Fenton was right there not two steps away. "Sorry, I couldn't help but overhear. Look, I'm sorry if my presence causes you discomfort."

I swallowed hard. "Look, I didn't mean to make you feel bad. It's just… I like my space."

He sighed. "But you recognize I'm just trying to help."

I tried to choose my words carefully since I was now outside, alone, with a man who made me uncomfortable. "And it's kind of you to be so helpful. Dexter thinks the world of you." There I was, doing it again. Making excuses for him, always trying to smooth the way. But he'd just left me. Like I was nothing.

"Why don't you let me take you home? You know Dex. He's had too much to drink. We can try to figure out a solution for him."

How exactly did one say fuck that noise politely? I was sure there was a way to do that. "That's all right. I think I'll just call an Uber."

He chuffed a laugh. "You know, Dex told me what happened. That you got mugged after the event. I was horrified. If you had just listened, did as I told you and took my car or let me take you home, none of that would have happened."

No, but something much worse would have. Something I needed to avoid now.

"Possibly. But I don't think one is related to the other. And I just want to go home and get to sleep."

He took my upper arm in a tight grip. "Let me help you. You never take my help. Never say thank you for what I've done for Dexter. It's distressing. It's like you don't understand how much I've done for you."

Bile churned in my belly. "Mr. Mills, you're hurting me."

He stared down at his hand, brows knit tight. "Stop being melodramatic. I'm not hurting you. I'm just trying to explain to you how it could be. Just let me take care of you. We're all a family here. I can give you what you need."

"I have what I need, Mr. Mills, thank you." I tried to pull my arm free, but he just tightened the vice. "Ow. I really need you to let me go."

His eyes roamed over my face. "So beautiful, but so ungrateful."

He pulled me closer, and I recoiled from the stench of gin. I hated that smell. Stale gin on the breath, there was nothing worse than that. "Let me go. Now."

His gaze narrowed. "You're such an ungrateful—"

"I think the lady told you to get your hands off her."

Goosebumps prickled my skin. I knew that voice. Did I dare pray.

"Mind your business, mate." Fenton spat. "My lady friend and I are having a conversation."

Ben's voice lowered to a growl. "Well, considering she works for me, she *is* my business."

I whipped my head around to find Ben taking long strides along the sidewalk.

He *was* here.

For me.

"She's asked you nicely to let her go. If you don't, I will do the asking. I'll be less than kind about it."

Fenton's fingers dug deeper into my flesh, and I winced. "Mr. Mills, let me go."

And then Ben was on us. Where Fenton held my arm, Ben's palm engulfed his hand. And then gently, I felt the pressure loosen.

Fenton's eyes went wide, and his mouth hung open in pain. "Ah, let me go, you piece of shit. There will be repercussions for this."

Ben scowled at him. "Yes, there will. For you. Not for me." He then wrapped an arm around me, pulled me tight to his side, and scuttled me along the sidewalk.

"What are you doing here?"

"I had a meeting scheduled. He was a no-show, and I was headed back to the office. I almost took the car, but I'm glad I decided to walk."

"Thank you."

"Looks like we keep saving each other."

I tried to blink away the impending tears. I was not going to let him see me cry.

"Where am I taking you? And let me be really clear. You're not going anywhere Fenton Mills will have access to you. Or knows about."

"Uh, I'll call Telly. I'll go to her flat."

He gave a terse nod. "Fine, call her. The car is up ahead. I'll take you there."

"Ben, you don't have to."

He paused and turned me to face him. "I think you and I both need to get on the same page here. For some reason, we are linked. You came barging into my life three weeks ago, and neither one of us has been able to shake the other. So stop apologizing and stop asking me to not take care of you. It seems you're mine now. Like a wayward kitty."

"Is that because you licked me? Now I belong to you?"

His quick grin was merciless. "I haven't even licked you yet. When I do, you'll know."

@

Livy

As it turned out, Telly couldn't find a fuck at the fuck store left to give when it came to Dexter. "He left you with Fenton?"

"Yes." This was the third time I'd had to recount the story. Telly grew more and more incredulous each time. She paced back and forth. Carmen watched her and just sat there rubbing my back and made sure I sipped the tea they'd given me.

"He fucking left you with that creep, Mills?"

"Yes, Tell."

"And then Fenton tried to attack you?"

"I wouldn't exactly use that word. He tried to make me go with him, and I told him no. And he was just gripping me so tight." Why wasn't I able to come out and say the word? It had been an assault. He'd put his hands on me without my permission. That's what had happened, but I felt like I couldn't say the ugly thing.

That was when Carmen frowned down at my arm, at the bruises now starting to turn purple on my flesh.

Carmen, as far as I could tell, was a pacifist. She was sweet and kind and never really raised her voice. With her long hair and her penchant for wearing flowers, I always considered her kind of a hippie. She was a doctor though and had already applied salve. She pulled out the bandages as she spoke. "If I find him, I'll kill him myself."

Telly met her gaze. "Carmen, you're beautiful, and you are amazing. But I will fight you for that right."

Oh God. Things were taking a turn. Before the night was out, Telly might form a posse like in the American old westerns she loved so much. "Turns out neither one of you has to do it. Ben already did." I hadn't really explained much when I'd rung up, Just the Dexter and Fenton part.

Telly stopped pacing and raised a brow. "As in sexy office Ben?"

I sighed. Must I really play into his arrogance with that nickname. "Yes, as in sexy office Ben."

A slow smile spread over her lips. "Uh-huh. So why were you and Ben there together?"

"No, I was not there *with* Ben. He had a meeting nearby."

"And he just rode into the war to save you?"

"Well, you know to be fair, he was the reason I needed saving in the first place."

Telly crossed her arms. "Explain."

I quickly ran over the incident at the office. Throughout, Telly and Carmen stared at me as if I had seven heads. "Say something, you guys."

Carmen just laughed. Telly, for once in her life, could find no words. Finally, she said, "So you kissed your boss?"

"No, *he* kissed me. But I kissed him back."

Telly counted out the points on her fingers. "Okay, so he kissed you, you kissed him back, and then you went to tell Dexter?"

"I don't know what I meant to tell Dexter if I'm being

honest. I just knew what I did was wrong and terrible, so I don't know, I wanted to lean into my relationship. It's no surprise that things have been difficult with us. I wanted to recommit or something dumb like that."

"But remember him and that redhead. I promise you your instincts are spot on there. Don't ignore them."

"I don't have any proof he did anything with her." My brain, oh so helpfully, replayed the night's events for me. "The things he said to me, Telly, it's like he hates me. And I don't understand what I've ever done to him."

"All you've ever done is try to help him. Sometimes people don't want to be helped."

"Tonight was horrible. And I know I can never see him again. And I know I deserve better, but there is this tiny part of me that feels awful, like I'm abandoning him."

"It's not abandonment when someone you care about puts you in a dangerous situation. Then it's called survival. And you are a survivor, aren't you?"

I swallowed nodded. "I am."

"Then yeah, I think you have your answer right there."

I tried hugging my knees in hopes that it would help me feel more whole instead of more fractured. "Yeah. You're right."

"I know."

"So, what do I do about Ben?"

Carmen had the perfect answer for me. "You shag him so good his dick falls off. It's been a long time since I've shagged a bloke. I don't normally miss it. But if he's that fit... Telly, you fancy a third sometime?"

Telly's laugh was rich. "Only if he looks like her boss. Because, wowsa."

I laughed so hard I snorted. "Oh my God. I wonder if I can break it from overuse?"

Telly nodded. "Hey, why don't you try it out and tell us."

I couldn't believe I could even laugh right now. "I'm not *shagging* him. I don't know, it's like we've sort of become friends. And then well today happened."

Telly nodded. "Are you sure becoming friends with the hot man you want to shag is a good idea?"

"I'm not shagging anybody. If Dexter and I are done, I need to put it to bed and then deal with my own shit before I bring anyone else in. I'm still grieving mom, I have a complete wanker for a boyfriend, and I just got a new job. I have a lot going on."

"Good point," conceded Telly.

"I know. I need to deal with it and soon."

"And then you'll be free." Telly took my hand and squeezed. "I promise you. None of this will kill you."

I wished I could believe her.

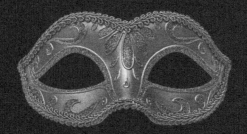

CHAPTER 17

Ben

B lake Boynton, the little shit, had cancelled on me last night. And good thing too, or I couldn't have been there for Livy.

Just thinking about that fucker, Mills, with his hands on her made me want to murder him. I'd never put in a name for a sanction, not once in the ten years I'd been in the Elite. But I was going to put Fenton Mills' name in, and I didn't give a shit.

If an Elite member called for sanctions, they had the option of stating their reason or not. Throughout a member's tenure, they could only call one no-disclosure sanction. All other sanctions needed to be disclosed to the members. Since I never wanted to drag Livy's name into the Elite, I'd call for a no-disclosure sanction.

But who will you call it against? Her idiot boyfriend or his idiot boss? It was a close one, but Fenton was the one who'd had his hands on her, so he would be the recipient of my sanction, and it wouldn't be pretty.

With a sanction, the membership systematically dismantled someone's life. Secrets revealed. Affairs leaked. The only exception would be if they had children. Children were off-limits.

Yesterday and last night had been a complete clusterfuck. I needed to get back on an even keel. I'd head out for this run to meet Blake in the park. The run would do me good. Let me clear my head.

Because there was still the little matter of me wanting to shag my operations director, and keeping my distance was getting more and more difficult.

I took the tube down to Regent's Park, not even concerned about the crowd of tourists. I knew my way around enough to avoid them entirely.

But there was something about the energy and vibe of London that was just what I needed. It was an unusually warm spring morning, and it felt good to have the nip of the air flowing to my lungs as I ran.

When you became one of the Elite, it was expected that you learn about things from military strategy to self-defense. Once you were tapped in secondary school, your training began in earnest. Then, over the course of five years, you became Elite in all ways, but you could specialize in certain areas.

Those who wanted to go into politics chose their path and received more strategic and diplomatic training. That's where my father would have preferred I go. But I'd followed Bridge and East into business with side training in security and clandestine service. I never actually got to be James Bond, but it helped knowing I could kick ass when I needed too. But I'd chosen the money path.

From the beginning, we'd known money was power. After all, the three of us had been controlled by it. And for me it was both a big fuck you to the old man and a step to freedom. Not to mention, I could be with my mates. We'd been given the best business internships with letters of recommendation from Elite members who were titans of industry. My father was right; as much as I wanted to believe we'd done it without the Elite, everything I had couldn't be separated from what I'd been given.

So many of us were in the foreign service, politics and clandestine services. The good news was my mates and I were well trained and well versed enough to be able to look out for ourselves. The bad news was so were the people we were determined to take down. Nothing had changed. If we had gone on with our lives without really knowing our culpability or the culpability of the other Elite members concerning Toby's death, things would have been simple. But I did know. I knew that for ten years Toby hadn't been able to rest. For ten years, the people who had killed him walked free. For ten years I'd been blind.

But that was over now. And there was a reckoning coming.

With my lungs burning, I made a left at the York Bridge entrance and proceeded west before turning at Ormond Terrace and making a loop around Primrose Hill. The views never ceased to amaze me. The yellow, red, and white primroses bloomed merrily along the paths.

Judging by where I was, I'd already run about four miles, and the meet point in question was in clear view. But no Blake.

I checked my phone to make sure I'd gotten the meeting location right, and I had.

After forty-five minutes, I knew he wasn't coming. Something wasn't right. Why take the meeting and not show? Had Bram gotten to him already?

I ducked off a path to run under a bridge, and cement chips flew out toward me, a piece grazing my cheek, making it sting.

What the fuck?

I ducked automatically and then heard that tell-tale whizzing.

That was a bullet. My brain did a mental calculation of where I was and where there would be cover.

I could run back along the path I'd come down and duck into a restaurant.

I made a quick right along the bicycle path and running path. Right next to it, there was a darkened pathway I recognized as a classic way to double-back and get to safety. Down here I was too exposed. And I'd be damned if I was going to die today.

But two dark figures at the end of the path blocked my way, and I knew I'd misjudged. There would be no easy way out of this. I'd have to fight my way out.

"Lads, you don't want to do this. I'm really sweaty and knackered. You don't want to try and hit me. Your fists will slide right off. It's going to be bad."

The two guys at the end of the short pathway smirked at each other.

"Okay, so you don't really care about your own well-being. Fair enough."

"I'm happy to kick your arse either way." The taller one said.

He was my height but bigger. He was swollen with muscle, and he meant to make quick, efficient work of me. Except, I wasn't going to be an easy target.

The one on the left, the darker-haired one, approached first. He was smaller but looked like he moved well.

"Now, before we get started, just put your guns down. Let's see if you're really up to the task."

The one on the left smirked at me, while the one on the right looked like he didn't like that idea at all. He was all business. His friend, though, took pleasure in their assignments.

Note to self: Do the one on the right first.

The one on the left made his approach, and I circled around, keeping my eye on the guy with the lighter sandy hair.

Sandy hair reached for his weapon, and I shook my head at him. "Uh-uh. No, no. Where's your sense of sport? Tell you what, if I can beat your friend here, you can kick my ass. Does that sound like a fair deal?"

He chuckled. His accent was all South London. "I'm going to kick your arse anyway, bruv."

"Ahh, just a moment ago you looked like you were going to pussy out and shoot me. Let's at least make it entertaining." Taunting the guy with the gun when I was unarmed was possibly not my best idea to date.

But it was all I had. This likely would get into the open street.

I thought it would be the dark-haired guy, but it was the other one who pulled me in. He launched at me first with a quick flurry of fists. Some I managed to duck; others landed too low. My side burned and I coughed.

But as he aimed to kick me, I swiftly turned, grabbing his foot and then delivering my own kick straight to his groin.

His eyes went wide and then slightly crossed. He cursed at me, and I released him, rolling out of the way. Quickly, he was back on his feet.

His mate lunged for me. He was slower. Less trained. But he was still fast enough to make me worried. It was one thing fighting with Martin, my trainer, or with Bridge and East and Drew. These guys were looking to kill. The dark-haired bloke lunged for me again. I took one to the face, but I landed a few of my own. A quick succession of two jabs and a hook.

His friend on the ground started to make motions like he was getting up. He was reaching for something. His gun? No thank you, I wasn't getting shot today. I landed another quick uppercut and grabbed the nearest thing to me.

Anything to use as a weapon. In this case, it was a pipe. I was going to do whatever I had to do to survive. These wankers weren't going to kill me on the streets of London and call it a random mugging.

Fuck no.

With my fingers wrapped around the pipe tight, the dark-haired one lunged at me, but I deliberately kicked, and he staggered back and fell. Before his mate could get up, I swung that pipe, hitting him on the back of the neck. The crunching sound made my stomach turn, but now wasn't the time to get queasy. I had a feeling I wasn't supposed to walk away from this today. Well, they were in for a surprise. I didn't go down easy.

The other one pulled me in, and I delivered a series of knees then a straight jab to the nose. I waited until he sagged to the ground before I let up. He was out. A quick pulse check told me he was still alive, but there would be no answers forthcoming from him. So I picked up his mate by the shirt collar and asked, "Who sent you?"

"Fuck you."

"Oh, brilliant. While you're not exactly my type, I applaud you for giving it a shot." *Jab.* "Who sent you?"

"Like I said—"

"Yeah, yeah, yeah, I heard you the first time. Fuck you." I hit him again, and his head just lolled back. I didn't even bother looking at my hands. I knew they'd be covered in blood.

I'd known when we agreed to go after the Elite this was going to be messy. I'd known it was going to get worse before it got better. But I hadn't known that it would be an open battle in the streets.

But now that I knew, I had the upper hand. I'd be ready. They wouldn't catch me unaware again. I just had to warn the others and make sure that I could keep Olivia safe, because she didn't know she had walked into a viper's nest.

Ben

I opted for my townhouse for our little regroup. It somehow felt more private than my suite at the hotel. After my adventure in Regent's Park, I'd gone straight home and sent out the SOS to everyone.

The starkness of Covington House surprised even me. Was it always this cold? And why the hell did I care? It had never bothered me before. I had loved this place so much when I first purchased the townhouses and renovated them. I'd done it for Lila. But then, while standing in the house I'd bought for her, she told me she was going to marry my father instead. She'd broken me right there by the fireplace. But I couldn't bring myself to sell it even though she ruined me here.

Bridge was the first one to arrive since he lived nearby, and he chuckled when he took in the sparse decor. "You're not here much, are you?"

I frowned at him then immediately winced when the skin above my eye protested. Those motherfuckers had gotten a few good shots. He knew I preferred staying in the loft. "Why do you say that?"

"It's beautiful, but there's nothing warm about this place. No one *lives* here."

I shrugged. "You're down the street. You can use this as your *pied-à-terre.* Your bachelor pad if you need it."

He shook his head. "I don't need to escape Mina."

I ground my teeth, mostly because it helped me keep my mouth shut. He was one of my best mates. I wasn't going to say a damn thing about his fiancée. I knew better.

East arrived next through the kitchen entrance. He made himself a drink before heading to the living room and ran his fingers over the island in the kitchen. "Jesus Christ, you have a nicer kitchen than I have. And you don't cook."

"I cook. I only said I don't know how. But there's no point cooking at the hotel, and I'm never here, so…"

"Waste of a beautiful kitchen."

Drew showed up last. I was surprised he showed up at all if I was being perfectly honest. The moment he walked in, he whistled low. "You look like shit, mate."

I nodded my chin at him. But even the small motion caused my head to thump as if an elephant just kicked me at the back of my skull. "Well, mate, you look just as lovely as ever."

Drew grinned and rubbed his jaw. "For once, I'm prettier than you are."

"Fuck off, I'm still prettier."

It was Bridge who got to the point. "What the fuck happened?"

"Well, I went on a run this morning to meet Blake Boynton and got jumped by a couple of professionals."

East's brows furrowed at that as he glanced up at me, but he didn't say anything.

"They must be watching me because I took a route that I don't run often. I took the tube to Regent's Park. I was pushing myself pretty hard, and they knew where to find me and ambushed me."

Bridge cursed. "This smacks of the Elite."

I shrugged. "I don't know. No one else I know wants me dead. I sent you lot pictures already. I don't recognize them as any of the fixers on the payroll. Judging from their accents, they're from South London."

East ran a hand over his face and then rubbed at the stubble on his jaw. "Okay, let's just go through it. They know someone accessed data but have no idea who. Why would they even target us?"

Bridge rolled his shoulders. "Unless this isn't about *us* at all. Maybe it's just about you, Ben. Van Linsted thinks you've gone unchecked for far too long. This might be his retaliation for the dustup at the fundraiser."

"What, with murder?"

He shrugged. "Or maybe they do know we're after them, and they're going to pick us off one by one. Together we're too powerful, but if they just take aim individually, make us weak, they could have a shot."

I scowled into my glass before draining it. "Unless it's only certain members of the Elite."

Drew's gaze ping-ponged between the three of us. "Do you lot hear yourselves? I know your focus was strategy and business, but you're talking about murder here."

We all lifted our heads to glance at him. I had no idea why he was shouting. East looked perplexed. And Bridge, well, Bridge had no expression. But that was normal.

I was the one who asked him the obvious question. "What are you talking about, Drew?"

"Mates, you're casually talking about how someone tried to take Ben out." He put the 'take Ben out' in air quotes. "When did this become us?"

We all continued to stare at him. My anger rose closer and closer to the surface. It was only mostly toned down because I'd used up most of my adrenaline earlier.

"You're kidding me, right?" East asked.

Drew shook his head. "No, I'm not kidding you. Not at all. This is the point when we all take a moment to stop and consider our fucking families. Someone went after Ben... with a *gun*. I have a family. Children. I have to protect them."

On the one hand, Drew was a pussy. The night we made our decision to go after those responsible for Toby's death, he'd been the last one to join in. Whenever there looked to be trouble, he was the first one to side with the Elite, and now, he was the first one to jump ship.

I wanted to call him on his bullshit because, out of all of us, he'd been the closest to Toby. But in this instance, when we were talking about real combat in the streets, I didn't for a second begrudge him for the concern about his family. Because that was a very real threat. Until that point, we were going after their money. Civilized things. We'd learned to defend ourselves, but that was meant as a precaution for a very distant possibility. We'd gone after money and secrets. But who had secrets worth dying for?

It could be anyone.

And just what the hell was on that drive? Because clearly, we had hit the jackpot.

I glanced over at Bridge. "Maybe he's right. We've been a bit cavalier about this, but now that we're talking real guns, maybe Drew has a point. He does have a family to protect."

East scowled at me. "What? You want to back down?"

"Fuck no. I'm not backing down. But Drew should probably sit out because these lads weren't there to fuck around. And it's likely going to get worse before it gets better. And you should probably back off too, Bridge. Watch your backs and let East and I handle most of this."

The corner of Bridge's lip turned up in a snarl. "You're really telling me to back the fuck off?"

I knew he wouldn't. "I know it's not like you. I know it's not in your vocabulary. But mate, today could have been my time. You have Mina to think about. Drew has Angela and the kids. It's serious. No one is playing around anymore."

Bridge shook his head. "Drew can do what he needs to. I get it. There are children involved."

Drew scowled. "Are you going to sit there and judge me, Edgerton?"

Bridge shook his head, and his voice was like ice. "No. I'm not judging you. All I'm saying is that Toby didn't get to have kids. He didn't get to get married. He didn't have any of that. Fucking Van Linsteds. They forgot him. They *made us* forget him. We can't let them walk away free on this."

Drew chewed his bottom lip. "Look, I'll give you all the support I can, but guns are where I draw the line. They're coming for us."

I nodded. "It certainly feels that way, but I can't stop. If they are willing to kill, there is something deep they are trying to hide. So I'm still in."

East shrugged. "You don't have to ask my vote, mate."

Bridge clenched his jaw. "You already know how I feel."

Drew sighed. "So now I'm the git who doesn't want to get vengeance for his friend?"

"No one is calling you a git, Drew." I was too tired for this conversation.

Bridge shrugged. "I mean, I might call you a git."

I gave him an admonishing glare that said *shut it*. "Drew, if you want out, then you're out. We can pull this off with three."

"So what, just like that?" He frowned, but the look in his eyes said he was torn.

"You have children to protect. We will get vengeance for Toby."

I just hoped I was right about that, because after the day I'd had, I couldn't help but worry about the safety of Olivia.

I rubbed my jaw. "We have another problem. If they're coming after us, it stands to reason that they're coming after Olivia Ashong too. We need to protect her."

Bridge nodded. "You're right. But the real question is how is she going to take that?"

"Oh, she'll hate it and fight me every step." And I was *persona non grata* with her after that kiss, but it couldn't be helped.

CHAPTER 18

Livy

I didn't remove my sunglasses until I was within the safety of my office.

Carmen had helped me with my makeup that morning, so I looked less blotchy and my eyes didn't look as red. But anyone who knew me well would know I'd been crying. I'd spent half the night trying to figure out where everything had gone wrong with Dex, and the other half crying about how badly I'd messed up with Ben.

Neither one of those scenarios meant a bright eyed and bushy-tailed morning. But I was at work, and I would just go about my day and pretend that my boss hadn't made my body hum. Hadn't made me want—things. Hadn't had me ready to beg.

I could pretend, right?

But before I could get on with my pretending and my delusions of everything being great, there was a knock at my door. I looked up to find Ben with several paper bags in tow. "Good morning. How are you feeling?"

I tried to give him a brave smile. "I feel fine."

"You recognize you're going to have to stop saying fine to me, right?"

"That's how I feel. *Fine.*"

He laughed. "Fair enough. If that's what you're going with. I brought you a couple of things."

"What's all this?"

"You know, just a few things. Some eyedrops. An energy shot. I figured you didn't sleep much. And, some beignets."

I grinned at him. "Beignets? Where did you find beignets in London?"

"Well, a friend of mine used to have a restaurant in New Orleans, they were famous for them. So I called him at his café and asked if he'd make some up this morning. So, here you go, beignets."

He felt bad for me clearly. Crazy woman who had thrown him in a trough of water, then moaned at his kisses while I had a, though absentee and rubbish, boyfriend. "You don't have to be this nice to me. I know I'm a disaster."

"You're not a disaster. Yesterday was a...long day."

"Yeah, tell me about."

He shoved his hands in his pockets, the motion highlighting his thick, toned forearms. He'd worn a gray vest today, making his eyes look stormier than usual. "And I know I *should* apologize. If I made you uncomfortable yesterday..." His mouth said the right things, but his eyes were focused on my lips. And that kind of direct scrutiny by him made heat pool in my core.

That was the thing. I *hadn't* been uncomfortable. I'd been a little *too* comfortable.

"I just, I could have sworn I was feeling something between us, and then I acted on it. I shouldn't have."

What did I say here? There was no handbook for I really enjoyed my boss kissing me. "You're my boss."

He nodded slowly. "I *am* your boss. Technically your boss's boss."

"I have no intention of being one of a revolving door of women. I'd rather not get sheet burns on my ass."

He huffed at that. "I do not have a revolving door. And I would take very good care of your arse."

An image flashed in my mind of just what he could do to my ass, and I flushed.

He muttered a curse. "Jesus, I didn't mean that how it sounded."

"I know. We have an *unconventional* working arrangement."

"You can say that again," he muttered. "The point is I don't do relationships. And as a result, I don't generally shag anyone I'm required to see the next day."

It was so easy to slide into the usual banter with him. "Performance that disappointing, is it? Are you embarrassed? I promise. I wouldn't laugh at you."

He opened his mouth to speak, then closed it. He tried it again, and a crack of laughter spilled out. "You're such a pain in the arse."

"I know." I snagged the bag of beignets from him. They really were best eaten hot. "Did you try one yet?"

"A beignet? I may have had one or two."

"Split one with me?"

He looked like he wanted to say no, but he nodded instead. Again, the focus of his gaze was on my lips. But he seemed to right himself and pulled out the little boxes inside then set them out on napkins.

I picked one, dipped it in the jam and took a bite. Christ, I moaned. "That's almost better than sex." I spoke around a mouthful of dough, sugar and jam.

"Then you have not been having sex with the right person. I mean these are good. These are excellent. But still, sex is sex. Even bad, it's good."

I laughed. "Sex is only always good if you're a guy. Not the same for us of the fairer sex." I took another bite. "I don't know. I feel like I could eat beignets every day for the rest of my life and be very happy."

"Note to self, bring you beignets every day."

"Oh my God, no. I mean, I go to the gym, but not enough for a beignet habit. Please."

He frowned as he took another beignet and sat in the seat across from me. "Why do women always do that? I think you look great."

"Do what?" A flush crept up my neck, and I couldn't help but run my teeth along my bottom lip. I could still *feel* his lips on mine, his tongue sliding over my own. I could *taste* him still. I shook my head to clear it.

"Act like they're not already fucking perfect. I promise you, whatever imperfections you see on your body, we never notice. We're just thrilled we're about to shag."

Now I would be thinking about him shagging. *Damn it.* I didn't need that visual if I ever wanted a good night's sleep again. "Right. Um, thanks for breakfast."

He pushed to his feet. "Of course. There's another thing too."

"Yeah?"

"We have corporate housing. And I don't want you staying on your own or going where your boyfriend would be."

I noted the way he said boyfriend. "Yeah well, he's not my boyfriend anymore. I just need to find time to tell him that."

"That's good. That's great. I still don't want you over there. I want you safe."

"I have a perfectly good apartment. I just need to find him, break up with him officially, and then get my keys, change the locks, that sort of thing." Although I had no idea which one of us would get to keep the flat if I was being honest. And Fenton knew where it was so I didn't exactly feel safe there.

"Right, and all that takes a little bit of time, so in the meantime, corporate housing. I can get you on the list today. If you can stay with Telly for the time being, I'll get you in."

My hands shook as I wiped away the sugar on my fingertips. Now was not the time to freak out. I could have a crisis later. When I was alone and could cry on the tube like a normal person. "I haven't really thought much further than notify him he's a horses arse. I suppose I can keep sleeping on Telly's couch. I'll look into the corporate housing thank you. But I know how expensive those flats can get. I'll start looking for a flat mate I guess too.

He teeth grazed his bottom lip, and this time it was my turn to be riveted. "Okay, listen, don't be weirded out."

I grinned. "Guaranteed way to weird me out."

"I have a place for you to stay. You'd basically have your own wing of a giant loft."

"Here in London? Whose first born do I need to slaughter first?"

"Yes, here in London. After the mugging and attempted second mugging and that bollocks last night, I'm concerned about you."

"About what? I'm perfectly safe." Even I realized how dumb that sounded as the words came out of my mouth.

"Do you really feel safe? With Fenton Mills running around?"

I frowned. He had a point. "I don't live with Fenton."

"But you *do* live with Dexter. Who doesn't seem to heed your concerns when you say you're worried or scared."

I sighed. "Fair point."

"I don't want you back over there until I can go with you myself to get some of your things."

"You sound like Telly. I don't need a babysitter."

"No one's saying you do. But the way Fenton grabbed you last night proves he's dangerous."

"I know. I get it. I'm not an idiot. I just want my life back."

"I know. In the meantime, for a few nights stay somewhere safe where you have privacy. I don't know what the situation is with your friend Telly."

"The couch is comfortable."

"While we wait on corporate housing, you will have your own suite, and your own bed."

"Where?"

"It's a double-suited loft at the hotel property next door, so you would basically have your own wing. And your own key to a door." He cleared his throat. "With me."

I blinked. Then when I couldn't think of anything to immediately say, I blinked again. He couldn't be serious. "And we're just going to be what, roommates?"

He nodded. "Yes. No funny business. Just for a few days. Until we get your flat sorted."

I wanted to fight. I didn't need him taking control of my life. "You recognize I can take care of myself."

"And no one's saying you can't. I think you're incredible. Jessa can't stop talking about how amazing you are. And you single-handedly saved me from a lorry."

"I did save you, didn't I?"

He grinned. And the smile melted my insides and exploded an ovary. Hell, that smile could make every ovary in this building explode. "Just for a few days. Until we get you squared away."

"This feels like I'm taking advantage of your generosity."

"You're not. I'm offering."

"You make it hard to fight you when you've already seen me at my lowest."

"And do I judge?"

I coughed a laugh. "Only a little."

He spread his arms. "See? Then say yes."

All I wanted to do was get a decent night's sleep and not be afraid or worried. "I don't want to intrude on your space."

"My loft is 1000 square meters. You're not intruding."

Wow. "Oh, okay then. Are you sure?"

He nodded. "Yeah, I'm sure. It's nothing permanent, obviously, but it gives you a chance to figure out what you want to do."

"I don't even know how to say thank you."

"Just say yes so that we can get back to work."

"And just when I thought I knew you, you completely change."

"Yep. I have to keep you guessing, don't I?"

@

Ben

You have it bad, you twat.

Saving Olivia from Fenton Mills had been a happy accident. It gave me just the excuse I needed to keep her safe. Without having to tell her everything. Fully disclosing everything about the Elite would only put her in more danger. So I was dong what was best for her.

By lying.

Sometimes lying was necessary. *You're sure about that?* Yes. I was bloody sure. And I certainly wasn't going to argue with myself about it any more. What was done was done and I wasn't going to apologize for it. She didn't need to know anything about the shooting. Or the likelihood that the muggings hadn't been random.

She'd be scared and worry. And I couldn't take any more of that blank terrified look she'd given me at the end of the Jack the Ripper tour. So I was going to keep the lid on the real reason her life was imploding. To protect her.

How are you pussywhipped without the pussy?

Christ I was a mess. My bullshit reasoning for not telling her everything notwithstanding, I *wanted* to be near her. Putting myself in charge of her safety accomplished that.

It's not like I was any good at pretending I was immune to her anyway. Now that she was in my space, it was only getting worse.

Easy does it, she's not yours.

The fuck she wasn't.

Whatever she needed, I wanted to be there for her. So there I was at Montgomery Airfield, staring at what looked like a tiny helicopter. More like a tiny flying sardine can.

My gut tightened. I was there because I couldn't stay away, because she should have someone who cared about her in times like this. I was there because she was mine. She just didn't know it yet.

I had it bad.

For a woman you can't have.

I just needed to keep telling myself that. I also needed to keep telling myself that I wasn't going to kiss her again. At least not until she asked me.

"Uh, we're not flying that, are we?"

She grinned. "Yes, we are. It's called an Ultralight."

I nodded at her as if any of the words she was saying made sense. "Uh-huh. Still, no."

"You don't like to fly?"

"No, I love to fly. Private plane, comfort, and all the liquor I can drink. But this… This is not that." I shook my head. "This is a flying death trap."

"It's not so bad. I happen to have my pilot's license, so I

figured we'd take off, you know, fly a little, see the countryside, and right before we land, I'll spread Mom's ashes."

"Yeah, sure. Why can't we do that in a real plane? I'll even take a propeller plane, but not this."

She chewed her bottom lip. "You don't have to go. I can do this myself." The way she tilted her chin up made me want to slam my lips over hers, coaxing her tongue with mine, as I reminded her that if she was doing this, I was doing this. No way in hell I was letting her do this alone.

"Nope. *We're* doing this."

She smiled. "Are you sure? Obviously, you really don't have to. I appreciate you just even coming."

"Look, I said I'm going with you, so I'm going with you. Now, why don't you tell me all the things you really love about flying?"

The smile she gave me was another poleaxe to the chest, and I knew right there that woman had me by the balls. From the moment she'd been pressed up against me in that closet, to the way she moaned when we'd had to cover what we were doing. From the kissing, to the way she'd handed me my ass in that meeting and never backed down. She had me and she had no idea.

Livy

I didn't mean to text him. I didn't even *want* to text him if I was being honest.

You're not being honest.

Okay fine, I wanted to text him. He was all the way on the other side of the loft, and I was lonely. Telly and Carmen were out on date night, and I needed a friend.

Tread carefully. Ben Covington isn't the kind of friend you want.

No, he wasn't. Men like that weren't capable of being anyone's *friend*. Men like that were capable of being every woman's wet dream. I shouldn't even be having wet dreams, but he starred in so many of them.

But, I wasn't going to be *that* woman, so I had to put my phone away. As soon as I did though, my phone buzzed.

Ben: *What happens when Batman sees Catwoman?*

I frowned.

Livy: *I don't know.*

Ben: *The Dark Knight rises.* <wink>

I couldn't help myself. I laughed. Sue me. It was funny.

Livy: *Oh, that's mature.*

Ben: *Well, truth. What do you call it when Batman skives off church?*

I rolled my eyes because I could almost see where this is going.

Livy: *I don't know. Why don't you tell me?*

Ben: *Christian Bale.*

I snorted a laugh then.

Livy: *Let me guess, you've got a million of these.*

Ben: *Yup. Are we in trouble for being up so late?*

Livy: *No. All good.*

There was more I wanted to say, but that was dangerous territory, and I wasn't going to go there. I liked Ben. And as it turned out, he was a half-decent friend.

That man is no friend. That man is dangerous.

But Ben wasn't the problem. I was. I needed to put him in the friend category and keep him there. No fantasizing, no nothing.

I watched the little dots flicker back and forth for a moment, and then he replied with something.

Ben: *What position did Bruce Wayne play on his baseball team?*

Livy: *What do you know about baseball?*

Ben: *Answer the question.*

I laughed even as I tapped.

Livy: *He was Batboy.*

Ben: *No fair, you've heard that one.*

Livy: *Maybe. These are kind of lame.*

More little dots.

Ben: *Oh really? How about this one? When is Joker not plotting murder?*

I frowned then trying to think of the answer, wanting to see if I could slide one by him again. But I didn't know the answer.

Livy: *I have no idea.*

Ben: *When he's riding his Harley.*

I frowned at that. What did a Harley Davidson bike have to—Suddenly, I snorted, finally understanding. *Harley.* God.

Livy: *Do you only know the dirty ones?*

Ben: *Would you expect anything less?*

Livy: *No.*

Ben: *Okay, one more and you can go to bed.*

Livy: *Okay. Do your worst.*

Ben: *What's Batman's favorite part of a joke?*

Livy: *I have no idea, but I suppose you're going to tell me.*

Ben: *You are in luck. I am going to tell you. It's the punch line. Get it?*

I laughed a genuine laugh. He was sweet and funny and knew I'd been sad all

day. He was doing what he could to cheer me up. God, men like him existed in the real world. Women like me barely stood a chance. But Ben wasn't mine. If he wanted to be friends, then I was good with that. I had to be.

Livy: *Thank you for everything today. It meant a lot.*

Ben: *What are friends for?*

Then that was it. I turned off my screen, ignoring that part of me that was empty

and lonely and sad. This wasn't how things were supposed to work out. I also wasn't a fool. Ben was my friend because I was someone unattainable. It worked, our little exchanges, because as a long-term prospect, he didn't have to deal with me. But I knew men like him. The moment I became available, he'd become emotionally unavailable. So I needed to not get my hopes up. I needed to be wary.

He was not the balm to my broken heart. That job would have to be mine alone.

CHAPTER 19

Livy

Ben and I were friends now?

It certainly looks that way.

At least friends was the word we were using. It felt odd. Outside of Telly and a couple of work acquaintances here and there, I somehow found myself without as many friends as I'd once had.

Surprisingly, Ben was easy to talk to, but he wasn't the kind of friend I wanted. He was far too good-looking for me to ever be completely comfortable, and yes, I knew his distinct taste. But he'd been kind and nonjudgmental. Bossy too. And a pain in the ass. Basically, he was just like Telly except with very broad shoulders, abs I wanted to lick things off of, and from what I remembered of our kiss, had a really big... smile.

So our odd friendship notwithstanding, I wanted to do something nice for him.

I'd gone online and scheduled the grocery store to deliver the groceries an hour earlier than I normally would have left work. And then I went to the loft to start prepping. Ghanaian food took a long time to prepare, but my mother always said that because it took so long you could tell that love was cooked into it.

What was funny was that in my mother's language of Ga, there was no real word for love. It was sort of an emphatic version of the word *like*. Even though I was keeping it simple on the cooking, it still took a while.

I made my perennial favorite, jollof rice, which included a tomato-based stew with a fragrant rice cooked together. Then I cut up a few ripe plantains and fried them lightly. Ben had some fancy air fryer thing, but my first few attempts came out wrong so I did it the old-fashioned way, seasoning them with ginger, garlic, onions, and cayenne pepper and tossing them together with just a hint water to get them to coat before doing a light fry on the stove.

His housekeeper would hate me for the speckles of grease everywhere, but it was worth it. For the meat dish, I kept it simple. Just chicken, seasoned the way my mother would have with enough spice to clear out your sinuses and make you weep at every bland piece of food you'd ever eaten in your life.

When Ben walked through the door, he blinked and frowned. "Christ, what smells so good?"

I had just started to plate dinner and wiped my hands on my apron. I turned with a smile, "Hey. I made dinner."

Nose in the air, sniffing, he made a beeline for the kitchen. "Oh my God, why has the house never smelled like this before?"

"Probably because you don't know how to make Ghanaian food."

"You *cooked*?" His eyes went wide.

I nodded. "Yes, I cooked."

"You know how?"

Why did he look so damn confused? "Yes, don't you?"

He shook his head. "I mean, I can make basic things but nothing complicated. Besides, there are chefs on staff for that."

I rolled my eyes. "You have the best chefs around, but there's a certain satisfaction in cooking for other people."

"You've been here for days. Why haven't you cooked before?"

"Well honestly, I didn't want to mess up your kitchen. And we have a complicated relationship."

His gaze dipped to my lips, and I licked them automatically. I watched his Adam's apple bob up and down as he nodded. "Yeah. Complicated is a word for it."

"Anyway, now that we're *friends*, I wanted to say thank you for looking out for me."

"You don't have to thank me, Liv. You were in trouble, so I helped."

"Well, my mother taught me that when someone does something nice for you, you do something nice in return. So dinner. Go on. Wash up and we'll eat."

I carried the plates into the dining room where I'd lit some candles and set the table. As he returned from the bathroom, he whistled low. "Seriously? This is gorgeous. Where did you get all of this stuff?"

"You have the most amazing place settings. Some of that stuff is worth thousands of dollars."

He shrugged. "I rarely eat here."

I could only shake my head. "Yeah, I noticed. Why is that?"

"When I'm having dinner, it's usually served up in the East's penthouse. So I just go up there."

"And if you have a date?"

He coughed on a laugh. "Oh, I don't bring dates here."

My brows lifted. "What? Why not?"

He shook his head. "I like my space. I don't need anyone poking around or snooping or thinking she's going to stay."

"Wow, okay. So then why isn't this place at all decorated or anything?"

His shrug was dismissive. "I'm never here."

"So you have this beautiful loft with views of Soho. I can see the London Eye from here. And you don't spend any time in it?"

He shrugged. "I can see the London Eye from the East's place too."

I set the plates down and then went back into the kitchen for the wine. The sweet stuff for me; he got the adult wine.

I took off my apron and deposited it on the back of a chair. I'd kept things somewhat casual, but still, I wanted him to enjoy himself, the food, and the company.

You're hoping he kisses you again.

No. That was *not* what I was looking for.

When he sat, his gaze lifted to mine. The icy-blue depths of his eyes warmed to a more cerulean color, or maybe that was the effect of the candlelight. Either way, his voice was soft when he spoke. "This is perfect. Thank you. Is it odd I've never had a woman cook for me before?"

My brows lifted. "What?"

"No. Not in an intimate setting like this."

My face flamed at the word *intimate*. "This is nothing. Just a thank you."

"This is *not* nothing. When you cook for someone, it shows you care. I knew you'd come around to caring about me eventually."

I rolled my eyes even as I laughed. "Forever arrogant I see." I held my breath when he took his first bite. Some people didn't like spicy food, so I was worried. What kind of food did billionaires eat anyway? I had no idea.

His first moan made me break out into a grin.

And then he sat back and nodded and did this kind of shimmy in his seat. Ah, a happy food dance. I watched, grinning as he tucked in, too preoccupied with his reaction to my cooking to eat myself.

Five bites in, he stopped and glanced over at me. "You're not eating."

"Well, I'm enjoying watching you eat."

He narrowed his gaze as he lifted another forkful to his mouth. "Did you poison me? I have to say it's too delicious for me to care."

"Are you kidding? I wouldn't dare ruin good jollof."

"Is that what I'm eating?"

I nodded. "The rice is a standard across West Africa, and everyone has their own version. You'll find the Ghanaians and the Nigerians are in a constant battle for who makes the best jollof rice. The Senegalese, who claim the origin of the dish, aren't even in that fight."

"A fight over rice?"

"You have no idea. We take our dishes seriously. Of course, being Ghanaian, I know we make the best."

He guffawed. "It's hard to argue when my taste buds are exploding with joy. Is that plantain?"

I nodded. "Yeah. I made it into kelewele. Chopped up and spiced."

"Oh God, I used to live on plantains when I lived in Jamaica. But they were sweeter, not as spicy."

"Yeah, same sweet plantain, but this particular recipe is just spicier."

For the next couple of hours we ate and laughed, and things were easy between us. Too easy.

"How has no one cooked for you before? Mom always said the fastest way to someone's heart was through food. I'm surprised some socialite hasn't figured it out yet."

"Socialites are busy figuring out what's in it for them. They want all the trappings of the money, so they wouldn't put themselves in the kitchen."

"I guess they want that sterile life. Like a hotel."

He laughed. "Yeah, they do. And they want that lifestyle where they never actually live anywhere and never actually form real connections with people. "This is probably the nicest thing anyone's ever done for me."

I shifted uncomfortably in my seat and tucked one foot under myself. "Well, Ben Covington, you and I could both probably use some new friends."

He raised his glass, leaning over to clink it with mine. "To new friends. To the best kind of friends who cook for you."

"Somehow I feel like this is going to bite me in the ass."

He grinned. "I knew you were dirty. I'm happy to bite you anywhere you like."

"You are incorrigible."

"I know you'll be shocked, but I've been told that before."

I wasn't shocked in the least.

@

Ben

I'd made a grievous error in judgment.

When I suggested we come down to the theater, I hadn't thought through the whole alone-in-the-dark scenario where it would be difficult to think about anything other than getting Livy beneath me.

I hadn't thought about how close she would be or the smell of her shampoo. Or that I'd be feeling warm and happy and really mellow from her cooking for me.

So I was sitting next to the woman I wanted, who more than likely needed time, and I had a raging erection.

When I got the text from East asking if I was coming up to watch the Tottenham match, I just texted back.

Ben: *Busy.*

His response was instant.

East: *Busy doing what? Long night of wanking? Get your arse up here.*

Ben: *Told you, busy. Plans.*

East: *Found someone new to shag did you? You're using one of the rooms?*

Ben: *Stay out of my business.*

East: *You're in the movie theater. What the hell are you doing in there?*

Ben: *Why are you stalking me?*

East: *Because you're being cagey. And I see you have a guest. I will immediately*

turn off the surveillance. Because nobody needs to see that.

Ben: *You're an arsehole.*

East: *I know. Have fun with the woman you're not into.*

I turned off my phone. I didn't need my mate getting into my head. Besides, this was about Livy. I'd told her cook's choice on a movie. We had thousands available. What she chose surprised me.

"Crouching Tiger, Hidden Dragon?"

Her grin was sweet. "I love this movie. And the screen is so big. I've only ever seen it on TV."

"Your pick, you can have whatever you want."

She snuggled into the seat next to me. "Ugh, I should have brought a blanket. Can we pause so I can go get one? I might pick up some sweet and salty popcorn too. You want any candy or anything?"

"Oh, you're adorable. Hold on." Did she really think I was going to send her upstairs to concessions?

I pulled a remote out of the side of my chair and tapped in a request.

She frowned at me. "What are you doing?"

"You said you wanted a blanket and popcorn, right?"

Her brows lifted. "Seriously?"

I grinned at her. "Owning the place has some perks."

"Jesus. What's it like to get everything you ever want? Doesn't that get boring?"

I shook my head. "Nope. And I don't always get everything I want. Some things I have to work for. And it's better when I work for them."

Way to be obvious.

"But it must be odd to press a button and have blankets appear out of nowhere."

"Well, I pay people to make sure that those things happen for anyone who stays here. I want people to know comfort. To have a sense of being taken care of. Like you have family even when you're far away."

Her smile warmed me from the inside as she grinned up at me. "So you do this at all the hotels so that people have a sense of family?"

Heat started to creep up my neck as the embarrassment hit. "A little. When I was a kid, I would watch people bend over backward to make sure that my father had everything he needed exactly how he needed it. And eventually they got so good at their jobs that he didn't even have to ask; whatever he needed would just appear. But then I noticed at school and other places that most people didn't have that, and I wanted to provide that kind of experience for people."

"Why, Bennet James Covington, you *do* care about people."

I brushed off the sentiment. "It's my job."

We were interrupted by one of the bellhops. "Mr. Covington, here are your popcorn and blankets."

Olivia grinned up. "Thank you so much."

Tucked into her blanket, she scooted closer to me. But the arm of the seat was in the way. I hit a button on the remote, and the arm retracted down, forming a love seat of sorts.

Her eyes rounded. "What? That's insane."

"It's great, huh? Come on. If you want a cuddle, let's do this."

"You're spoiling me. How will I ever return to normal life?"

It was on the tip of my tongue to tell her she didn't have to. *What is wrong with you?* "Oh, I'm sure you'll manage."

She grinned. "Or I can just bring my normal life back to you, and therefore, I shall not be tempted by such extravagances."

"Sweetheart, I have no idea what normal even is."

"No you wouldn't, would you? Is it lonely? I mean you live in the hotel. Before I turned up, it looked as sterile as a hotel. You have no personal touches in the loft. Don't you want that?"

I thought about East's place with his photos and art and that lived-in quality. "I guess I don't put the effort into that. I focus on other things. You don't realize how lonely you are if you're always doing something else."

"Well, not to worry, I shall add warmth."

I smiled down at her. She was so close, smelling sweet and inviting. Where had she come from? How had she found me? Why was she already changing the shape of how I thought, what I wanted, what I needed from my life?

"You're staring at me."

"I'm aware. I'm trying to remember that you're my friend right now."

"It shouldn't be hard."

All I had to do was forget that I knew exactly how she tasted. All I had to do was pretend that I wasn't desperate to taste her again. Should have been easy, right?

Except it wasn't. Because I wanted her. I wanted *more* from her. I wanted to kiss her, taste her, remind her how combustible we were together. I could do all of that. But she hadn't finished dealing with the git she'd been involved with, and I could tell that she wasn't ready.

But when I kissed her again, I wouldn't stop myself. I wouldn't stop until she was mine. And she wasn't quite ready for that. "Watch the movie."

"Yes sir, Mr. Covington, sir."

"God that sounds so sexy. Can you say that again?"

She threw popcorn at me. And just like that, the tension eased. The monster clawing at me from the inside, demanding me to take her, to mark her, to make her mine, receded just a little so I could focus on the movie. I wanted her to be comfortable around me, not forever running for the hills. After everything she'd been through, she needed time. So I could be patient.

Are you sure about that?

CHAPTER 20

Ben

I saw him the moment I entered the hotel. Marcus Van Linsted. It wasn't like he was subtle. There he was, at the bar in the lobby, sitting on the throne as if he owned the place.

No motherfucker. I do.

I took my time striding over to him. "Is there something you need?"

Around me, bartenders and waiters clamored to get to us, and I waved them off. I wasn't having a drink with that fucker. And he wouldn't be staying.

"Covington, is that any way to treat a guest? Remember, a gentleman above all."

"Right. But power is king and it's my hotel, so what do you want?"

"I know what you've been doing."

"And what's that?"

"I know you've been skulking about asking members to vote against my son."

"Why would I do anything like that? To vote against him, they'd need someone else to vote for."

"Like you're not making a play for Director Prime."

I frowned. "I'm not."

To the average person, Marcus Van Linsted might have seemed affable. Friendly even. But I knew better. I knew that this was merely a showing of his teeth. "You won't win this, Covington. My son *will* be the next Director Prime. And you and your friends *will* fall in line, or there shall be dire consequences."

"That sounds like a threat. What happened to a gentleman above all?"

"Yes, well, as you said, power is king. And it's good to be king."

"Marcus, if you just came here to postulate about rumors and innuendos, I can't help you."

"How is your new operations director? What is her name again? God, it's so hard to remember these things. It's something foreign sounding. Ashong, is that right? I've heard that you two have gotten quite *cozy*."

I lifted a brow. "You're paying such close attention to me? Then you should know I'm not a threat to you or coming for your seat. The last thing I want is to be Director Prime. I just want to make sure your son doesn't get it."

"Wouldn't it be better to turn your sights to making sure that your pretty little operations director doesn't get hurt? She has a penchant for getting into trouble."

My brow snapped down. "*Gentlemen* don't go after civilians."

"Who said I was going after her? Come on now. I would never do such a thing. I am, above all, a gentleman."

He was nothing of the sort. "It sounded like you just threatened her."

"Well, if we are breaking rules, then you should remember that secrets whispered are never to be revealed. How did you find out who the Five were?"

Fuck. He knew that we knew. They knew someone had access to the files we'd copied onto the drive.

I kept my face impassive. "I'm not one to share secrets, but I will tell you this; If you go after my operations director, I will forget that I'm a gentleman."

He grinned. "You forget, my specialty was strategy and politics. I wouldn't have to lift a finger. I could just as easily ruin her life from the background. Her boyfriend, the one you so conveniently forget she has, just the wrong word here or there would tip him into making different decisions, putting her just out of your grasp. Don't play with me, Covington. I will win."

"Who said anything about playing?"

"If you must do this, just remember, enemies and friends are of the same coin. Loyalty is a fickle bitch. You come for my family, and I'll come for you. How much are you willing to lose?"

I met his gaze levelly. "Everything. I am willing to lose everything just to make sure Bram pays."

He stood and gave me a nod, then he stalked out.

So much for the secret approach. He knew, and he was ready for a fight.

@

Ben

I rubbed the back of my neck as I started to plan. "So, the whole plan to get to Downs is in jeopardy now?"

Bridge nodded. "Van Linsted's trying to get to Downs first. Downs isn't usually close and is notoriously cagey. Bram can't exactly go all the way to Australia to see him because there's been bad blood in those two families for years. And Downs rarely makes an appearance, so while he's in Paris, this is his chance… and ours, too."

East nodded. "I found an elusive art piece by Pierre Bonnard. Downs is crazy about his work, so I arranged for a viewing and auction. He's definitely coming."

I rubbed my jaw and tried not to let the frustration get to me. "It's like we take one step forward and then two steps back. So I have to get to Downs, but somehow *not* let Van Linsted get to him?"

Bridge nodded. "Yup. That's the crux of it. It's a two-man job."

East shrugged. "Can you take a date?"

"I don't trust a date. But I guess Jessa is an option."

East looked hopeful. "Maybe your cousin will let her come out?"

I laughed. "My cousin Roone is extremely protective of his wife." Without seeming to recognize that Jessa, while a princess, was first and foremost a badass and could take care of herself. "But I just remembered, she's on vacation. Working while they're traveling, but still, on vacation. Last I checked they were in Thailand. There's no way she'd get here quickly enough."

Bridge rolled his shoulders. "Well, there is always your new employee."

My brows snapped down. "Livy? No."

"Oh, so she's 'Livy' now? Actually, I kind of like the idea. She's charming, certainly elegant enough. And, since she's your new flatmate, you can ask her easily enough." East went full Benedict Arnold.

"She's not my new flatmate. We all agreed I need to keep her safe. That's what I'm doing."

Bridge grinned. "Yeah, right down the hall from where you sleep."

"I'm not trying to bang her."

My mates just laughed. They didn't get it. I actually *liked* her.

She was smart, funny, and had a vulnerable side that she showed to so very few people. Unfortunately, she'd shown it to me.

"Okay, fine. I can take her with me and explain the trip as being one for work."

East nodded. "Okay, good. We'll provide extra security. It'll be discreet, just to make sure there's no funny business. I don't want you guys taking some wrong turn down a Parisian alley and not coming back to us."

Unfortunately, he wasn't entirely wrong about how things could go. "You make it sound like people are trying to kill me every day." It was so funny because it was true.

Bridge just raised his brow. "Oh, someone can actually make jokes now."

"Sorry, just trying to ease the tension. None of this is funny. But I'll get it done. I'll bring her with me."

"If anything seems off at all, call it off."

The hell I would. "I'll make it happen."

After our meeting, I found Liv in her office on a call. She gestured at me to have a seat. When she finished, she turned to me. "Hey, I was going to text you. What do you want for dinner? Sushi?"

We'd developed an easy routine over the last week. We ate together, and she forced me to watch television and play Scrabble. I had her work out with me in the mornings. *Just like a real couple.* Nope. Like friends. Because that's what we were.

"That works. You doing all right?"

"With Jessa technically out of the office, I'm handling a lot of what she usually has on her plate. So it's a learning curve, but I've got it."

"About that. There are a couple of client meetings that I need to handle in Paris. Normally Jessa would come with me, but since she's on vacation, would you like to come?"

She stared at me. "Paris?"

"Yup, Paris."

"Now is not the time to play with me."

"I shit you not, Paris. So, are you in or out?"

"When do we leave?"

"In a couple of days."

She grinned so wide her dimple peeked out. Christ. I wanted to do everything in my power to make her that happy all the time.

"Thank you. You won't be disappointed."

"I don't think I ever could be."

"While we're there, there's an event. Black tie. I might need your help keeping a competitor occupied while I close the deal with a client."

She lifted a brow. "Dare I ask who?"

"Bram Van Linsted."

She arched a delicate brow. "Let me guess, he's going to try to stop that meeting from happening."

"He is. So we'll need to go covert."

"I've always wanted to be Bond," she said with a sly grin.

CHAPTER 21

Livy

I 'd finally managed to get Ben to stop hovering and let me go back to my old flat to pack for Paris. His idea that I could buy clothes there was bullshit. I could, but it was a business meeting. I needed to have my things.

Having familiar things would also help me feel a little more like me. Since meeting Ben, I'd been on my back foot. Or at least it felt that way. Like I was just a little bit unsteady all the time. And no wonder. Since that fateful moment in the closet a month ago, I'd gotten a new job, gotten mugged, lost my boyfriend, moved in with my boss, and found out that someone might be trying to kill me.

The tell-tale *ding* of the front door told me that Dexter's code had been punched in, and the pit of my stomach dropped. *Shit*. It was way too early for him to be home. What the hell was he doing there? I hadn't anticipated a fight.

Technically he still lives here.

Ben had sent me back to the flat with Todd, who doubled as a bodyguard and driver. Ben said he'd get dropped off there after he was done and we'd ride to Heathrow together. I should have had have Todd come inside with me, but I'd thought it would be a relatively quick trip.

I quelled the irrational instinct to hide as I heard his footsteps on the hardwood, but I tried to hurry my movements.

"You're home."

I paused but didn't turn around. "Not for long. I'm just packing for my trip."

"You don't come home for days, and when you do, you're going away? Can I even ask where you're off to?"

With every word out of his mouth, I could feel my blood pressure rising. "Paris."

"You're going to Paris?"

"For work."

"Why is an admin being taken to Paris for work?"

I stopped trying to cram my boots into my bag and turned to face him. "Seriously. How is it you don't listen to a single word that I say?"

He swallowed hard. "Liv, I—"

"Nope, you don't get to call me Liv. That is reserved for people who love me. You humiliated me, tried to make it seem like it was my fault, then put me in a potentially dangerous situation. I'm done taking your bullshit."

I moved faster, scrambling around and shoving things into my bag.

He was quiet for so long I thought he'd left, but when I hurried out of the bathroom, he was still there. Our gazes locked, and he pleaded with me. "I fucked up, Olivia."

Well, at least he hadn't called me Liv again. "I don't have time for this."

"Look. The other night got way out of hand. I was out of it. I know. And I get that Fenton makes you uncomfortable. I've been a complete twat. I never..." He let out a long breath. "I never should have spoken to you that way. I was out of order, and I shouldn't have left you alone with him."

I shook my head. "Dexter, I'm leaving. I can't have this conversation with you. Not right now. I have to go."

Stepping forward, he took my hands, stilling me. "I am sorry about the other night. I had just taken a pain pill."

"That's your excuse? That's not good enough anymore, Dexter. I've made excuse after excuse for you. You can't be there for me in the way I need because you're not looking after yourself. I need a *partner* Dexter."

"I know." He licked his lips. "And I can be that. I just started an outpatient program. I want to kick the pills and the booze."

I tried to pull my hands out of his. Tears stung my eyes. "I'm happy for you. And I'll support you in any way I can, but we..." My voice trailed as he got down on one knee, and my eyes went wide. "What the hell?"

"I know I don't deserve you. I know I've broken your trust. But I'm kneeling before you a changed man. I will give you my everything. I love you so much. Please don't leave me. Marry me instead."

"What? Are you mad?" He had to be insane.

"No. For the first time in a long time, I'm thinking clearly. I haven't had a drink or any pills in a few days. I'm lucid and steady. I want to be better for you." He reached into his pocket and pulled out a blue velvet box.

Oh God, no. My head swam. "Dex—"

"I love you. I want to be by your side. Always. Will you marry me?"

This wasn't happening. Couldn't be happening. Everything about this was all wrong. "Dexter, stand up."

"You have to give me an answer."

I blinked in surprise. "You're doing it again, Dexter, trying to force my hand. And now you expect me to believe you really want to marry me?"

"I need you."

And that was the crux of the problem. "You want me to look after you?"

"Yes. No one does it better." My brows drew into a tight line, and he rushed to add, "I want to look after you too. I'm a selfish prick, but I'm serious about changing."

"Christ, I have to go, Dex. This is not the time to do this." I managed to finally tug my hands free.

"Okay, think about it. Take the weekend. I'll wait for your answer."

"What? Just the weekend? You've sprung this on me."

He ran a hand through his hair and started to pace. "I know. I just miss you so much and can't live without you."

I could feel myself caving. Feel myself wanting to do what I'd done since the accident. Trying to fix him. Trying to fix *us*. But I stopped myself. "I told you I'd think about it, and I will. But you will not pressure or guilt me. This is still my decision, isn't it?"

He blinked at me rapidly. "Of course. You know I love you."

My watch vibrated, letting me know I had five minutes.

I left Dexter sulking in the bedroom and rolled my bag downstairs and into the hallway where I did the final passport check in time to hear the doorbell.

When I opened the door, instead of the driver, Ben stood on the doorstep. "I was just coming out."

"Let me get the bags."

I hadn't put my sunglasses on yet, and I was sure he could tell that I'd been crying. "I've got it."

"Nonsense. I might force you to work over the course of a three-day bank holiday, but chivalry is not dead." Brushing past me, he stepped inside to the living room and grabbed hold of my weekend bag. "You are the only woman I know who packs light for Paris."

I tried for levity. "I mean, you said there was shopping to be done, right?"

He rolled his eyes as he chuckled. "Leave it to you—" Dexter's appearance at the top of the stairs cut him off.

Ben glanced up, and his shoulders tensed. Dexter froze then went pale. I could feel the slow-motion train wreck before it happened.

Dexter recovered first with a flash of a smile that reminded me of the old him. "You must be the famous Ben Covington. Dexter Ford. I swear Olivia spends more time with you than she does with me."

Ben's demeanor was cool and professional, but I knew him well enough to pick up on the gaze that narrowed imperceptibly. "Olivia," he said deliberately, not using Livy like he did at work, "works very hard. I'm lucky to have her."

Dexter gave him another smile that somehow felt like he was visually marking his territory. Then he sauntered over to me to *actually* mark his territory. "Were you leaving without a kiss?"

What the hell was I supposed to say to that? "I—uh—"

What I didn't expect was Dexter wrapping an arm around me and pulling me into him. I hadn't prepared for Dexter's lips swooping in to capture mine and refusing to let them go. He didn't give me the kind of sweet kiss I'd have expected from the old Dexter. This was all possession and branding, bruising my lips.

When I gasped in surprise, he shoved his tongue in, sliding it along the roof of my mouth. I couldn't help the claustrophobic need to flee, to escape. I fought his hold a little and pulled back, my eyes wide.

Dexter set his jaw. "I love you. I'll see you when you get back." He then very deliberately placed the ring box on the table that sat under the mirror where Ben couldn't help but see it.

I stumbled backward and stared at him. In the end, it was Ben who saved me by breaking the not-at-all-sexual tension by clearing his throat.

"I'll put this in the car and let you say your goodbyes. Not to worry, Ford. I'll look out for her."

I glanced back at Ben and then at Dexter. "What was that about?"

Dexter shook his head. "You didn't tell me that was your boss."

I shook my head in bewilderment. "I've told you his name a million times."

"You failed to mention he was good looking."

I lifted a brow. "Because it didn't really register." *Lies.*

He flushed. "When you get back, we'll hash this out. Just know that I do love you."

I turned to leave, and he grabbed my arm and planted another kiss on my lips. It was even more forceful than the first. The kind of kiss that a year ago I would have said I wanted from him. But it felt cloying, needy, wet, slobbery, and I had to fight not to jerk my face away. When he released me, I staggered backward and wiped a hand over my mouth. "What the hell are you doing?"

"I just want you to remember we're good together."

"Next time you feel the urge to kiss me, ask my permission first."

I left him at the doorway staring after me and slid into the open door of the Tesla Ben was driving, surprised to see that he must have sent my driver back to the office.

When my gaze met his, his expression was surprisingly soft,

and his eyes had warmed from ice blue to something closer to navy. It was as if he understood everything that had just happened better than I did.

Ben

That twat was her bloody boyfriend? The same arsehole I'd seen shagging the redhead in the conference room at the fundraiser? Fucking hell. And had that been a bloody ring?

You're too late.

No, I fucking wasn't. She could see through his bullshit, right? I prayed that she could.

He'd endangered her safety.

She was smart. She had seen what he was like. I had to believe that. But she likely didn't know about the fundraiser. And if I told her now, it was going to hurt her.

I couldn't help but think I was making a mistake.

The last thing on earth I'd wanted to do was involve her. But our plan required two people, or it wasn't going to work.

And the sooner we were rid of Van Linsted, the sooner she'd be safe.

I knew I was on shaky ground. I was definitely bullshitting about this trip being work-related, and I should have told her the truth. But I was protecting her and knew the truth would make her less safe, so I rationalized that it was better if she stayed in the dark.

The things you tell yourself.

"Are you sure about this?"

She gave me a courageous nod. "Yeah, I've got this. I'll keep Van Linsted distracted. You talk to the client or whoever it is you need to see."

"You make it sound so simple." Fuck, I didn't want this for her. But here we were. "If he makes any move toward Rowan and me, what are you going to do?"

She grinned at me and reached for her skirt.

My gaze automatically scanned over the long slender expanse of her legs. *Jesus.* I swallowed hard and dragged my gaze away. "What are you doing?"

Suddenly, I heard three taps in my com device.

She grinned at me then lifted the hem of her skirt a little higher. "Look what I did."

I frowned. "You put it there?"

"Well, my hair is up, so this is more covert. He would be able to see the device in my ear, so I just placed it under here. I used double-sided tape."

I placed my hand on her bare knee like a rookie. God her skin was so satiny soft. Touching her was a mistake. Letting my index finger trace the silky patch under her knee. I stared at her legs, trying not to picture them wrapped around my waist as I fucked her. I forced myself to swallow before I started drooling. "Uh, you certainly thought of everything." She was right. Bram might see her communication device in her ear, which could make it extra dangerous for her.

Just thinking about that possibility made my stomach coil and sent a bolt of fury through my blood. My fingers gripped her knee a little too tightly, so much so that she winced.

"Ow."

"Sorry. I'm sorry." I immediately released her.

She blinked then licked her bottom lip, and yep, I couldn't help but stare. "You're staring at me."

I swallowed. "You look nice."

She grinned. "You think?"

With most women, I'd assume a fishing-for-compliments

situation, but she was being real. Just as guileless as usual. "Yeah, I think. Remember, just engage in a conversation and get out. Don't be extra."

"I don't know what you mean by 'extra.'"

"Don't do anything else. Don't try and get him to confess to anything. Don't record anything. Just talk to him and keep him the hell away from Downs for a little bit, okay?"

"I got this. Don't worry."

"I'm not worried. I believe in you."

She grinned. "And I believe in *you*."

"Do you have to be so cheery all the time?"

"It's my most lovable trait."

The use of the word love made my heart squeeze. Did she know I was falling for her? That she was on my mind at all times.

Know what, you twat?

Jesus. I started to sweat without even realizing it. I wanted her more than I'd ever wanted anyone.

Let's not forget she knows nothing about you.

I kept trying to shove that piece of information out of my head. The reason she wouldn't be with me, the reason I couldn't have her. The secrets I was keeping.

Not to forget what you know about her boyfriend. Ex? Christ, I hoped he was her ex.

I could tell her. Claim her. Make her mine and never think about it. But the way she was looking at me and smiling... I didn't want to hurt her.

And you're scared.

If she was going to me mine, I'd rather she chose me on her own.

All right, suit yourself. Don't tell her. Suffer.

I shoved all those thoughts out of my head. I had a job to do, and it was going to get done. "All right. If you're ready..."

"I've never been more ready in my life. Let's go, James Bond."

I shook my head. "You're a loon."

"Possibly. Also, another reason you think I'm brilliant."

I swallowed as her words found their mark.

CHAPTER 22

Ben

The limo pulled up to the auction at Tousant Ball-room. When the chauffeur opened the door, Olivia grinned at me, giddiness written all over her face. The peek of a dimple was almost too much. I almost caved and leaned forward to kiss it. As it was, my fingertips dusted her shoulder, and the way her eyes dipped to the slight touch... I could feel it, the tension between us. The pull and push of need and attraction. But she couldn't act it on, and I wouldn't ask her to.

Even if you have something that would free her.

I wasn't going to use it. I didn't want to see her hurt. Not on my watch. When she moved to get out, I stopped her. "I'll help you out."

I exited and went over to her side, opening the door for her. She placed her hand in mine. I had to grit my teeth against the charge of electricity. This time, she couldn't hide her response from me. She gasped and tried to remove her hand, but I shook my head at her. "We're friends, remember?"

She blinked up at me and nodded. "Yup. Friends." She dragged in a shivering breath and released it slowly. Well, it was nice to know I wasn't the only one.

I ignored the photographers and headed straight inside. "Do you remember what Van Linsted looks like?"

"Oh yeah, I remember." She tapped her temple.

Despite myself, I wanted to laugh. "God, just be cool."

"I am being cool. And let's not forget, I'm your badass operations director and master distracter."

"That's not a thing. You're also a complete goof."

"I'm not a goof. I'm efficient. I mean, I talk a lot, a mile a minute, but I know what I'm doing. Relax."

"Fine. Stay out of trouble. If anything happens, you come find me and we'll get the hell out of here, okay?"

"Got it."

I proffered my arm. "Okay. Show time."

We walked in together, playing the part of a couple besotted. Nodding at familiar faces here and there. Once well into the ballroom with champagne in our hands, I pointed out her mark. She grinned at me and then stood on tiptoes and dusted my cheek with her lips.

Circuit. Fucking. Overload.

I couldn't form a coherent thought. I could only stand there and stare at her.

"You okay?"

I shook my head to try and loosen her effect. "Yep. After you."

She sauntered off, hips sashaying through the crowd. I wasn't the only one watching either. Several men turned to watch her as she glided forward with the elegance of a swan. I couldn't talk. I couldn't fucking think. Why was I there again? What was I doing? God, one touch from that woman and I was a completely useless piece of shit.

Focus. Get in the goddamn game. Downs, he is your concern.

Her scent knocked me on my arse. I was barely functional.

For fuck's sake. Get your shit together.

Fortunately, locating Downs was easy. He even smiled when he saw me coming.

I left my empty glass on a waiter's tray, then he asked Downs if he'd like a drink.

"Yeah sure, mate. Scotch."

His Australian twang was so subtle now that I had to listen closely to hear it. But I knew better than to think that he wasn't Aussie through and through. "Rowan, you look well."

He grinned. "Are you going to butter my arse?"

"Does it need buttering?"

He laughed and shook his head. The waiter brought our drinks, and Downs laughed as he scrutinized the ball. "You traveled quite a distance to see me."

"A happy coincidence. Paris is only a weekend trip. We're building a hotel here."

"Ah yes, your hotel interest brought you here."

I grinned. "Oh, you thought I came to woo you? I promise you, you're not my type."

His grin was quick. "Shame, since I'm so pretty." He took a sip of his scotch. "Speak plainly, boy. I'm tired of dancing around it."

So direct was the way to go. "I think the Van Linsteds have had too much power in the Elite for too long. For the last fifty years, save four years, a Van Linsted has been Director Prime. I want to see that change."

His lips tipped into a bit of a smirk. "Somehow you found out I'm one of the Five?"

"I'm not sure it's as much a secret as you think it is."

"Only the Director Prime at any time should know who the Five are."

"Hard to keep secrets in a family as small as ours. The rumors are that you have opposed the Van Linsted cabal before and lived to tell the tale."

He drained his glass then. "Get to your bloody point."

"I'd like you do it again." I knew the plan, how to work him. "The Van Linsteds have held too much power for too long. You know that to be true."

There was that famous Downs smile. "And you want something for nothing?"

"Of course not." I pulled out the envelope from my breast pocket. "I know your daughter had a difficult time last year. I hope these files find both you and her some peace. These are the only copies in existence, and it's been scrubbed from the inter-webs. Even the news outlets that initially reported the story before you could stop them have had an unscheduled data breach. She is free to continue her life as she pleases."

He stared at me for a long moment then took what I offered. "You are proving yourself a formidable adversary."

"I'm no one's adversary, merely an interested party."

"And if not Van Linsted, then who? You?"

I shook my head. "Politics have never interested me. Neither have bullshit games. I just want Van Linsted out and someone else made Director Prime."

He whistled low. "You must really hate him."

Yes. "On the contrary. I have no feelings toward him. I just want what's best for the Elite."

His gaze was assessing, his shaggy salt-and-pepper brows furrowing. "You are your father's son. Politics might not suit, but you are certainly skilled enough to play in that sandbox if you choose."

"Not interested."

"Pity. If you wanted to, you'd do well as Director Prime."

"If and when the time comes and we have your support, there will be another candidate."

He lifted a brow. "And who would that be?"

"We're keeping it under wraps until it's needed."

He nodded as he chuckled. "Secrets whispered."

"Exactly. Secrets whispered. Do I have your support?"

He seemed to think it over. "You have done me a great service, and I am indebted to you, but not enough to vote for an unknown Director Prime."

Fuck. Downs was a slippery fucker, but he was also the most influential of the Five. I had nothing else to offer. "And just knowing a Van Linsted won't hold the seat of power isn't enough?"

"Afraid not. Your Prime might be worse."

"He's not."

"So say you."

Across the ballroom, I watched Olivia chat animatedly to Van Linsted. There was much smiling and handwaving, and it made my lips twitch. She could only keep that up for so long though. "And if new evidence came to light of Van Linsted acting in a way that was contrary to the Elite? His culpability, his crimes..."

"Look, most everyone in the Elite has a skeleton somewhere. Something they don't want coming out into the light of day."

"Except for you. You seem to be clean. So tell me, what do you want? What can I give you to have you on our side?"

Rowan Downs met my gaze. "I want the Canary Jewel."

I frowned, certain that I hadn't heard him correctly. "What?"

"The Canary Jewel."

My mouth unhinged. "That massive yellow diamond that April Van Linsted trots out at all her charity functions? That thing is the size of my fist. You want the Canary Jewel?"

He sniffed. "Yes, I do. What nobody knows is that jewel actually belongs to the Kimberly Downs Mining Conglomerate. It was a gift from my great grandfather to his fiancée. On the eve of the night they were supposed to wed, she vanished. She'd been having an affair with Harrison Van Linsted. She took the jewel and ran. She couldn't very well be prosecuted because it had been a very public gift for her birthday. But she married him, taking our prized jewel with her. I want it back in my family. If you bring me that jewel, I will sway whoever the fuck you want."

I stared at him. "How would you suggest I get it? That thing is priceless."

"Well then, it is handy that you're a billionaire, isn't it?"

"You know full well April Van Linsted is not going to sell that."

He shrugged. "I've given you my price. If you can do the impossible, you'll have my support."

Impossible was right. "You'll have it. Before the vote."

He gave me a brusque nod. "I look forward to it. I want it home. I don't care how you get it or what means you have to employ. But I want it back at Kimberly Downs."

I didn't know how, but I was going to have to make it happen. *Good thing you happen to know a jewel thief.*

Bridge and East weren't going to be thrilled about this development. I heard the three taps in my ear, and it startled me. "Rowan, always a pleasure. Thank you for taking the time to speak with me."

He nodded. "I look forward to our partnership."

I turned just in time to see Livy angling her head awkwardly toward the door. The three taps meant Van Linsted was on his way. I ducked out the side door and met her in the hallway.

"Are you okay?" My gaze swept over her several times.

"Yeah, I'm fine. He is dreadful. He talks about himself in third person. He seems to think he's God's gift to women. Do you know he propositioned me? Slid his hotel key into my purse and told me to come and see him later."

222

I scowled. "He what?" *Arsehole.* I could kill him. That would solve everyone's problem.

"It's fine, I handled it."

The idea that Van Linsted could put his hands on her... I started for the door, and she held me back. "I thought the idea was *not* to be seen."

"Fine, let's go."

Her hand slid into mine easily. We were the perfect picture of a couple slipping out into the night for some fresh air. She turned her face up to me with a sweet smile. "Did you get what you needed?"

I swallowed because no, I did not, in fact, have anything I needed. But I gave her a tight smile and nodded. "Yeah, he's going to help me."

"That's fantastic. What did he ask for in return?"

I shook my head. "Something I'm not sure I can give."

"I'm sorry. But maybe this can help." She pulled a black phone from her purse.

"What's that?"

With an impish grin that showed a hint of dimple, she said, "Bram Van Linsted's phone. And bonus, I watched him enter the code."

I froze. "Y-you stole his phone?"

"Yeah. He was touching me, so I figured I could touch him. Though we probably want to copy or clone it, or whatever it is you do, before he notices it's gone."

"Woman, I think I love you."

"Sorry, you'll have to join the queue. I'm pretty brilliant."

"Yes. Yes, you are."

"I didn't really do anything special."

"You did more than you know. I mean that. And as a reward, tomorrow I'm going to show you Paris."

She treated me to another showstopper of a smile. "What?"

"I'm serious. I know we planned two days of work, but I want to be able to show you the city."

She grinned and threw her arms around my shoulders. Then she stood on tiptoes and gave me a complete toe to chest to shoulder hug. I could feel all her pulsing points pressed against me, hot, warm, and soft. The scent of lime and honey wrapping around me, cutting off my oxygen supply so that I couldn't think rationally. I don't know where the low moan came from, but the moment it was out, I released her immediately. "Let's go."

When she stepped back, I noticed the high flush on her cheekbones. Yeah, I wasn't the only one affected. Too bad neither one of us could do a damn thing about it.

@

Livy

Golden orange rays of sunlight streamed through the blinds in my room, breaking through my sleep solitude. I started to drag the pillow over my head until I remembered that Ben had promised to show me the city that morning.

So instead, I cracked open an eyelid and stretched. It was only when I noticed a shadow looming over me that I squeaked and jumped back.

"Morning, sunshine."

"Oh my God, Ben, you scared the hell out of me."

He laughed. "Rise and shine, princess. We have the perfect Paris day ahead."

I turned to glare at the clock. "It's six-thirty."

"I know. But we only have one day. We have to get a lot in. Wear something comfortable that you can walk in."

I wrinkled my nose and grumbled, "Comfortable isn't cute."

"Come on. If you must see Paris, this is the way to do it."

"Okay, but can we get room service first?"

He turned back to glare at me with a mock expression of horror. "What? You don't eat a hotel breakfast when you're in Paris."

"We did yesterday."

"That's because we had a meeting to go to. But today we do it right."

"Oh God, why can't someone just come and dress me and wash my hair and all of those things?"

He chuckled and leaned over me. Strong hands gently gripped my shoulders and he pulled me to a sitting position. "Come on, out with you."

"What if I was indecent under here?"

"Then I would have gotten the image of a lifetime."

The way his voice pitched low and his gaze hovered at where my breasts lay under the giant duvet made me quiver. "No peeking."

"I promise not to look."

Everything about the cheesy smirk on his face said that he would *definitely* look.

"Turn around. I'm not—Oh, just get out. I'll be out in ten minutes."

"Make it five, or I'm back coming in."

I groaned and flopped back into bed. This was what happened when you became friends with your boss.

He knocked at the door again. "Seriously, get up or I'm coming back in there. I can dress you if you want."

"No, I'm fine. I can dress myself."

He chuckled. "Okay. If you say so. Just hurry up."

I was ready in five. I brushed my teeth, washed my face, and then secured my hair in a bun. He had picked out my favorite sundress, but the sandals he'd laid out were not comfortable, so I switched them out for my Adidas. When I came out, his gaze slid over me, stopping at the Batman pin on the dress. "You brought that with you?"

Heat sneaked up my skin, flaming my cheeks. "Um, sort of out of habit."

He frowned but nodded. "Right. Anyway, let's go."

"Where are we going?"

"First, we are going to have breakfast."

"Where? It better be good because I'm starving."

"This is Paris. It's all good. We are headed to *Ble Sucre*. It is on *Rue Antoine Vollon*. God, the *pain au chocolat* will ruin you for any other croissant you'll eat in your life. I promise."

He took my hand. I was tempted to pull it back, but he was so enthusiastic I didn't want to ruin it.

You're sending mixed messages. And you still have a complicated situation.

God, did I still have a boyfriend? I had a lot to sort through, and I didn't need feelings for Ben to complicate things. Discreetly, I pulled my hand back and tucked it into the pocket of my dress. Ben didn't say anything though. Instead, he tossed an arm around my shoulders as he directed me toward the smell of the most amazing bread in my life. "This better be worth it."

"I promise you it is."

And he was almost always right, which was annoying. It made me want to hit him in his smug face. But the croissants were well worth it. We carried several along with us as we continued to walk. We headed across the Seine and decided to see what was remained of Notre Dame. There were still parts of the structure left. My heart broke as I thought of the fire we'd all seen on television. But like most things in Europe, they would rebuild and restore. Maybe one day I'd get to see it in its former glory. *Jardin des Plantes* was our next stop. "Is this the botanical garden?"

He nodded. "Yeah, it's the main one. It dates back to the 1600s or something. Come on, let's go. We're taking a quick walk."

I groaned. "Can't I just sit down and gorge myself on this delicious bread?"

He laughed. "We can walk and do it. I didn't realize you were such a morning person."

"You know that's funny, because on workdays I am. I'm up early in the office doing stuff. But on days that I have to myself, I would sleep till noon. It's like I can switch off that part of me that has to follow a timetable, you know?"

He nodded. "You are definitely a mystery."

I grinned at that. "I aim to please."

He pointed. "Now, there's a national museum in that building, but we have a lot to cover so we're going to skip it today."

"Okay. Let me buck up. Hey, stop hogging the croissants."

Paris had a certain charm with its old buildings and narrow winding streets. They were lined with bistros and boutiques and cozy bookshops. When we hit *Rue Mouffetard*, Ben stopped. "Okay, grab that lamppost. Wind yourself around it. Look happy."

"What, are we doing, an impromptu photo shoot?"

"Of course. You have to prove you were in Paris, you know for the 'gram."

"Oh my God, please don't say 'the 'gram'."

"What? I'm hip. I'm cool."

"I'm not sure hip and cool is what I would refer you as."

"Oh my God, don't you know I am a London Lord? We're notorious for an overabundance of fun."

"You know, I could see that… in your heyday."

"My heyday? You are a dead woman."

I squeaked as I bolted away from him. He caught me easily, wrapping his arms around me and tickling me until I squealed.

It was so easy to be with him in the spring sunshine. And fun. It felt light and happy. We stopped at a few spots in the market, and Ben bought me a scarf and cheap jewelry. I couldn't help but smile. "You know, you didn't have to do this."

"Yes, I did. You helped me. I owe you at least this much."

"No, I think you've already done enough for me."

"No, not nearly enough."

We passed the Pantheon, and I stared up in wonder. "Aren't Marie Curie and Alexander Dumas entombed there?"

He laughed. "Yes, along with many other religious, political and cultural figures, but it was originally a church before being secularized during the French Revolution."

"God, I know we don't really have time to go in, but just the history, you know? My mother would have loved it."

"She never came to Paris?"

I shook my head. "She did, but she was always working. She never seemed to have time to really explore. Not until she got older and quit work. And then she was always bothering me to live life and experience all the things I could experience, spread my wings, and fight for justice."

He laughed. "Like Batman."

"So to speak. But yeah, it was long after she retired that I think she really understood that she'd spent too much of her life crammed into an office and meetings, you know?"

"How long did she have before she got sick?"

"Oh, we had a good solid five years. Every opportunity we had, she was like, 'Livy, let's get on a plane.' And we had some wild adventures, but we never did Paris together. I wish we had."

"Well, I think her spirit is here." He reached for the pin. Even though it was only the back of his knuckles that touched my arm really, my skin flamed.

Jesus. Get your shit together, Livy. No more emotionally unavailable men.

We headed down to Luxemburg Gardens then and had fun exploring. Ben was the perfect guide. Knowledgeable and patient as I found spots to scatter Mom's ashes. He didn't ask any questions when I asked for a minute, just gave me space and didn't make me feel weird when he caught me with a misty eye.

We scarfed the last croissant that Ben actually had the nerve to fight me for. He learned very quickly how far I was willing to go for pastry. The tulips were blooming, and I could see why everyone raved about springtime in Paris. We passed the *Palais de Justice* where Marie Antoinette was imprisoned before going to the guillotine, then we just wandered through the elegant buildings, charming streets, and picturesque squares of the 5th. And the shops… the shops full of antiques, clothes and things that I couldn't afford, called my name. But oh God, I would have loved to window-shop and touch.

Then Ben stopped me. "Right here. *Café de Flore.*"

I laughed. "Oh boy, I bet you're feeding me again. I'm going to not fit in my clothes by the time I get back to London."

"Oh, I think you're going to fit just fine."

He came back with two steaming mugs of hot chocolate. "Here you go. This is the best hot chocolate in Paris."

I took a sip and moaned sweet chocolate and whipped cream soothed my soul. "Oh my God. You are so right. Okay, where to next?"

"Well, we are in Paris, so obviously, the Eiffel Tower."

I couldn't help but squeak. Just the idea of it made me excited. "I know it's touristy, but I really want to see it."

"Are you sure? It's a bit of a walk, but if you're up for it, let's go."

He pulled out two tickets to the Eiffel Tower. "You ordered tickets early?"

"Of course. I don't want to waste our day standing in a queue."

And he was right. The queue for the Eiffel tower was insane. But we went straight to the top.

I didn't care if it was cliche, the views alone were worth the disdain of the locals.

I couldn't believe I was in Paris, taking in the sights with him, and it was so easy talking to him. I learned a bit about his life at Downing Street, his father, boarding school, and how he'd met Bridge and East and Drew. I didn't think I'd met Drew yet. And then he talked about his friend who'd died, Toby. Their adventures, their misadventures. Mostly surface things. Maybe it hurt too much to talk about him. But he also talked about his cousin Roone, who had inadvertently married into a royal family.

"Your life is crazy."

"Believe me, I know."

We walked and talked and walked some more, and my feet were on fire. Luckily, we were close to *L'Epoque,* and we stopped to rest for a moment and have a coffee. Ben looked at me across the table and asked, "How are you liking your perfect Paris date so far?"

Date? "It is absolutely perfect."

"I thought you'd appreciate a break before we hit the Louvre."

I just grinned up at him. "You don't have to do any of this you know."

"I know. But at least I can show a girl a good time in Paris of all places."

I shoved him. "There's that ego again. And let's be clear, the only reason I'm so happy is because of Paris."

He rolled his eyes. "Yeah okay, if you say so."

He knew the truth. I knew the truth. He was the reason. We could have been in any ordinary place, and I still would have been just as happy to be with him. Because I was completely done for.

CHAPTER 23

Ben

She looked... happy. All day she'd been a chatterbox, asking me questions, wanting to know more about me and how I'd grown up. And for the first time in a long time, I felt light. Content. As if nothing could touch me.

But it's not real, is it?

No, it wasn't real. And I had to live with that because someone was following her. Because of me she was now a part of this. It was my fault, and there was no taking that back.

But for now, she looked content.

"Why were you hiding in that closet that night?"

She sighed. "I was hiding from Fenton."

I frowned. "That git I pulled off of you at the bar?"

"The same one. He's always too close. Too inappropriate. He always seems to find me."

I ground my teeth, speaking through them as I tried to bite back the flare of anger. "Define 'find you.'"

"It happened at a work thing for Dexter the first time, about a year and a half ago. I'd never seen him before, but we were making chit-chat. You know me. Then Dexter came and put his arm around me and... I don't know, Fenton got this look on his face. It looked like fury. As if one of us had done something to piss him off. I didn't really understand it." She shrugged.

"Did he try to get closer to you?"

"Not really. But he started making Dexter work longer hours. Then one day he turned up at my office. And this was before mom got really sick. I was leaving to go and have lunch with her and there he was. He just *happened* to be there. He called it a happy coincidence and insisted on following me to lunch."

I cursed under my breath. Every invented curse I could think of. "Hell, he stalked you."

"I'm not sure if I'd call it stalking, but every now and again he's there, right when I don't want him to be. He insisted on lunch that day, forced himself on me and my mother and paid for everything. I, of course, tried to decline. And then Dexter asked what the hell I'd done to his boss because the guy was so upset that he changed Dexter's job and made him directly report to him."

I frowned at that. "This is only getting worse." For a month, we'd been worried about an unseen enemy, but this toad sprocket had been right under my fucking nose all along.

"I kept telling Dexter I hadn't done anything. I didn't know why he was being like that or what he wanted, but Dexter was happy to move up. He's the kind of guy who was always ambitious and wanted more, and he just didn't want to see it. But every time we had a date night or something planned, we'd have to cancel because he'd have to work. It was weird. One day I finally stopped listening to Dexter and didn't put our date nights on his calendar. When the next couple happened as planned, I figured that Fenton had been having a look at his calendar and stopping our plans."

"Did you report him?"

She shook her head. "I don't really have any proof."

"Why didn't you tell me?"

She shrugged. "We haven't talked about any of this stuff. You know about my mom, but I mean, it's not like you know who I lost my virginity to when I was eighteen."

My scowl deepened. "We'll talk about him later. And as soon as we get back to London, you need to file a restraining order against Fenton Mills. That's an order."

"You don't get to dictate my life."

What kind of utter bullshit was that? "Yes, I do."

"Why?"

Why? Because for the first time in a long while I was allowing myself to care about someone. "Because I care about you. You're the best operations director I've ever had."

"I'm the only one you've let yourself have. Jessa told me you like to stay hands-on."

"Yeah, well, if you want something done, do it yourself. So what's your plan for pencil dick?"

She sighed. "I've been trying not to think about it."

"I saw that kiss he gave you when he said goodbye."

"Yeah, I'm pretty sure that was for *your* benefit, not mine. Things just got really bad for us about six months ago right after Mom died. I was driving one night and we had a bad accident. He broke his hand in three places and required a lot of physical therapy. We've never really recovered from it. He blames me."

I was going to kill him. I was going to kill both of them, Fenton and Dexter. Fenton because I now had a feeling that he was the one following her or having her followed, and Dexter because he was just a pure arse.

He was cheating on her. But I couldn't tell her any of that because she would want to know how I knew. It would hurt her, and my sole aim was to keep her from hurting.

"We're friends, remember? So, let me help you with this. This shit can't go unchecked. You have to tell the police."

She frowned. "Now you sound like Telly. She's been saying for ages that I need to just report him."

"I agree."

"I wish I could explain it, but I sort of feel like I can't, like my hands are tied and that no one will believe me."

I took her hand, dangerous rookie move that it was, but I couldn't help it. I needed to touch her. I needed to feel her soft palm in mine. "I am your friend, Livy. I'm not just your boss. I will help you. I know people in the police department. They'll take your report seriously. He'll be forced to stay away from you. People like that are dangerous. I don't want you hurt, get it?"

She nodded and withdrew her hand from mine. I was bereft at the loss of her warmth, but I couldn't really force her to hold on. "Thank you. It's like my whole life is in a twisty-turny shamble and I don't have a clue about what to do."

"Listen, I'll help you. Whatever you need. I don't want to overstep, but you have to do something about him. He forced you to hide."

"I know. I feel dumb."

"Don't feel dumb. That's how he wins. That's what he wants you to feel. Like, 'Oh, maybe you're making this up.' You're not."

"Why are you so amazing?"

"Tell that to my mates, would you? They're not always sure I'm amazing."

"Why do you do that?"

I frowned. "What?"

"Diminish the good qualities about yourself. You act like all you are is a facade, but you're so much more. Why don't you want anyone to see that?"

The woman saw me too well, and that was dangerous. But despite the danger and my pounding heartbeat, I met her gaze. "Because sometimes it's easier to pretend than to let them see the real you."

@

Livy

I had been dreading this moment all night. All day really. I had known there would be a moment when it was time to say good-night. Put an end to the day. Put an end to pretending that I was carefree and happy and had not a care in the world. "I should probably get to bed."

He nodded and took the wine glass from my hand and sat it on the coffee table along with his. Then he stood and reached out a hand to me. I glanced up at him. He was so tall and broad, and sex appeal oozed off of him in waves.

The connection to him was ever-present. From the moment I'd shared a closet with him, it had been like the gears of a clock clicking into place. Like every moment of my life had led me to him. He was more than familiar. He was home.

He'd spent his whole day showing me everything I wanted to see in this glorious city. I hadn't even asked, and he'd done it. I didn't even know what to say to that.

"Thank you for everything. I wish I had the words to say thank you properly, but I've never in my life dreamed of a day like this. I won't forget it."

He flushed slightly, and ducked his head. "I'm glad you had a good day. It was my pleasure to show it to you."

"And thank you for letting me spread more of my mother's ashes. You're probably sick of that process by now. I get weepy and all that sad shit."

His smile was soft as he spoke. "No, actually." He dug his hands into his jeans, tugging them lower on his hips and showing just a hint of hip bone, making me swallow around the saw dust in my mouth. When I lifted my gaze, he was watching me closely. When he spoke, his voice was thick. "I feel like I know her. I feel like she and I might have been great friends."

"You know, you're probably right. She always said she liked a man who was a bit of a rogue."

He grinned then. "Well then, resident rogue at your service."

"You really didn't have to do all this, and I don't just mean a day in Paris. What you've given me in the last few weeks, a new job, a roof over my head... I don't have any way to say thank you properly."

"I didn't do any of those things for you. I did it for me. I *like* being near you. I *like* your obsession with Batman. I *like* your teasing. I love your smile. Being with you reminds me that I have been living in a shell of myself for too long. I haven't had a woman I trusted in a long time. Everything about this is completely crazy, and every single day you make me want to keep up. So spending the day exploring with you was absolutely my pleasure."

"Goodnight, Ben."

He frowned, his voice hoarse when he whispered my name. "Livy—"

He reached for me, and I automatically stepped back. "I should go to bed."

"I just wanted you to have the perfect day."

"And it was perfect."

He opened his mouth to say something and then shut it again. I shouldn't have been desperate to know what he wanted to say, but I was.

He wasn't the kind of man for lazy Sunday lie ins. He wasn't the relationship type. Hadn't I already learned my lesson?

I turned, and he reached out for me. His touch a light graze on my skin. A caress of two fingers sliding over me like satin, making me forget a simple thing like breathing. When I turned, the muscle in his jaw ticked.

"This is a bad idea for a lot of reasons."

I blinked up at him. "What?"

"This." He pointed his finger between us. "It feels like you're mine."

When he said it like that, with that low growl, I believed everything he said. And my body was being pulled to him like the reverberation of elastic that had been pulled away too tight. I was coming back to him at high velocity speed, and we were going to collide. But there was no stopping it. No chance that I was going to escape. It was happening. It was a matter of how long I could put it off. Heartbreak was coming for me.

You're insane if you think you can put it off.

He stepped into my space and wrapped his arms around me, his hands settling on my hips like a brand. "Ben—"

His lips latched onto mine in a crash and a caress, and it was like something broke inside me. I was the elastic snapping back. I was careening out of control, and I didn't give a shit.

I leaned into the kiss, digging my fingers into his T-shirt, pulling him closer and needing to feel the press of his body against mine. I was going to hell. I prayed I could stop time, to have this moment, this taste, before doing what I knew I had to do. I could just pause that moment and be the woman he wanted me to be. Be brave and wild and fun and adventurous. I could be her. I could let go of safe me, of the Livy that followed the rules, that did the right thing always.

For once I could follow passion, and I finally understood

what my mother had been trying to tell me about making sure that every moment was lived with that kind of passion. That life was so short, and if you weren't looking, you'd lose threads of it. I finally understood what it really meant to be alive. Just to have someone who would kiss me like I was everything to him, like I was the only thing that gave him breath, that gave him life.

Ben's hands were in my hair. I could feel the press of his heavy ring against my temple as his fingers twined in my curls and pulled. He angled my head swiftly and devoured my lips, his tongue sliding in, not in a gentle, slick motion, but in torrent of need and desire and strong licks intent on igniting a new rapture. He was owning my mouth. With a groan, one hand released me and wrapped around my waist, slid over my ass, and pulled me in close. I could feel the hard press of his dick against me. Thick. Bulging. Insistent.

Holy hell. He was *huge*. And I wanted to feel him filling me up, claiming me, making me *his*. Who was I kidding? I was already his. Anything he asked, I would give. Anything he wanted, I would break every oath and vow to give it to him.

Against my lips he moaned. "So fucking beautiful. I need you so much."

Unable to form any coherent thought, all I could do was whisper against his lips. "Ben."

It must have been enough because his lips went back to devouring mine. And there was a muffled cry as he dragged me down to the couch. At first, I laid on top of him, but then with a grunt, he rolled us over and his body lay over mine, hips between my spread legs, and all I could do was hang on for the ride. His kisses were taking me high, dragging me along with them in a wild Icarus ride. With his tongue, he drove me closer and closer to the sun, and I didn't give a fuck that my wings were on fire.

I just wanted more. I wanted to be closer to him. I wanted his skin pressed against mine, to feel the heat of his skin under the press of my fingers.

We tugged and pulled at each other's clothes. Muffled moans, low groans, desperation chased need as we fought each other free of our clothes. He dragged the strap of my sundress off my shoulder and then groaned when his eyes took in the strapless bra I wore underneath it. "I need to see." His lips kissed along my jaw, my collarbone, and down my chest as his fingers played with the other strap, dragging that down as well. "Can I? Can I see you?"

He was normally so forceful, so demanding. But he lifted his gaze, his hair falling over his brow, and he was so vulnerable. Pleading.

I nodded. "Yes."

With his teeth, he dragged down the red satin covering my breast, and he groaned.

"Christ." And then his mouth was on me. But there was no frenzied, pulling need. No. This was tender. Softer. Gentler. And the soft tugging of his lips made my hips arch into him.

"Ben, please..."

Instead of hurrying, he pulled the other strap of my sundress down further and tugged the satin down with his fingers. When I was completely bare to him, he pulled back and watched my breasts as I dragged in breath after breath. I just needed his mouth on me. His hips pressed into mine, but it wasn't nearly enough pressure. Not where I needed. I just wished he would touch me more. Use his mouth, his fingers, anything. The fire was burning in my soul, and I didn't give a shit. The things I couldn't take back, the apologies I couldn't make, I would deal with those later, but I needed relief.

He finally touched my right peak, and his gaze met mine as

he ran a thumb over it. "I love your nipples. I want to cover them with fucking chocolate."

My eyes fluttered close, and I threw my head back. "I don't know, just... just... I need something from you."

"I know, baby. And I'm going to give it to you. But first, I need to taste. I've been so desperate to know. Just a little taste."

His words were so gentle. They were nearly whispered against my breasts as he lowered his head. I arched my back, trying to rush him, hurry him along. Get his mouth where I needed it. And there it was. His lips wrapped around my nipple, and his tongue was a tease. I cried out needing more. The pull at my belly was deep and throbbing, and God, it held such promise of everything I had ever been looking for.

With his free hand, he cupped my other breast, rolling the nipple between his thumb and forefinger, tugging gently as he suckled on the other one. "Fuck."

Reaching a hand behind me, he unsnapped my bra and kept tugging on my sundress, kissing the skin that was bared to him. His fingers were still playing with my nipple. He tried tugging the dress all the way down, but it wouldn't budge.

"There's a zipper."

He shook his head. "Fuck." He shoved the material up over my thighs, and then adjusted his position. When he kissed my belly button, I squirmed. "Oh my god. Ben, God, please..."

"Shhhh... I will make you feel better, okay?"

Why was he being so gentle? I expected this to be hot and fast and dirty and...

But instead of giving me the thing that would sate the crawling need, he was giving me more. He was giving me gentleness. He was giving me feelings and emotions, and I didn't know what to do with all of that.

One of his fingers traced the edge of my panties. "Can I touch you?"

I nodded. "I'm yours."

"I know. Since I saw you in that closet, you've been mine. You just didn't know it yet."

He was right. I hadn't known it. I didn't even know as I fought that truth. There was a part of me accepting it. Part of me willing him to do what he needed to with me, to give him whatever the hell he wanted. When his finger slid under the elastic, I moaned. He released my breast and then tugged aside my panties. His moan was low and throaty. "God, you're so pretty."

"Ben, please... I need you."

"I'm getting to it. I'm just going to take my time."

"No, not okay. Now."

His chuckle was soft. "No. I've been waiting for weeks. No way am I rushing this. You and I, we're happening. And before *we* happen, I'm going to make you feel so good you will never again question who you belong to."

I nodded up and down. I would have agreed to anything at that point. Anything at all. His thumb slid over my clit, and I yelled out. "Oh my God."

He did it again, slower this time. Applying more pressure to my clit, and my hips bucked up off the couch. "More... please."

"You're gorgeous." He parted my folds and slid a finger inside me. "So wet. Have you ever been wet like this before?"

My head thrashed back and forth. "Ben...."

And then his mouth, oh God, his mouth, he planted it over my clit as he added a second finger, his fingers making shallow thrusts as his mouth worked on my clit, sucking, teasing, pulling me deep down under the abyss. Oh fuck, I was going to die. I was going to die just like this. With Ben Covington owning me.

And that should've terrified me, but it didn't because I was ready. Any way he wanted to have me, any way he wanted to own me, I was his. And I had known that long before I had gotten on the plane and come to Paris. It had just taken that moment of his raw need to make me realize it.

He pulled his fingers from me. "How do you like it? Soft? Hard? Gentle presses? Hard presses?"

"I don't know. Just anything... something."

He slid another finger back in. "Like this?" His thrusts deepened, but the single penetration of one finger wasn't enough. My inner walls pulled him in, and he gave me a devilish smile as he glanced back up at me. "Do you like it like this? Or do you like it like this?" He slid another finger inside me, and I arched my back.

"Like this. Like this, God."

"Now do me a favor and come for me once, because I need to see it." His voice had taken on this smoky quality.

And then his mouth was back on me. Sucking, licking, taking me to the edge, making me feel alive. Begging me to fall, begging me to come apart and give him what he needed from me.

And I was close. So close. Writhing on his big palm and underneath his mouth as he owned me. I reached for freedom. Reached for the new me. The woman he promised was underneath everything else. I reached for her and she danced on the edges, hair wild, smile bright, hips swaying, calling to me, telling me that I could be free. I could have everything. All I needed to do was fall. She may have been wearing the devil's own wings, but I didn't care. I just wanted everything he could give me, and God, I was so close. "Yes, right there—"

Somewhere in the room, music started to play. The sounds of Lizzo asking why men were great till they had to be great filled the room, and I froze.

Ben didn't seem to notice at first because his mouth kept working. Sucking. Licking.

And he almost managed to drag me back under and make me forget. But Lizzo's voice only grew louder, talking about how she'd just taken a DNA test and turned out she was a hundred percent that bitch.

And I knew who was calling. Telly had changed my ringtone for Dexter. I shook, my orgasm within reach, so damn close. But instead of all-encompassing bliss taking over, a feeling of dread settled over me.

"Ben, wait."

His snapped his head up. "Livy?"

I scooted away from him and he released me immediately, his finger sliding out of me, as he groaned.

"Stop. Please stop." I scooted to the edge of the couch and covered my face. As if that was going to solve my problem.

Ben backed off immediately, allowing me some space but not too much. "Hey, you're okay."

"I'm such a mess."

"No, you're not." He inched closer. "Let me hold you."

When I only bit my lip in response, he gave me a soft smile. "I'm only going to hold you. It's okay if you're not ready yet."

"I'm sorry."

He took my hands and tilted my chin up, so I had no choice but to meet his gaze. "Don't be. This is happening. And when it does, it's going to blow the bloody roof off of both of us. You left things a little unsettled back home. So you come to me when you're ready."

"I—"

"We're happening. I've come to terms with that. Now it's your turn. I should also warn you that I'm impatient, so if you take too long, I'll be forced to remind you how good we are together."

I shook my head. "You are so damn arrogant."

"I know. It's why you're going to fall in love with me."

I froze. L-O-V-E. Did he just say that word to me? He didn't seem to even notice. He just grabbed the blanket and pulled it over us as he tucked me into his side, seeming so sure that I belonged there.

CHAPTER 24

Ben

A s rain pelted the windshield, I held my fingers entwined with Livy's for most of our trip back. Waking up with her was the most relaxed I'd been in years maybe.

This was a dangerous game.

I knew the stakes. But once everything had aligned in my mind, I couldn't fathom giving her up. Like it or not she was mine. Mine to protect. Mine to cherish. Mine to love if she'd let me.

You sound as crazy as Fenton.

That wanker was getting slapped with a protection order as soon as we settled back at the hotel. I was done with her being afraid. And I was done keeping things from her. I'd tell her everything tonight. I first needed to tell the lads about Rowan, because we needed to set plans in motion. And I'd warn them. My secrets unfortunately were their secrets. I had to tell them first.

She turned her head to smile at me. "You know, you've been holding on to me like you think I might run."

"I'll find you if you do. "

"And if I don't want to be found?"

I lifted a brow. "Do you want to be found?"

She laughed, the sound so light, it elevated me out of the darkness of my thoughts. "That's not the point."

"I already told, you. We are happening. I can be only so patient."

She licked her lips, and I watched her tongue with rapt interest. "I'll deal with Dexter and the house and all of that. You're right. It does seem like we are inevitable."

I lifted my brows. "Did I hear that correctly? Did you just say I was right?"

"You're incorrigible."

"I know. It's my best tra—" The car hit a slick patch and we fishtailed. I immediately tightened my hold on Livy's hand and the hand grip above the door. Livy gasped, then squeezed her eyes shut tight. Our driver muttered what sounded like an expletive as he fought to control the car.

We finally came to a stop at the side of the road, bumping into one of the guard rails. The mini collision jostled us in the back seat enough to make my teeth rattle.

I reached for her immediately. She had her fingers to her temples and rocked back and forth. "Livy! Livy, you all right?"

Todd, our driver, turned around. "Sorry about that. Let me just get quick photos for the accident report. I'm sure it's minor, but still."

I wanted to rip him a new arsehole, but right now my concern was her.

She kept holding her head. "Ben…"

I unlatched my belt so I could pull her close and rub her back. "Yeah, I'm right here. I will have him severely reprimanded just as soon as we get you back. Let me call a doctor and have him wait for us at the hotel."

She shook her head. "No. I'm fine. I just—" Her dark eyes met mine. "I remember."

"Remember what?"

"The accident. Just now. We started to spin, and I could see it."

"Fuck, I'm so sorry. The last thing I wanted was to have you triggered."

Livy grabbed my arm. "No, it's a good thing. I wasn't driving. *He* was."

My eyes went wide. "Just when I think he couldn't be more of an asshole he surprises me."

"Can you take me home?"

"Over my dead body. You need to get checked out. And I'm not letting you near him."

"Ben, I'm fine. You're fine. At most, we have a few scratches on the car. It was more a scare than anything else."

I ground my teeth. "I'd like to be sure."

"And I'd like to take care of this once and for all. He's stolen enough of my life from me. I want this done."

"Fine, but I'm staying with you."

"You will do no such thing, Ben Covington. You were right. We are inevitable. But you have to let me do this my way."

"If you think I'm going to leave you behind, you've grossly underestimated my desire to keep you safe from harm. Not bloody happening."

Her lips pressed together, and I could sense that she was going to unleash her barely contained rage. "I won't be able to do this with you there. Can't you see that?"

I could but I didn't care. "Answer is still no."

She dragged in a deep breath. "Fine. Leave me with Todd here. He doubles as security, right?"

He did, but clearly, he was a git who couldn't drive. "No. Not him. He clearly doesn't take enough precautions with your life."

"For the love of God. It was an accident." She crossed her arms and I could see the gears in her brain working. She wouldn't let any of this go until she'd dealt with pencil dick.

"Fine. I'll call and have someone meet us there, and Todd can take me back to the hotel. Call me when you're done, and I'll pick you up myself."

She threw up her hands. "You are the most stubborn, obstinate, pain in—"

I lifted a brow and took one of her hands in mine. "That's a yes."

"See was that so hard?"

I'd said yes, but it didn't sit right by me. What if, after everything, she still chose him?

But then I looked down at our entwined fingers. No. She was mine. She just had to admit it to herself.

@

Livy

I knew what I had to do. There was no point in putting it off any longer. At the end of the day, I couldn't accept that ring.

I'd known it before I left on Friday.

I knew it even more now. Dexter was a liar. He'd used my guilt to manipulate me. I didn't even recognize the man I used to love. He was gone.

And as much as it had something to do with how much our relationship had deteriorated, it was more about me. This wasn't about my feelings for Ben, though they were there and unavoidable and intense.

Somewhere along the line, I had changed, and he'd changed. And there was no going back. No recovering from that. He'd broken us.

I let myself in the flat, and Dexter was waiting for me. "Oh, I didn't realize you'd be waiting."

His brows rose. "I didn't expect you home. I figured you'd send Telly over to get your things."

My fury choked against my leash of control. "Dex look, you probably know what's coming, and I do need to talk to you. I think this conversation had been coming for a long time."

He raised a hand. "Look, I know you're probably angry, and I don't want to get into a huge fight. But I need you to hear me out."

I was so tired. And I regretted insisting on coming alone. I wanted Ben's strong arms around me right now. "I'm done, Dexter. I'm done hearing you out. I'm done listening to your excuses." I frowned. "You made me believe I was driving that night."

He went pale. "Y-you were."

"No, you asshole. It is not the time to double down on that lie."

He licked his lips. "Okay, look. It seems bad, but I've had a drunken driving offense before, and I couldn't have another one. You were out of it, and I just put you under the wheel."

"For six months you've lied to me. Made me feel guilty. Used me."

"That's not what it was. I just, I messed up. You weren't drinking, so it just looked like an accident. They didn't even investigate closely because you were clean. There was no harm."

"There was harm. *You* did me harm every time you tried to blame your injuries on me. God. Were you ever even injured?"

"I did hurt my hand."

"Clearly not very much because you were able to move me to the driver's seat."

He started to pace and ran his supposedly injured hand through his hair. "It just all got away from me. Fuck. Everything was bloody fine until you took that job. This is Ben Covington's fault. I knew he wouldn't be able to resist poisoning you against me."

I could see it so clearly now. The blatant narcissism. The delusions of grandeur. Had he always been like this and I'd just been too dumb to see it?

Suddenly, all I felt was utter exhaustion. "Dexter, I'm not angry. I'm numb and empty. If I'm being honest, I think I always knew. I just didn't want to see it, admit it."

He glared at me "How can you not be angry? That's the problem, you don't care enough."

I blinked at him. "W-what?"

"The accident. The fact that I've been sleeping with someone else. You can't even muster the energy to give a shit. How am I supposed to feel loved and desired like that?"

His words were a punch to the gut. "What?" I hadn't said a thing about him sleeping with someone. Sure, that pretty redhead from his office had given me pause, but had I missed some obvious sign?

"What? Like Covington didn't tell you?"

My brain whirled, and I shook my head, trying to get some kind of handle on the conversation that was happening. "I don't understand what the hell you are saying."

My stomach churned. Then nausea threatened to take over. Dexter stood then and started to pace. All I could do was drop my bag where I stood and then sink down onto the ottoman.

"You're telling me, he didn't tell you?"

"Tell me what?"

He ran his hands through his hair, tugging. "He didn't fucking tell you? Why wouldn't he? He clearly wanted to fuck you."

My stomach squeezed as I thought of what we'd done last night. "Back the fuck up, Dexter. What is going on?"

"What do you think I'm talking about?"

I stared at him. "I have no idea. I thought you were talking about the fact that I can't accept that engagement ring and that we haven't been right in months. But you're talking about you cheating on me? And what the hell did Ben have to do with this?"

He shook his head. "I—"

"The cat is out of the bag. You might as well just say what you need to say."

He paced and ran his fingers through his hair and then over his face. "Okay look, I thought he'd told you. I just need a second."

"What, a second to lie? No, say what you're going to say."

He stopped and glared at me. "Fine. You were so depressed all the time. You were always moaning about your mom, and you really weren't there for me."

"Wait, so you're blaming me because my mother died and I'd been grieving? She died six months ago. So you decided you should cheat on me?"

"No, it wasn't like that. It was not like a decision I made. It was just—it just happened. I missed so much work because of my hand. And—"

I couldn't believe the words that were coming out of his mouth. First, he told me he cheated on me only because somehow, he thought Ben would have told me. And then he blamed me. And now he thought that I was going to overlook this and just let it go? I stared up at him. On the outside, he was still the same tall, handsome man I'd fallen in love with. It wasn't so much that he'd changed; it was that I was seeing him more clearly now. "Why don't you tell me exactly what happened, and why in the world do you think Ben knows anything about it?"

He sighed. "Look, why can't we just move past this?"

"We can't move past anything until you tell me the truth."

He sat across from me on the couch and took my hands. "Okay, look. Things were so messed up after your mom died, and I didn't know how to help you. You were just so sad. Then, I messed up with the promotion, and it was just a mess at work. You weren't really there for me, and then we had the accident. You didn't remember how it happened, and you know, you had your injuries and I had mine. Then I started physical therapy, and Andrea, she used to really get me, you know? It was wrong, and I shouldn't have done that to you, but I was grieving too. And I didn't handle it the right way. I should have talked to you. We should have gone to more therapy or something. Taken it more seriously But here we are."

"Why do you think that Ben knew anything about it? He's my boss, why would he know anything?"

He swallowed hard then. He gripped my hands tighter, and I could feel the clamminess of his skin. All I wanted to do was pull my hands out of his, but he held on too tight. It was like a poison he'd created around me. "At the fundraiser, I didn't think you were coming. And Andrea was there. He caught us in the conference room."

There was nothing for me to do but blink at him. "My boss, Ben Covington, caught you screwing your girlfriend at the fundraising event?"

He inhaled sharply. "She's not my girlfriend. It was just a fling."

"You've been sleeping with her. Shagging her. Fucking her. Whatever you want to say. But you have the nerve to stand here and accuse me of something happening with Ben?"

"Oh, come on, I could see how he looked at you."

I smiled at him. "Maybe you're right about how he looks at me, and you know what? Maybe you're right about how I look at him."

He nodded. "See? I told you. You slag!"

The insult rolled off of me like I was teflon. "The difference is I *didn't* shag him. Because I thought I owed you the respect of tying this off because of our relationship, and I wanted to make sure that I had a clean slate before I did anything. But I guess none of that was necessary."

"Don't act so fucking spoiled. People have affairs all the time. It's no reason not to get married. I want to build my life with you."

I pushed to my feet, tired and numb. But the more I thought about it, the look on Ben's face as he assessed Dexter when he first met him, the way he'd wanted to make sure I had a perfect day in Paris, the tender way he held me when he kissed me, he'd known all that time. And he'd lied just like Dexter had.

But why? If he'd told me the truth, I might have given in. Why couldn't one person in my life tell me the goddamn truth? It was that lie that broke my heart, not Dexter's. Because the truth was I'd been done with Dexter long before I'd gotten on that flight to Paris. This was just a technicality. The one I'd wanted out of the way before I could really explore what I was feeling for Ben. But in that moment, what I felt for Ben was nothing but pure rage.

"I want you out of here."

"You can't kick me out. My name is the one on the lease. Or did you forget?"

What was he talking about? "Yes, I can. I was on the lease when we got this place."

"You *were*, but you were so busy with your mum when we renewed you told me to go ahead and sign it. *You* are no longer on the lease. So I won't be going anywhere."

Fuck. Me.

You don't want it anyway. "I'll be back later for my things. Preferably when I don't have to look at you." I left my bag where it was, but I grabbed my purse and walked right back out the front door.

CHAPTER 25

Ben

I was so raw from Paris that I'd completely forgotten that Bridge and East would be waiting for me when I got home. I don't even know what made me go to the flat. It was like I was going on autopilot.

But sure enough, when I arrived, my mates were already inside. I was too exhausted and depleted to even be pissed off or confused.

Bridge scowled when he saw me. "What the fuck is wrong, mate?"

"What are you doing here?"

East and him exchanged glances. "We're here for an update on Downs."

Oh yeah, Downs.

I dropped my bag by the stairs then shrugged off my jacket and tossed it at the back of the couch. East, the good mate that he was, had already poured me a glass of scotch. Two fingers. Oh, I guess he anticipated the news was bad. I lifted my glass in cheers and then downed the whole thing.

More glances.

Bridge sat forward. "What the fuck happened? How much trouble are we in?"

I shook my head. "On the contrary, we're not in trouble. No one really knows yet that we're attempting a coup. Downs suspects only because we're the only ones in place to make a play. And we're the only ones who have been vocal in voicing our displeasure with Van Linsted."

East drained his glass before leaning against the back of the couch. "Okay, so what does it look like?"

"Well, the good news is Downs is willing to help us."

Bridge rocked as he fisted one hand into his other and nodded. "All right. All right, we're on play. With Downs backing us, we're on the fence. We can do this."

East grinned but sobered when he looked at me closely. "Yeah. Mate, why don't you look happier?"

"Well, because Downs wants something. Something I'm pretty sure we can't get."

East stood up then and crossed his arms. "What the fuck does he want?"

I laughed as I went over to the bar and poured myself another scotch. I downed it again, letting it burn down my throat, and then the warmth spread to my gut. "He wants the fucking Canary Jewel."

Bridge frowned. "What the fuck is the Canary Jewel?"

East, however, was more in-the-know. He whistled low. "You know that big fuck-off rock that sits on April Van Linsted's wrist every time there's a charity event or a big important meeting meant to spoil her son?"

Bridge's eyes went wide, and he ran his hand through his hair. "The fucking yellow diamond?"

I nodded. "Yup, that's what Downs wants."

Bridge started to laugh then. "We're fucked. We're blown."

I laughed. "Well, we might be, but that's the thing he wants."

East started to pace. "But why does he want *us* to get it for him?"

I shook my head. "It seems Grandpa Downs made a fatal error back in the day. He gave the jewel as a gift to his sweetheart and then she backed out of the deal and took the jewel with her and married a Van Linsted, which is why their relationship has been so testy all these years. Past generations have tried to mend those fences by brokering deals, but Downs isn't interested in that. He wants the jewel back by any means necessary. If we get that for him, he'll vote with us and sway whoever else we need."

Bridge laughed and shook his head. "Well, we're done then. What, we're to rob her on the street? It's impossible."

I laughed and poured myself yet another glass of scotch. My lids had started to feel loose and my tongue slightly numb. The alcohol was taking swift effect. I hadn't eaten a goddamn thing all day. So yeah, I'd be feeling this shit in no time.

East, on the other hand, was clear-headed and calculating. "Well, it's not entirely impossible. We could attempt it."

Bridge turned around and stared at him. "Are you mad? Corporate raiders, yes. Ruthless billionaires, sure. But we're not fucking diamond thieves. This isn't some James Bond flick. If we try and steal from them, we're dead."

I shrugged. "Well, possibly. Or, maybe we happen to know a diamond thief who can steal it for us."

Bridge's gaze snapped to mine, and East laughed. "Of fucking course. If we ask for help, our chances of survival go up twenty-fold, but would he do it?"

Bridge stared at me. "You're really going to ask for help from the goddamn prince of the Winston Isles?"

"Before he was a prince, he was a con man and a thief. I happen to know he's pulled off a jewelry heist before."

Bridge laughed. "Are we really considering this?"

"Look mate, I've just told you what the price is. Whether or not we're going to risk it is up to us. If we don't, Van Linsted gets away with what he's done. He becomes the most powerful man in the UK, and then he will be absolutely unstoppable politically. He can do anything he wants."

East rubbed his jaw. "I say we can do it."

Bridge glared at him. "Are you insane? We are going to steal one of the largest diamonds in the world?"

East shrugged. "Look, with the right plan, it's possible. I have the tech we might need, and with Prince Lucas, we could do this. We just need the right plan."

Bridge turned to me. "Are you in on this?"

I was distracted. My mind was on Livy and what she was telling Dexter right now. Was he going to go quietly? I was also worried about her safety. He had already proven he made poor decisions that had bad repercussions for her. *You left her with security. Focus on this.*

My mates were all in. I needed to be too. Before I'd started to fall for Livy, I had another priority and I needed to see that through. The difference was now I had something to lose. "I'm in. But we all have to be in, or we don't do it. That includes Drew. We're probably going to need his help."

Bridge cursed and sat back, staring at the ceiling. "So which one of us is calling Prince Lucas?"

As I downed the rest of my fourth scotch it went down smooth, and I said, "I'll do it."

@

Livy

I had considered going to Telly's, but I couldn't get over the fact that Ben had known. The entire time we were in Paris, he had known about Dexter's affair and he'd said nothing to me. What, he'd thought I wouldn't find out? Why keep that from me?

Think harder. That's not why he kept quiet.

I shook that voice of reason off. I was in no mood to be reasonable.

The numbness had given way to anger by the time I rarely drove so I pulled into my usual parking spot at London Lords. The low simmer had turned into barely banked flames. As I got off the elevator, I ground my teeth as I marched. I had no idea what I was going to say. No idea what I wanted the outcome to be, but I wanted the goddamn truth, and I wanted to know why he'd kept those important facts from me. He was my friend, no, more than just my friend. And he'd let me be humiliated. He'd *lied* to me.

I tracked him down at the loft and followed the lights until I found him in his bedroom, in his closet. I'd never been in his room before. Even so I only barely registered that his closet was the size of the dining room and living room of my flat. Correction, old flat.

I didn't bother knocking, just shoved open the door. I was so furious, not even the floor to ceiling windows with the stunning view of Soho could distract me.

His back was turned as he removed his watch and his head snapped around when he heard me come in. "Jesus, what the fuck are you doing here? You were supposed to call me to pick you up."

I glowered at him. "You knew?"

His whole body sagged. "He told you?"

"You fucking knew!!"

Those embers under my skin became white-hot as I marched up to him and shoved him in the chest. My heels sunk into the soft plush carpeting and made me unstable so I stepped out of them and shoved him again.

He didn't budge.

"You knew. You stood there, knowing what he'd done, humiliating me, and you kept it from me?"

His eyes were soft as he searched mine. "I didn't want you hurt."

"So you kept it quiet?"

"What was I supposed to do? Hurt you myself? That was the last thing I wanted to do."

I didn't realize I was crying until I tasted the salt on my tongue. "I was humiliated walking in there with no idea what he was going to hit me with."

His brow furrowed then. "I'm surprised he told you. I expected him to lie. Get you back somehow.""

"He told me everything. He said you caught him at the fundraiser? Was it Andrea?"

"I don't know her name. I didn't know until I walked into your flat on Friday who he was or what he meant to you. It took me a second to even register it. And I didn't want to be the one to break your heart if you wanted him. I wanted you to have what you wanted."

"Bullshit. You're a coward. You just said all this bullshit about being my friend, caring about me, but you let me walk into an ambush."

He scrubbed a hand over his jaw. "I didn't know he was going to tell you like that. And it wasn't my place to tell you."

I knew he was being truthful. But it wasn't right. I knew why he'd done it. He cared about me, and he did not want to see me hurt.

"So you lied."

He shook his head. "I never lied to you. Not once. I didn't lie about my feelings for you. I didn't lie about what you mean to me. I didn't lie about you being mine. I didn't lie when I said that *you* had to choose. You had to *choose* me. I didn't lie; I kept something from you that would have hurt you. It wasn't my place to tell you something that you wouldn't have believed anyway. Maybe I should have told you. I don't know. It was impossible to know the right thing to do. And it was impossible to let you walk in that door without me, but I did it because you needed to make your own choices. Your own decisions."

I knew my anger was irrational, as were my tears. I shoved him again, but this time, he caught my wrist, his fingers gently pressing into my pulse. "I didn't want to hurt you."

"I walked into the flat feeling so guilty, knowing that I needed to put the final nail in the coffin because I hadn't felt about him, ever, the way that I feel about you."

He closed his eyes and released a long breath. "What do you want from me, Liv?"

I didn't know what he was asking, and I scowled at him. "You don't get to ask that. Not when you messed with me."

"I have *never* messed with you. From the moment we met in that fucking closet, you owned me." He gripped my hips. "Tell me you're done with him."

I nodded. "He cheated. And he lied about it. He made me think I caused the accident and I didn't. He tried to lay his addiction at my feet."

He gently released my hand. "Say the words, Liv. I need to be sure you're done with him."

I shook my head. "I am never ever going back there. Unless it's to pack myself up."

"I'm sorry you're angry."

I could see the muscle in his jaw ticking. He was carrying his own anger and holding back from me. "You're sorry? We spent that whole day together in Paris. You could have told me. You could have said something. *Anything*, like 'listen, I don't know how to say this, so I'm just going to say it.' You should have told me."

"As if that would have changed anything. You needed to make your choice. You needed to choose me." His hands went up and gripped my shoulders. As big as he was though, his touch was still gentle, and I felt it, that tension coiling tight between us, pulling so taught it was on the verge of snapping.

"How do you know I wasn't going to choose you?"

"I couldn't take that chance because the moment you do make that choice, you and I are going to need to do something about it."

"Oh yeah? Like what?"

His grip tightened ever so slightly. "You and I have unfinished business. So tell me right now, are you *choosing* me? Come what may, are you making that choice?"

I knew he was right. I'd known it when I came here.

Despite my anger, despite him keeping this from me, despite the humiliation that burned in my chest, I had already chosen. Over the course of the last month, I had *been* choosing; I just hadn't known it. I met his gaze and licked my lips nervously. "I'm choosing you."

"About fucking time."

CHAPTER 26

Ben

I'd wanted her for so long, I had no idea where to start.

But she was standing in front of me, her lips slightly parted, and something in me shattered.

Your self-control.

My fingers digging into her flesh as I pulled her closer. "You are so fucking beautiful."

"Ben…" Her voice was pleading.

"Fuuuck." A groan ripped out of my mouth seconds before I crushed my lips to hers. We were far beyond exploratory and had tripped into desperate territory. A spike of electricity wound around my spine and I knew I wouldn't be able to stop until I'd had my fill.

Livy moaned, molding her body against mine. Her lips were so damn soft, her tongue meeting mine tentatively at first. It wasn't until her hands tightened in my shirt that I lost full handle on the situation.

I growled, sliding my hands into her curls, tightening my grip and angling her head so I could sink in deeper.

She accommodated me by parting her lips. That angel that

had been on my shoulder before, the one telling me I couldn't do this, telling me where the line was, telling me to keep her safe...well, the devil killed that angel. One deep and stroking lick into her mouth, and I eviscerated the line.

She tasted so good. A little spicy, and a little sweet, and all Olivia. The little mewling sound she made at the back of her throat just drove me further. And I couldn't think. I couldn't process that she was really mine now.

My lips refusing to leave hers, I backed her up out of the closet and into my room. I'd never had another woman in here, but I knew just how many feet it was to my bed. My mouth still owning hers, my hands slid down her back, over her arse, and then I hoisted her up onto my bed.

God, she was so tiny and delicate in comparison to me. So soft in comparison to my sharp edges. I had to remind myself that I had to find some bloody control. It didn't matter how much I shook with need, I needed to take my time.

Yeah, good luck with that.

My cock throbbed as she parted her thighs to make room for me. Christ—yeah, right fucking there. Behind my zipper, I throbbed, begging for freedom. Desperate to seek out her heat.

Her tongue met mine in a slide of wet, silky warmth as she rocked her hips into mine. Every tick of her hips was a call. Could she feel how hard I was. Could she feel just big I was? Was she wondering if I'd fit?

Jesus Christ, why was she so—The moment she scored her nails in my hair and over my scalp, a shiver of need rocketed through my body. The molten lava spread through my veins, singeing nerve endings as it went. When she sucked on my tongue, I bit back a curse.

My hands dug into her flesh. I needed more. *Wanted* more. It was either touch her or spontaneously combust. Sliding a hand under the soft cotton of her top, my fingertips skimmed the supple flesh of her belly. *So soft.*

With every brush of my hand, she trembled then arched her hips.

We'll get there, darling.

But she had to be ready first. And while she thought she was there, I needed her clawing and climbing the walls first.

When my fingertips traced over the edge of her bra, she arched her back, giving me better access. I teased the underside of her breast and her breathing came in shallow breaths as I stroked closer to her nipple.

She tore her lips from mine. "Damn, it, just—"

I shut her up with another soul-searing kiss, my thumb tracing over her nipple in slow deliberate circles.

When I finally pulled away from the kiss, it was to nip at her jaw with open-mouth kisses. "You can try to drive this train all you want, Liv, but I'm at the wheel, and I plan on taking the long way around. I've been dreaming about this since I met you."

"Ben—"

"Hmmm?" Gently, I rolled her nipple between my thumb and forefinger.

"Please…"

"It's only fair that I torture you half as much as you've been torturing me." Kissing along the column of her throat, I murmured, "Do you know that all day I've been thinking about you, your tits, your taste. They are the perfect color of honey."

I kissed down her neck, to her clavicle. "I need you to do something for me, Liv."

"Anything," she whispered on a groan.

"Strip," I barely managed to grind out. "If I strip you, you won't have any clothes left."

Livy dragged heavy lids open and blinked up at me before licking her lips. "You take them off."

I narrowed my gaze. "You don't like that pretty blouse?" It was a simple white tunic with long sleeves that cuffed with a delicate pearl button at the wrist and a neckline that was almost indecent. Certainly not office attire. But fucking attire, absolutely.

I smirked down at her as I gripped her thighs. I forced myself to loosen my grip. I didn't want her having bruises on my account.

"I don't want you holding back from me. We've had enough of that."

"Suit yourself," I said while undoing my buttons quickly. I lost a few to my impatience before tossing the shirt aside. Studying her blouse, I tried to find a simple way to take it off, but there wasn't one. "Fuck it," I muttered as I ripped it.

The flimsy fabric tore in my hands like it was nothing, bearing her mauvy pink lace bra. There was no finesse left in me when I leaned over and dragged one of the cups down with my teeth.

As I trailed an open-mouth kiss over her collarbone and down the center of her chest, she kept trying to hold me in place.

When my lips finally wrapped around the sensitive tip, sucking it deep, she threw her head back and groaned. Livy's hands threaded into my hair, holding my head in place. Then she scored her hands down and over my back, leaving a trail of desire on my skin.

I swirled my tongue over the milk chocolate tip of her nipple, and she arched her back on a low moan. "Ben, oh my God." Her hands fisted in my hair and tugged enough to give me some pain with the pleasure.

"Fuuuck. You naughty thing."

Releasing her breast with a pop, I backed out from between

her thighs. When she protested, I hooked my hands behind her knees and pulled her forward, bringing her to her feet.

My voice was guttural and hoarse when I spoke. "Bend over."

@

Livy

Holy hell.

The ice blue of his eyes were now a searing electric blue. My eyes were wide when I met his gaze, but then I turned slowly and complied.

Impatiently, with rough hands, he dragged down my leggings and lace panties until they slid over my hips, dragging them down my legs. "Step out of them."

My hands shook as I slowly tried to turn around. "B-Ben?"

"Shhhh, bend over kitten. I might die if I can't taste you. What do you say? Can I have a little taste?"

A shiver ran over my body as I leaned over his enormous bed. I felt vulnerable and exposed and... *sexy*. The way he looked at me, I thought I might combust. It helped knowing I wasn't the only one feeling this way. I'd seen his hands tremble.

He caressed my back gently, sliding over my skin, then possessively palming my ass. "Open for me, love."

A flush of heat cascaded over my body, but I did what he asked, widening my stance for him.

The first brush of his tongue had me gasping. The next pulled a moan from deep inside me. But when his hands dug into the flesh of my ass and he lapped at me, my sounds became unintelligible. Who needed words, honestly?

He made this moaning sound of satisfaction as he licked and sucked. His thumb stroked my slit, coating it in my juices.

When he pressed on my clit, I stopped caring about what I sounded like. I only cared about this moment, right now, with him.

Expertly, he sucked on my clit as he sank two fingers inside me. "Jesus Christ, you're so tight. The way you're gripping my fingers. You're going to be a tight fit. "

All I could manage was a week plea of, "Ben, please." The wave built deep inside me, and I knew it was coming. But God, I was so in a hurry for it to come *now*. I thrashed in his hold. "Ben, I need —"

"That's it, kitten," he crooned. "Come for me."

It was so close. I could almost taste it, but it was still so far away, still just out of reach. "I can't."

"Shhh, I know what you need." On his next upstroke, he licked higher...where I'd never been touched. *Holy flipping Christ.*

I squealed and wriggled away. With a growl, he hauled me back against his mouth and gave me a stinging swat on the ass for my trouble. The bolt of electricity went straight to my clit.

The sharp crack stunned me, even more than his roving tongue and I screamed. "Jesus, Ben!"

When he twisted his fingers around, hooking them ever so slightly and pressing on that deep bundle of nerves, he added another resounding crack over my tender flesh, and I broke in a not-so-silent scream.

White hot heat froze me in position, mouth open, back arched, eyes screwed shut shaking from the force of my orgasm, unable to form coherent thought or action. I was broken. Definitely broken. The few brain cells I had were completely obliterated.

All I knew was I could stay there like that for likely hours.

His voice was a soft chuckle. "All right, love?"

How the hell was I supposed to answer that question. Okay was so not the right word. "I—I'm not sure I've ever been okay in my life."

Ben smoothed his hands up my legs, then followed the trail with his lips, only stopping along the way to give a tiny love bite to one of my butt cheeks. When I squeaked, he kissed the tiny injury. "Come here."

Move? The man wanted me to move? I made a feeble attempt, but then collapsed back on my face. Moving required so much work.

Gently, he pulled me to my knees, then turned me over. Then he made making quick work of the rest of his clothes and the tattered remains of my top. I still couldn't move much. My muscles refused to function properly. "Do you know how much those little sounds you make turn me on?"

I bit back my smile. "Maybe."

When his trousers fell to the floor I glanced down and gasped.

©

Ben

My cock twitched at her at full attention. Or maybe it was the way her tongue peaked out. "See something you like?"

"I—" She licked her lips. "Jesus, you're huge." I could hear the nerves behind the chuckle.

Dipping my head, I planted kisses along the hollow her neck then up to the shell of her ear. "Still sure you're mine?"

She nodded without hesitation or reservation. Which was a relief because I was steely hard, nearly to the point of pain.

Scooping her up into the center of the massive king-sized bed, I climbed over her, kissing my favorite spots along the way.

I guided her hands above her head and restrained her wrists with one hand.

She arched her back into each kiss and caress. The more she asked for, the more I wanted to give her. I wanted to bloody give her everything.

"Woman, you're trying to kill me."

Her head thrashed back and forth on the pillow. "Ben, please. Don't make me wait."

I nipped at her neck again before easing the burn with a kiss. From the nightstand I retrieved the box of condoms I'd bought when she moved into the loft. Not at all presumptuous. More like damn good planning.

To my chagrin, my bloody hands shook. As I ripped the foil, she blinked up at me, lips parted, showing no hint of self-consciousness. She kept her gaze on mine as I ripped the foil and sheathed myself.

Stay in control. Easy.

Bullshit.

Along her skin, I used my tongue, making her wiggle and squirm as I explored each hollow and dip. The scent of coconut and lime drove me mad.

I cupped her breast with one hand as the other traveled a path over her belly to the juncture between her thighs. Her eyes fluttered shut. My cock nudged her thigh, and I whispered against her skin. "So fucking beautiful... can't think... making me... so hot..."

I slipped first one finger inside her, and then another. The only sounds in the room now were our comingled deep breaths, groans and moans. Livy dropped her head back against the pillow and wrapped her legs around me as she attempted to draw me in. "Oh my God. Oh my God."

"Fuck, you're so wet. Does my kitten want more?"

Livy lifted her hips. "Yes."

"Yes, what?"

"Please,"

"Remember what I said about being mine? Who's pussy is this?"

"Please...I need...." I started to retreat and she whimpered. "What are you doing?"

I gave her an evil grin. "Tell me what I need to hear first."

"Oh God. It's yours. Is that what you want to hear?"

"It's a start, kitten."

Gently, I guided my cock home with the other hand. I needed to go slow. Take my time, but Jesus-fucking-Christ, she felt good. Too good. The tenuous hold on my control started to slip. Scorching bliss hit me like a blast furnace. With the first inch, I exhaled slowly and deliberately. *Easy. Easy.* Christ. It was too much. She was too tight.

With a trembling breath, I retreated, then slid back inside. *Inch by inch. Slide, retreat. Slide retreat.* My skin slicked with sweat and my muscles bunched.

I squeezed my eyes tight at the pleasure spiraling inside. She was small, but we fit. The easy slide made me moan. The feel of her silken depths milking my cock made my eyes cross. I retreated again. When I finally sank all the way in, I dropped my forehead to her shoulder. "Jesus Christ, I think you're going to kill me."

I penetrated her slowly, increasing the pleasure, then retreating.

The sheer effort of the concentration made beads of sweat pop on my brow. Her eyes widened on each slide. Leaning over, I teased her nipple. *Slide, retreat. Breathe. Slide, retreat. Breathe.* I kept that rhythm.

With my thumb, I stroked over her clit sending a shiver though her. With a long exhale of breath, she relaxed and I picked up the pace.

"Yes, God. Right fucking there."

I pulled nearly all the way out, then sank home again on one stroke, making her whimper. "I want to do this all night. Would you like that?"

"Y-yes. God, yes. Ben..."

I released her breast and slid my hand between our bodies, then used my thumb to tease her clit. Over and over I took her to the edge then back again, not wanting to push her over yet. I wanted to live inside her forever. Might make social gatherings awkward, but fuck anyone who had anything to say about it.

Her muscles squeezed around me. Her thighs quivered and I knew. She was so fucking close. Molten heat started to spread from the base of my spine making me grit my teeth. Nope. No fucking way. She was coming again first.

I changed up the pressure on her clit pressing harder, varying my rhythm.

"Ben, oh God. Just like that. Yes. Yes...so good."

"That's it. Come for me, Livy. Let go, kitten." She was so close. Right on that edge, but it wasn't until I nipped her ear and whispered, "I don't ever want this to end," that her body went stiff.

Her silken walls grasped me tight, and my release started at the base of my spine and built. Step by step, vertebrae by vertebrae, I fought to hold on.

She cried out and shook in my arms, and I increased the pressure on her clit, intertwining our fingers I drove home. With her owning my cock, her silken walls fisting me, all it took was three more strokes, and white-hot heat nearly blinded me as I came.

CHAPTER 27

Livy

Last night had been the kind of sex intended to make me forget my name and everything about anybody that might have come before Ben.

The sun was cheerily streamed through a window demanding I wake but I was pretty sure I couldn't move. And if I *did* move, my pussy would groan in protest. *Damn, I was sore.*

I tried to move a foot and then just groaned and flopped back.

"It's better if you try not to get up too quickly."

I couldn't help but smile at that voice. *Ben's voice.* "Good morning."

He was already facing me with a smug grin on his face. "Good morning, kitten."

"So, that happened."

He grinned. "And by 'that,' you mean?"

"I mean orgasms so good I'm certain my legs don't work right now."

He grinned. "Well, you know, I aim to please."

He shifted to pull me close and his shoulder blocked out some of the light. "Jesus, you're enormous."

"In more ways than one," he said with a wink. I bit back a laugh.

I tried again to get up, but he wrapped an arm around my waist and pulled me close. "Where do you think you're going, woman?"

"I just remember you saying that you don't do sleepovers, and here I am, sleeping over. I'll just go back to my bed across the hall."

His brows furrowed. "So, we're going to go ahead and establish that anything that happened before is not what's happening now. This, right now, it's different, yeah?"

I nodded slowly. "Yeah, this is different."

"Good, now that we've got that established, I will make sure that we are perfectly clear on this. I don't bring people here. I've never brought anyone to this bed besides you, just in case you had that visual going on."

I bit my lip, trying to fight my smile. "No, but thank you for making sure I'll never have it."

He nodded. "I like having you here."

I grinned at him. "You do?"

He nodded. "Yes, and just so there are no other doubts in your mind, I plan on having you here a lot."

"Define a lot. I mean, we do have to work."

He grinned at me then. "Oh, you must be having all kinds of ideas about afternoon quickies."

I laughed. "Oh my God, you're ridiculous."

"You're the one who brought that up. Don't blame me for letting my mind go there."

I stretched, and he immediately dove under the covers to kiss my belly. "Oh my God, Ben."

"Yes?"

"I have things I have to do."

He frowned. "Like what?"

"Well, we just got back from France. I have to prep all the files to meet with Peterman. I also have to do my status update for Jessa."

"Do that from here."

Tempting as that was, I didn't want to slide down that slippery slope. "I should probably go into the office. Get out of your hair."

He took my hands. "Look. I'm still worried about your safety. And I want you here with security. Working remotely is something my employees do all the time. Not just the ones I'm seeing. This is real, okay? It means friends and Netflix queues and all of that jazz. No hiding. No going back to him."

I scooted back. "No. Never. It's not going to happen. But I do need to move freely."

"Good. I don't share. But I understand. Let me do a security assessment, then we'll figure out your freedom of movement. Now, I need to get some work done with East and Bridge."

He did have a point. Someone had tried to hurt me. I needed to be safe. But how long could we shack up? "Do Bridge and East know?"

"About us?" He shook his head. "Not yet, but they're going to. Please rewind to earlier and what I said about this being real, friends and all. You're mine now. I'm not letting you go without a fight, so get used to being here."

I nodded. "Okay. It'll take some getting used to. This is, uh, new."

He laughed. "I know. I also know what I want. You and I have been dancing around each other for weeks. I knew exactly where I wanted you to be when I met you in that closet."

I lifted a brow. "On my back?"

He rolled his eyes. "And on your knees with me behind you, holding on to those perfect tits. Jesus Christ."

He gently nipped at my nipple and I giggled. "Oh my God, that tickles."

He lifted a brow. "Oh, really? This tickles?" He leaned down then and pulled that same nipple into his mouth, tugging forcefully enough that I could feel a pull low in my belly.

"No, that does *not* tickle."

"Oh, good."

His hands wandered down my belly, and his fingers slid over my sex, gliding to my folds, and my breath hitched. "Ben."

"Open for me."

I parted my thighs a little, and he slid right in. First one finger, his palm branding over my clit, and then he retreated. When he slid back in, it was with two fingers. The slow, teasing motion caused me to chase his hand as it teased pleasure but didn't quite satisfy.

Before I knew it, he released my nipple, kissed at my neck, and then the thick length of him slid right in.

We both groaned, and I hissed with a bite of pain. He immediately stilled. "Fuck, are you okay?"

"Yes, it's just... You really are Big Ben."

He nuzzled his face on my neck. "Oh my God, I'm so sorry. I didn't mean to hurt you."

"I'm not hurt. I'm just a little sore," I whispered.

"I should have just kissed it better."

"You did kiss it better, remember?"

"That was hardly kissing. I can do better."

He started to glide out, and my fingers clawed at his back. "Nope, you're already here. Why don't you start moving and make me feel better."

"Oh, is this kind of like kissing it all better?"

"Yup. Um-hmm. With your dick."

His movements were slow. Controlled. But now with the initial sting gone, I didn't want slow and controlled. I wanted hard and fast, and I slid my fingers into his hair and tugged him close.

It was his turn to hiss. "Jesus, Liv. I'm trying to go easy here."

"I don't want you to go easy."

"You'll be sore."

"I like being sore."

With a growl, he increased his movements. A wave of ecstasy rolled over me as I careened toward the edge of bliss. "Yes, that's it."

"Who does this belong to?"

"You. Always you."

"Don't let anyone else ever touch this again."

I shook my head. "Nope. No, never. Oh my God, Ben, right there."

"Do you know how long I've waited for this?"

"A month and three days."

He pulled back and peered down at me. "Do you know exactly how many days?"

"Yup, absolutely. That's how long I have been tortured too."

"Uh-huh." He swiveled his hips again, and I cursed. "Somehow I think I've been more tortured. I didn't even think you liked me."

I grinned then. "I'm still not sure I do."

"Well then, Miss Ashong, let me convince you."

And he did. He convinced me so thoroughly I had three more orgasms before he roared and spilled inside me. "Jesus, woman, I really don't think I can move."

"I really don't think I want to."

Three hours later, after Ben had convinced me to shower with him and he'd fed me, he headed off to a meeting with East and Bridge. I called Telly from the comfort of the bathtub.

"So you finally got laid, huh?"

"What?"

"Please, I can hear it in your voice. Was it in Paris? Shit, please tell me it's Ben and not Dexter."

I hadn't told her anything yet about Dexter. "Yeah, about that…" Once I got started, everything flowed out of me. I told her all of it. Even the part about how Ben's nickname really was accurate.

She paused me several times along the story for typical Telly reactions. When I finished, she asked, "When do we pack you out?"

I shook my head. "I need to plan for when he's not there. Maybe next week?"

"How is Tall Blond and Viking taking this. He says this is the real thing, and it feels that way, but I got so involved in Dexter's world I didn't even stop to think about what I wanted for myself. I'm not doing that anymore."

"Well, okay. I'm glad you're figuring it out. I do want to say something though."

"What, that you were right?"

"I mean, I was, but something else."

"What's up?"

"Have you heard of something called the Elite?"

I frowned. "No, I don't think so. Why?"

"Well, it's a secret society out of Eton."

I frowned and sat up straighter in the bath. "As in, the super posh all-boys school?" Ben and his friends had gone to Eton.

She nodded. "Yep, that's the one."

"I don't know anything about it. Why?"

"You know how my mate, Matthias, who's been working on decrypting those files from the flash drive you copied?"

"Yeah?"

"It's a list of names and dates. Some of the corresponding dates match to major world events."

"But why would that information be encrypted?"

"I have no idea, but I need you to be careful, okay? If Ben

had that information, it's worth something to him. Maybe he's in the group. I want you to tread carefully with him."

"Telly, are you serious?"

"At the risk of sounding cliché…As a heart attack."

"Fine, I promise." I hung up with her and got out of the bath and into my robe. As I padded into the bedroom, I considered calling Ben. All I needed to do was ask him about the Elite. He'd tell me.

Would he?

Would he lie? And then there was the slight problem of finding myself in close to danger since I'd met him.

Was I in more danger with him than on my own?

Last night, I'd let him screw me into complacency. He'd dickgasmed me. From the time I'd said yes and handed over the drive, I thought I'd been in control. But what if that wasn't the case?

Or you're paranoid and you're freaking out and want an easy reason to run.

Damn it. Last night had been some kind of out of this world sex. It had meant something. It was certainly a shift in or relationship. Especially after Paris. He cared about me, and I well…I was dangerously close to falling.

So then talk to him before you freak.

I would. We were certainly past the point of keeping secrets. He'd seen all of my dirty laundry.

When my phone buzzed, I rolled over on the bed, tugging the robe around me, and grabbed my cell off the nightstand. I assumed it was Telly following up with a text about something she'd forgotten, but I frowned when I saw who it was.

Dexter: *Where the hell are you? Where did you stay last night? Call me.*

I immediately hit delete. Then pushed out of bed to find

some clothes. I'd only managed a T-shirt and panties when the phone chimed again. Dexter again.

Dexter: *Just talk to me.*

I couldn't avoid him. If I did, he'd just keep calling and texting. And I was done avoiding. I called him instead of texting back.

He answered right away. "Oh my God, Livy, are you okay?"

"I'm fine. But you can't keep calling me. You can't text me. We're done."

"I made a mistake. Are you really going to throw away everything for a little mistake?"

"And therein lies the problem. To you, it was a little mistake. To me, you took everything that we were, and you ruined it."

"Jesus. Look, I'm just saying the wrong thing. If you would just meet with me, okay? I'll come to you, or just come back to the flat. We'll talk."

"I'm pretty sure I told you to get the hell out of the flat."

"You weren't thinking straight."

I sighed. "Let me make it perfectly clear to you, Dexter. I was thinking straight. I'm done with you. I never want to hear from you again. I never want to talk to you again. Do not be there when I come to collect my things. Matter of fact, I'll send someone to do that."

He cursed under his breath. "Fuck. Look we just need to talk this out. Where are you? I'll come to you. I'm willing to start over and give you whatever you need."

"What I need is not to talk to you again."

His voice took on a sharp edge. "Tell me where the fuck you are. I'm done arguing. You're acting like a spoiled bitch."

I lifted my brows. So this was him. This was the real Dex. "Bitch is it? Fine call me what you need to. The more you talk, the more you cement my decision."

There was a beat of silence. "You're with him, aren't you?"

"I'm not with Ben right now." Technically the truth, but still, I wasn't going to get into that with him. "Dexter, we're done. I'm in love with someone else."

Silence. "So, you shagged him then? To get back at me?"

Had he always been such a self-centered prick? *Yes. Absolutely yes.* "Everything I told you when I walked in the apartment yesterday was true. You're the one who's been having an affair."

"Well the way you're acting is making me wonder a few things too."

"Wonder all you want. Let's not forget, you practically threw me at your boss?"

Another beat of silence. "That's not what that was. You're overreacting. Typical. If you would just stop being so high-strung and listen—"

"Ah, and there's the real Dexter. Ready and willing to blame me and call me names. I'm done. I don't have to put up with that anymore. And while we're at it, I'm going to call the investigators in the morning and let them know I wasn't the one responsible for our accident. I'm not signing off on it."

"God, you're such a fucking cunt," he spat out. "Do you know how much I hate you right now? If you would just—"

I hung up without letting him finish.

For three long moments I started at the phone waiting for the guilt and concern. It didn't come. I felt so much better. *Lighter.* Like I'd taken charge of my own life again.

I was free.

I needed to find pants. I'd get dressed check in on work maybe, then give Ben a call. I heard a crash from somewhere in the house and I paused.

Frowning, I went to the door and listened. There was a loud thump coming from down the hall to the left. I opened the bedroom door and called out. "Ben, is that you?" I inched out, peering into the rooms I passed. Looking for signs of life.

It wasn't until I made a left toward the living room that I felt it. The hairs at the back of my neck stood at attention, and I whipped around. Instead of Ben, it was the one person I didn't expect to see. I opened my mouth to scream, but he grabbed me and planted his hand over my mouth. "You have been a very naughty girl."

To be continued in The Benefactor....

ABOUT THE AUTHOR

USA Today and *Wall Street Journal* Best Seller, Nana Malone's love of all things romance and adventure started with a tattered romantic suspense she "borrowed" from her cousin.

It was a sultry summer afternoon in Ghana, and Nana was a precocious thirteen. She's been in love with kick butt heroines ever since. With her overactive imagination, and channeling her inner Buffy, it was only a matter a time before she started creating her own characters.

Now she writes about sexy royals and smokin' hot bodyguards when she's not hiding her tiara from Kidlet, chasing a puppy who refuses to shake without a treat, or begging her husband to listen to her latest hairbrained idea.

Looking for a few Good Books? Look no Further

FREE

Shameless

Before Sin

Cheeky Royal

Protecting the Heiress

London Lords

SEE NO EVIL

Big Ben

The Benefactor

For Her Benefit

Royals

ROYALS UNDERCOVER

Cheeky Royal

Cheeky King

ROYALS UNDONE

Royal Bastard

Bastard Prince

ROYALS UNITED

Royal Tease

Teasing the Princess

Royal Elite

THE HEIRESS DUET
Protecting the Heiress
Tempting the Heiress

THE PRINCE DUET
Return of the Prince
To Love a Prince

THE BODYGUARD DUET
Billionaire to the Bodyguard
The Billionaire's Secret

London Royals

LONDON ROYAL DUET
London Royal
London Soul

PLAYBOY ROYAL DUET
Royal Playboy
Playboy's Heart

The Donovans Series
Come Home Again (Nate & Delilah)
Love Reality (Ryan & Mia)
Race For Love (Derek & Kisima)
Love in Plain Sight (Dylan and Serafina)
Eye of the Beholder – (Logan & Jezzie)
Love Struck (Zephyr & Malia)

London Billionaires Standalones
Mr. Trouble (Jarred & Kinsley)
Mr. Big (Zach & Emma)
Mr. Dirty(Nathan & Sophie)

The Shameless World

SHAMELESS
Shameless
Shameful
Unashamed

Force
Enforce

Deep
Deeper

Before Sin
Sin
Sinful

Brazen
Still Brazen

The Player
Bryce
Dax
Echo
Fox
Ransom
Gage